BEAST

MEASHA STONE

Copyright © Measha Stone 2018 All rights Reserved

Editing and Proofreading by Wizards in Publishing
Cover Design by Simply Defined Art

No part of this publication may be reproduced or transmitted in any form or by any means, electronic, or mechanical, including photography, recording, or any information storage and retrieval system without the prior written consent from the publisher and author, except in the instance of quotes for reviews. No part of this book may be uploaded without the permission of the publisher, and author, nor be otherwise circulated in any form of binding or cover other than that in which it is originally published.

This book is a work of fiction. Any resemblance to persons, living or dead, or places, actual events or locales is purely coincidental. The characters and names are products of the author's imagination and used factitiously.

The publisher and author acknowledge the trademark status and trademark ownership of all trademarks, service marks and word marks, mentioned in this book.

CHAPTER 1

"Not again."

Ellie Stevens stepped off the bus and into the thick humid air of the city to find a group of people milling around the entrance to The Café, her father's coffee shop. She pushed her sunglasses up the bridge of her nose and made her way through the crowd.

"It's locked again, Ellie," Jason, their full-time cashier, informed her as she reached for the handle of the door. The lights were still on, and the *We're Open* sign hadn't been turned off.

Which meant her father was inside.

And, if the door was locked, he wasn't alone.

"It'll be just a minute." Ellie pulled her saddlebag forward, unzipped the leather pouch, and dug out her spare key.

"I'm not sure you should go in there. Those guys work for Ash Titon," Jason said.

"Who?" Ellie asked, finding the key among the array of colored pencils littering her purse.

"Just—maybe wait is all I'm saying."

"Jason, the customers aren't going to wait around." She slid her key into the lock and turned the bolt, feeling the door give way. "I'll just go hurry them up. Dad probably just couldn't fit everyone in his office."

More than likely, he was begging for more time. A scene she'd been accustomed to growing up, but one that annoyed her as an adult.

"I'll be out in a minute and let everyone in." She opened the door enough to squeeze through and locked it behind her. If her father shooed the customers out, it meant he was either in dire negotiations for more time to repay a debt, or the goons cornering him wanted privacy.

She doubted either side would be happy with her presence.

"I swear, I'll get the cash. I promise." Her father's broken plea tore at her.

Coffee cups and dessert plates littered the floor where tables had been knocked over. The pastry case was unharmed, but all the countertop displays lay scattered on the floor.

She heard a grunt and knew the sound for what it was. Her father taking a fist to his belly. No matter how many times she'd heard him being roughed up by his creditors, it still turned her stomach.

Ignoring the mess, she ran through the small café to the back room, where she found her father pinned against the wall by two overgrown goons. A third man stood before him, rubbing his knuckles. As though he hadn't already grown callouses from the previous beatings he dished out.

"You've said that twice before, and yet, no money. Ash is tired of waiting. You're months behind, and your interest has compiled to the point you won't be able to repay in the timeline agreed."

Her neck tingled, signaling her heart to beat faster.

Months behind? How much interest? What the hell had her father gotten himself into this time? And who the hell was Ash?

Her father usually dealt with a man name Javier, not Ash. Had he started going to two different men to help cover his gambling debts? Borrowing from Peter to pay Paul?

"Wait. Stop." Ellie stepped into the scene, grabbing hold of the arm ready to deliver another blow to her father.

"Ellie? No." Her father groaned at seeing her, but she ignored him. He didn't want her involved. She got that. He wouldn't want her hurt. No matter how many times he'd put them at risk, the café at risk, their home at risk with his gambling, he never wanted her involved. But he also never saw how his actions dragged her into the fray every time.

Every time she had to sell another piece of her mother's jewelry to pay off a two-bit loan shark, or had to take a second job on the weekends in order to pay the rent on their apartment, she was involved. How could she not get involved? He was her father. It had been just the two of them for so long, she could hardly remember anyone else there to take care of her. And no matter his faults, his weaknesses, he loved her.

The goon shook her off his arm and turned to her, licking his lips like some sort of hungry, rabid dog. He was nicely dressed, and clean-shaven. Compared to the usual hired fists who came knocking on their door, he could be considered attractive.

"Ellie? Is this your daughter?" He jerked a thumb at her, while questioning her father.

"Ellie, just leave." Her father struggled, but he was no match for the two apes holding him. At nearly sixty, and after surviving a heart attack, even with a forceful struggle, he presented no real challenge.

"How much does he owe?" She tugged at her saddlebag, but took a step away from him. He towered her.

The man laughed, more of a snicker, and it came out forced. "You don't have it in your little bag, sweetie."

"How much?" she demanded.

"One hundred and fifty thousand." The man's eyes narrowed. "Before interest."

Before interest? What could her father have needed with that kind of money? She didn't glance at him, knowing she'd see a pitying expression if she did.

"Do you have it in your little bag?" he asked, pointing to where she gripped the zipper.

"N-no. But we'll get it," she promised him. The café would be lost. Her mother's dream gone. "We just need a little time."

"He's out of time." He nodded to the men holding him, and they dragged her father toward the rear door leading to the alley.

"No!" She lunged at them, but the big goon with the too-black hair and condescending smile shoved her with one hand.

"No need for you to come. You don't need to see this."

She fought against him as they hauled her father out. She heard him scream, heard the screen door slam before car doors did the same, but she couldn't get free. The man stood in the doorway, arms crossed over his chest, not letting her pass. He said something, but she wasn't listening.

"No! Leave him alone."

"I would suggest you forget him." Wheels squealed in the alleyway, and a car drove off, leaving only a cloud of dust and dirt to be seen through the open door.

She stopped fighting, gasping for breath, feeling hot tears welling in her eyes.

"Forget him. Run your little coffeehouse, and learn from his mistakes."

"Where did you take him?" she demanded, stepping away from him.

He raised his eyebrows but said nothing. After a moment of thick silence, he shot her a wink and started to whistle.

Once again helpless to stop him, she stood on shaky legs, struggling to breathe as he sauntered out of the café. Another car pulled up just as he pushed the screen door open.

Taking a deep breath, she yelled to his retreating form, "Where did he go?" But no answer came. He held the screen door as he closed it, keeping it from slamming. "Where are they taking him?" she tried again.

"Forget about him, Ellie. Just forget." His eyes met hers briefly before he climbed into the black car and drove off.

She stood in the silence of their coffeehouse.

Where did they take him?

What would they do to him?

She didn't know the answers, but she knew one thing.

She wouldn't just forget him.

ღ ღ ღ

"You can't really think to do this."

Ellie swallowed a sob when she stepped out of the cab up in front of the massive estate. Was her father inside? Did dungeons still exist in places such as this?

Gates surrounded the entire property. The only thing missing from the menacing property were perched gargoyles. And even those would probably lighten the atmosphere. "You can't think to do this. *Don't* do this, Ellie," Jason pleaded.

"Jason. Just take care of the café for me, okay?"

"Ellie. This is Ashland Titon. He doesn't mess around."

A lesson she'd already learned. After her father had been snatched right in front of her, she'd done a little digging. Ashland Titon owned a fair amount of the city's night life. Between bars, nightclubs, and stripper clubs, he had his hands in almost everything. None of which explained what he would want with her father, until she came across new articles showing him dealing with accusations of sex trafficking and loan sharking. Loan sharking. *Bingo.* It hadn't taken much more digging to figure out where Ashland lived.

"I know, Jason. I'm not attacking him. I'm going to ask him to let Dad go, that's it." It sounded naive at best, even to her.

"Let him go? Are you insane? The only way he's letting your dad go is if you have the money. And you don't." A heavy sigh came through the phone line. "Please. Just don't go in there."

Ellie peered up at the foreboding gates before her. "I have to, Jason. He's my father."

Another sigh. "Fine. I'll take care of the café. Be careful, and don't do anything stupid."

"Of course not." She ended the call and took a deep breath. She had passed stupid when she got into the cab.

Straightening her bag strap on her shoulder, tucking a few loose hairs behind her ear. She rolled her shoulders back and went for it.

The button made no sound when she pressed it. A bit of static and then a greeting came through the speaker.

"Uh. Hi. Uh. I'm here to see Mr. Titon."

"Your name and business?" came the reply.

"Ellie Stevens. He-uh-does business with my father." Mostly true.

A breeze whipped her hair into her face. The sun had

already started setting, making the estate even more ominous and chilling the air.

She stared at the metal speaker, waiting for a response. A sense of being watched struck her, and she scanned the house, searching the windows for a set of eyes. Nothing.

She let out a long breath and reached for the button again.

"Someone will be along to collect you," a deep voice rang through before she could press the call button.

Collect her? She wanted to roll her eyes. If they were trying to make her feel intimidated, they were about five hours too late. Seeing her father dragged away with a split lip and bruised face had worked well enough.

Loose strands continued to blow into her face, and she peeled her hair tie from her wrist and went about working the long locks into a braid. She couldn't very well be fidgeting with her damn hair while trying to bargain for her father's life.

The gates opened, and the man who had hurt her father descended the half-dozen steps of the house and followed the winding path to where she stood. In a hurry to get this over with, she dashed forward, ignoring his offered hand to stomp past him.

"You probably shouldn't want to rush this." He chuckled behind her, catching up and grabbing her elbow to keep her at his side.

He guided her up the stairs and into the house. The enormity of the beauty inside took her breath away—mysterious and foreboding, much like the outside, but the artwork appealed to her. Baroque. Every painting, every statue they passed came from her favorite era. Everything appealed to her, the music, the architecture, the paintings, so, after getting a taste of it during her coursework for her language arts degree, she'd immediately signed up for a class focusing solely on the Baroque period.

"I told you to forget about your father." His grave voice, though soft, interrupted her inspection of the pieces they passed and reminded her she wasn't in a museum, but in the home of a man willing to kill her father if it would send the right message.

She didn't respond, focused on what she would say when she spoke with Ashland Titon. There hadn't been many pictures of him in her search, other than a few old ones. He didn't appear overly threatening in the smiling photographs. A soft, forced smile giving little insight into his true mood. She doubted he'd be as happy to see her.

The emptiness of the house sank into her as they continued along the corridor. The dark carpeting gave way to deep-maple-stained wood flooring. The clicking of her sandals echoed through the hallway. Although her escort barely held onto her, she could feel him, invading her thoughts with his threatening presence. She held no misgivings about how dangerous these men were.

They came to a closed door at the end of the hall and he reached around her to open it, shoving it inward and exposing the interior.

An oversized mahogany desk sat in the center of the room. The décor mirrored what she'd seen of the estate so far: ominous coloring with dominating artistry. Large sconces adorned the spaces between the paintings, holding long white electric candles that lit up the room. The rich purple draperies were drawn back from each window, but the closed blinds didn't let enough light through to illuminate the area.

"Go on. You've come this far." The man gave her a little shove, and she stepped into the room. The door slammed shut behind her, signaling the finality of it.

She swallowed and took in the room where she stood. It was only when he moved from the corner, she saw him. Stepping out of a shadow, he advanced into the light. Her breath hitched, her heart all but stopped as she took in the massiveness of the man before her. He had broad shoulders, larger than she'd ever seen on a man, and stood taller than her by a foot, maybe more. His thick, dirty-blond hair was tied at the nape of his neck, exposing a scar above his left eye and another running from his right ear along his jaw, disappearing beneath his beard.

He took another step toward her, the muscles in his chest, beneath the black button-down shirt rippling with his movements. The rolled-up sleeves showed off black tattoos running up from his wrists and disappearing into the folds of fabric. Was his entire body covered with ink?

"Peter told me you're Dominick's daughter." His voice, so deep, shook her from her inspection.

"Y-yes. He's my father." She swallowed and thrust her chin forward. Allowing him to see how terrified she truly was would ruin everything, and having a quivering lip would most definitely give her away. "Your men took him this afternoon. I'm here to take him home."

His eyes narrowed, his jaw tensed. When his gaze moved over the length of her, she found herself rolling her shoulders back and swallowing a demand for him to stop. He didn't seem the sort of man who would listen to any demand she made of him, or one from anyone.

"You're going to hurt yourself if you keep twisting your fingers like that." She dropped her hands to her sides and fisted them. More to keep them from returning to a fidgeting state than out of anger.

"My father," she said again when he seemed content to keep staring at her. Her insides shook beneath his scrutiny, but she held herself straight, not wanting him to see how much she wanted to cower from him, how badly she wanted to run from the room.

"Your father owes me a lot of money," he said, striding to the desk and leaning against it. He crossed one ankle over the other and pressed his hands against the edge of the desk. How could a man appear so casual and dangerous at the same time?

"I know. We'll get it. I just need time. I'll have to sell the coffeehouse." It wouldn't be enough, though. She'd have to let go of the rest of her mother's jewelry and put their condo on the market.

"He asked for more time. Three times already. I granted it, but he's delayed and delayed. No more delay." He gave his dictate with a hard tone.

She didn't come to him a timid mouse, she reminded herself. It was her father she was trying to save, nothing else.

"He's not asking. I am. Let me sell the coffeehouse, or maybe you could take it as a down payment on his debt?" The idea seemed logical, an easy transaction for a man who had as many business dealings as he seemed to.

He laughed, a cheerless, deep-rooted sound that failed to add levity to the room. "What the hell would I do with a coffeehouse?"

"You could turn it into one of your clubs or keep it a café. We already have staff. All you'd have to do is collect the profits. Maybe Dad could still run it for you–"

His lips thinned and eyebrows rose. "What do you know about my clubs?" Of all the things she'd just suggested, that was what he wanted to know more about? His clubs?

"I know you own several." A dozen, to be accurate.

"And what type of clubs are they?" he asked, uncrossing his feet.

She regarded him for a long stretch before licking her

bottom lip and answering him. "Nightclubs and a few sex clubs."

"Well, strip clubs, to be precise, but yes, sex happens. A lot." He pushed off the desk and strolled around to the other side, opening a drawer. "Do you think your father would like me to turn his little café into a strip club? Maybe he could manage that? Help the girls with the blow jobs in the back room?" The sneering grin accompanying his crass words sent a tremor through her.

This was not a man with compassion.

A door behind him opened. She hadn't seen it at first; it was masked along the wall. Her father stumbled in and barely caught himself before falling on his face.

She rushed toward him as he straightened. Peter stepped in front of her father, blocking her attempt to help him.

"Move." She tried to get around him, but he thwarted her.

"It's fine, Peter. Let her see him," Ash said.

Peter moved to the side, and she stepped up to her father. His face was swollen, one eye completely closed. Reddish-brown dried blood creased his puffed lips.

"You shouldn't be here." Her father coughed and grabbed onto her shoulders. "You need to leave."

"No." She shook her head. "I won't leave you here. We'll find a way to pay him. There has to be a way." She kept her voice hushed, not wanting anyone else to hear. "We can sell everything."

He grasped her face. Years of hard work left his hands rough against her skin.

"It's not enough, Ellie. If it had been, I would have done it. I owe him almost a quarter of a million dollars. The interest compounded too quickly. You have to leave, go home. Please. I can't risk losing you."

She'd heard the regret in his voice before, too many times for it to register as truly authentic. Always on the lookout for the fast buck, the quick way to repay one loan or another. And, every time, she paid the price. She could be angry with him later, once she made sure he was safely out of Ashland's clutches.

"You're so much like your mother. Strong and loyal. Not weak like me, Ellie. Please, you need to go." He tried to push her away but started coughing again, grimacing. His ribs were probably as bruised as his face.

He was right.

She was strong. Much stronger than he. And the strong didn't let the weak die. The strong protected.

She turned away from him. Taking long strides, with her chin thrust out, shoulders pinned back, she moved to the desk, facing Ash who hadn't moved during their exchange. He eyed her with an arched brow.

"Let my father go. I'll pay his debt."

The corners of his lips curled upward. "And how do you think you'll do that? You've already admitted you don't have the money, and I've already denied your request for more time."

"What are you going to do with him? If you kill him, you get nothing." She waved in her father's direction, not facing him any longer. Not able to withstand seeing the torment in his eyes for another second.

"His death would be a message to those who think they can borrow and borrow and never repay." His sinister tone unsettled her, but she didn't cower. "I'm not a fucking charity. He owes."

"Then take me." She heard her father's gasp but didn't react. She focused on the man who towered over her, even with the desk between them.

"You?" His voice rumbled with the question.

"Yes." She gave a curt nod. "I'll work off his debt. In your clubs."

"No. Ellie, no!" Her father tried to get to her, but Peter grabbed him again.

"Do you know how long that will take?" Ash asked.

"I'll do whatever is needed, but you have to swear to let him go and never bother him again." Her nails dug into her palms, but she didn't blink, didn't turn her gaze away, even when his eyes narrowed.

He stepped around the desk, coming to stand behind her. His hands closed over her shoulders, and he tugged, turning her to face him. Her eyes came in line with his chest, but he gave a simple command.

"Look at me."

She tilted her head, dragging her gaze over the buttons of his shirt, past the swirl of a tattoo peeking out from where the top buttons were undone, along his thick neck covered in stubble, and across his beard before she came to his eyes. She'd been wrong. They were bright blue with specks of gray.

"You have no idea what you're offering me." The warning sang clear in his tone.

"I'll work off his debt. Take my life for his." She may not understand the workings of his mind, but she knew what giving up her freedom meant.

He studied her for a long moment. "You would give up yourself for him? Why?"

"He's my father."

After a prolonged moment, he gave a brief nod. But she doubted he understood. Men like him only understood loyalty to themselves. Only to him.

Releasing her shoulder, he ran his knuckle across her jaw until he reached her mouth. He ran the tip of one finger over her bottom lip then her chin, her neck, until reaching her chest. He didn't stop, and she made no move to make him, either. She sensed a test, and how well she performed would determine his willingness to accept her offer.

Her father yelled again for Ashland to leave her alone, but no one acknowledged him.

Ashland's finger trailed along her breastbone, into the dip of her T-shirt and the valley between her breasts. Her breath picked up, her lips parted—to beg him to stop?

He moved from her chest to the elastic band of her skirt. Instinct took over, and she put her hands on his, stilling him. It only took a raised brow to make her release him. If she stopped him now, he wouldn't consider her offer.

Unchallenged once more, he continued his descent, slipping inside the band then beneath the cotton of her panties and lower still until he tickled the narrow trail of hair there.

"Spread your legs," he whispered. She scooted her feet apart, just enough to give him room to continue. Her face heated, and tears welled, but she wouldn't tug away, she wouldn't give him the satisfaction. She had to make this deal in order to keep her father safe and alive. Ash could touch her body, but he wouldn't get gratification of seeing her unease.

"You're wet," he accused softly. His lips curled. "Danger turns you on." He kept his gaze locked with hers and pushed a digit into her entrance. She gasped, not having expected him to go so far. Her body stretching around him was only slightly uncomfortable. He pumped in and out half a dozen times before he withdrew and rested his finger against her clit. Humiliation over what he'd just done washed over her, stealing her breath and heating her face.

Keeping the tears back took more strength than she could have ever imagined possessing. Managing to stay upright and conceal the shaking of her insides, a damn miracle.

"You have no idea what you're getting yourself into."

Fatality resounded in the words he spoke, amplified by his solemn tone.

"He'll be safe?"

Ashland jerked back as though her skin suddenly hurt him. Steadfast gaze locked with hers, he pushed his finger into his mouth, licking it clean of her juices. Oh God, she'd been so wet. He gave his attention to Peter. "Let him go. Put him in a car and take him home."

"No!"

"If you so much as dial her cell number, your debt will be reinstated. Thank your baby girl, old man. Her tight little pussy just saved your fucking life."

Ellie tried to reach her father, to hug him, to promise she'd find a way to see him, but Ashland grabbed her arm and held her at his side.

"No! Ellie. Don't do this!" Her father continued to struggle against Peter, but he couldn't overpower him any more than he could in the café.

"I'll find a way. I promise." Tears rolled down her cheeks.

The door slammed, and her father's cries became only a muffled sound fading away. Ellie wrapped her arms around her middle, trying to suck in air. Wiping her cheeks, she settled a glare on him.

"You are a beast." Her voice shook with rage.

His lips curled again, exposing his perfectly white teeth, and he grabbed her chin, forcing her to hold still as he brought his mouth down on hers. She didn't struggle, but she refused to respond. It didn't matter. He pressed hard, biting her lower lip before straightening and chuckling softly.

"I am. And you are quite the beauty. But don't think for one fucking second this has a happily ever after." He gripped her face tighter. "Because this is no fucking fairy tale." He released her with a jerk and called his men.

The masked door opened, and the two men she'd seen earlier entered.

"Take her upstairs. Make sure everything's locked," Ashland ordered, and before she could argue, could ask him what he was going to do with her, they had her in their clutches and dragged her from the room.

She'd saved her father.

But what would become of her?

CHAPTER 2

"She hasn't eaten since she got here, Ash." Peter aimed the pool stick at the cue ball, lining up to take the winning shot.

Ash enjoyed playing with Peter. He never let him win. Unlike most of the other men in his employ, Peter never shrank from expressing exactly how he saw things. He never minced words. Ash trusted few men in his life, but Peter sat at the top of the list.

"She'll eat when she's hungry enough." Ash watched the eight ball roll into the far corner pocket and tossed his stick on the table. "I don't know why I play with you. I never fucking win."

Peter laughed and put his stick in the rack.

"Have you seen her?"

"Since she was put in her room? No." Ash strode toward the bar. He'd added the billiard room shortly after the house came into his possession. He was no pool shark, and hustling had never appealed to him. He just liked the game. The simplicity of it. Not much else in his life was so easy.

"What are you going to do with her?" Peter poured himself three fingers of whiskey.

She'd been in her room for nearly a full day. From what the maids told him, she hadn't slept in the bed. And now he had confirmation she wasn't eating, either.

"I don't know yet."

"You could sell her. Easiest way to get the money her father borrowed." Peter sank into a chair and sipped at his drink.

He'd already considered the idea. The wide-eyed, naive girl who had marched into his world and demanded her father's safety. No, not demanded. Traded. She had traded herself for her father.

Dominick Stevens. Ash had pegged him for an easy score. Lend out some money, ramp up the interest, make a tidy profit. When he hadn't paid the first installment, Ash gave him more time. But three strikes and you're out as far as he was concerned. Unfortunately, killing him wouldn't have made him any money.

Ellie didn't know what she offered when she bargained for her father's life. But Ash had accepted anyway. He remembered how wet she'd been when his fingers slid through her folds, how fucking tight her pussy had been when he thrust into her.

Her father standing nearby, yelling at him to stop, to leave his precious daughter alone, hadn't bothered him in the least. Nor the pleading in her eyes. She hadn't fought him, not with any willful strength anyway. Ellie was smart enough to know if she'd resisted him, he wouldn't consider her barter.

She'd called him a beast. And she was right.

He made his fortune off the misfortunes of others. He wasn't ashamed. It wasn't his fucking job to police the world. Adults made decisions and paid the consequences when they failed.

"Sell her against her will? Is that your suggestion?" Ash brought his brows together.

But wasn't she already acting against her will? She didn't want to be there in his house. She didn't want to be locked in the bedroom adjoining his. And she didn't want to say goodbye to her father forever.

Oh, she'd made the offer. She wasn't the first woman to cry for help, to beg him to forgive, but she was the first who had sought him out at his home. She was the first for whom he entertained the idea. And making her say goodbye to her father, making her stand in his office with his fingers up her pussy had felt fucking good.

"Ash." Peter put his drink on the table and leaned forward, his elbows braced on his knees. "Dominick could go to the police. He could raise suspicions. And the last thing we need is more attention."

Peter was right. They'd survived investigations into his companies before. Rumors spread he was trafficking women. Well, mostly rumors.

"He'd be a fucking moron to do something like that." Ash downed the amber liquid in his glass. "I'll have Charlie keep an ear on things."

"You have his daughter. Fathers do stupid things for their kids." Peter threw back the rest of his drink and stood. Peter knew exactly how much a father would do for his children, seeing as his had given his life to save Peter's. A bad deal, the wrong crew, everything had gone to shit and, to save his oldest son, Peter's father had taken the hit.

"Don't worry about Dominick. Or his daughter."

"You can't sell her."

"You were the one who suggested it." Ash made his way to the door, already set on his course of action.

"She's an innocent. The men who would want her—"

Ash opened the door and paused.

"Don't go getting soft on me, Peter. And don't mistake naiveté for innocence." He'd seen the fire in her eyes, felt the heat of her pussy as he touched her. She'd been aroused, at least her body had been. It might take some time for her mind to catch up. But, lucky for her, he could be patient when needed.

"I'm going to check on my—guest. We'll talk tomorrow."

ღ ღ ღ

Ash wasn't sure what to expect when he entered the room adjoining his through the connecting door, but what he found still surprised him.

THE WOMAN STOOD near the window, tying bed sheets corner to corner. He had to blink several times to be sure he wasn't seeing things.

"Those knots won't hold," he remarked, rounding the large four-poster bed to her side.

She gasped, eyes wide. She'd appeared less fearful in his office. But she'd been in protective mode then. Now, she was on her own and had spent a full twenty-four hours figuring out what she'd gotten herself into.

"You have to use a square knot. You've got slip knots there. You'll fall and break your neck." He picked up the sheets she'd stripped from the bed, and others most likely retrieved from the bathroom closet. "You've read too many books, I think."

She gripped the fabric until her knuckles whitened. Her hair, he noted, had been left loose around her shoulders. Long, thick waves fell in front of her face, curtaining her expression from him. That wouldn't do. None of this would do.

He wanted the hellcat back.

"Drop the sheets, Ellie."

She glanced toward the open window. He'd have to talk with his men. When he gave an order for everything to be locked, he expected it to be carried through.

"You know, if you managed to get down from here and through my security gates, your father's debt would remain unpaid."

Dark-brown eyes shot up to meet his. Good. The fire returned.

"And, I would have to add interest as well. A penalty for reneging on our deal."

She cursed and let out a grunt before throwing the sheets to the floor.

"There's a good girl." He kicked the mess away until nothing separated him from her.

She tucked her hair behind her ears and did her best to glare up at him. The fear still lingered there, a tiny speck in her expression, but otherwise her stubborn nature came through.

"I'm told you haven't eaten." A tray of roast beef and mashed potatoes sat untouched on a table in the corner.

"I'm not hungry," she said and stepped away from him. He went over to the table and picked up the plate. Still warm. Not as hot as when he ate his supper, but still edible.

"You need to eat. You haven't had anything since you arrived."

"I don't want to eat. I don't want anything from you." She sat on the bare mattress and crossed her arms over her chest. Taking the time to really see her, he noticed her generous breasts. Not too lavish. Breasts weren't meant to be overblown balloons, but gentle flesh of a woman he wanted to caress. Touch them.

Whip them.

"Too bad. Everything you get in the future will be from me. So, get used to it." He brought the plate over to her and put it on the bed. "Eat."

"I already told you—"

He pushed the plate aside and pressed his hands into the mattress, bringing his face down to hers, touching her nose with his.

"And I told you to eat. You're here, in my house, under my fucking rule. You will do what I say, when I say, and exactly how I say. Eat your fucking dinner, or I'll tie you to a chair and force it down your throat. And if I have to go to all that fucking trouble just to get food in your damn belly, I'm going to make sure I enjoy the process."

Her eyes widened; a little gasp escaped her lips. If she knew the details of what would make him enjoy it, she would do more than let out a puff of air.

"I don't make idle threats. Now, fucking eat." He picked the plate up and dropped it in her lap before jerking away from her.

She forked up mashed potatoes and brought them to her mouth. Her perfectly pink, pouty mouth. He'd kissed that mouth, a symbolic gesture really—acknowledging she'd given herself to him, but he wanted to kiss it again, do other things with it in a less symbolic and more animalistic nature.

He brought a chair from the table over. Propping his feet up on the bed and crossing them at the ankle, he observed her.

She took another bite of potatoes.

"Not much of a meat eater?" he asked when the potatoes were all gone and the roast beef remained.

"I'm done," she replied and put the plate on the bed.

He eyed her quietly for several long minutes, until she readjusted her seating. She still wore the skirt and T-shirt she'd shown up in the day before.

"Go take a shower. I'll have some clothes brought up for you. I'm sure one of Peter's girls will have something you can borrow until we get you more."

"I'll shower when you go." She shook her head, peeking up at him through lowered lids. If she thought playing the demure captive was going to work with him, make him feel sorry for her situation, she really didn't know who she was dealing with.

He took a deep breath and let it out slow, and loud. "Now, you see, that puts us in a bind. 'Cause I'm not going anywhere, and you need to get in the shower."

Those thick, kissable, fuckable lips pressed together in a thin line, and she raised her chin. Ah, he loved the stubborn ones.

Irritation gave way to anger. The soft edges of her chestnut eyes heated, and her cheeks reddened.

"Why does it matter to you?" Her clipped tone pleased him, more than she could possibly know. Wilted flowers weren't interesting.

"For one thing, you said you'd work off the debt in my clubs, right? Working for me? Well, if you can't even take your clothes off in front of me, how will you be able to do it with a room full of horny, drooling old men ogling you?" He crossed his arms over his chest.

The red of her cheeks deepened, and she nibbled on the inside of her lower lip.

"When will I start?" she asked.

He masked his surprise at her question. No argument, no pleading to get out of it.

"When I see what you can do. Stand up and strip." He hadn't meant to make her get naked in front of him. Not this time, at least, not at their first true meeting. But things had changed a bit when he caught her trying to climb out the damn window.

She took a shaky breath and seemed to come to a conclusion. She jumped off the bed and gripped the hem of her shirt. Before he had the chance to even enjoy the idea of her getting undressed, she peeled off the T-shirt, shoved her skirt off, and stood before him in a pair of light-purple lace panties and matching bra.

"Not one for seduction, I suppose." He grinned. "You're still dressed." He nudged his chin in her direction.

Her chest heaved with a sigh, and her hands moved behind her to unclasp her bra. With as little ceremony as she had given with her outer clothing, she shed her undergarments, dropping the bra on the pile with the shirt and skirt and shoving her panties to her ankles and kicking them off. When she stood upright again, one arm draped across her chest, and the other hand covered her sex.

He clucked his tongue. "Now, you see, that's not going to fly." When she didn't respond or make a movement, he raised his eyebrows. "First, look at me." He gave her a moment, and she didn't disappoint. Fiery eyes met his, and he grinned even more. Damn, she was more than he could have expected from such a weasel as Dominick. "Good. Put your hands at your sides."

"You're an asshole," she said with tension in her jaw. She seemed ready to spit at him. Delicious.

"True enough. Hands." He didn't move from his position. If she didn't comply, he'd have to step in. No sense in letting her think she could get away with directly disobeying him.

She fisted her hands and dropped them to her sides, still holding his gaze with her own. He couldn't be more pleased. While she had her eyes locked on him, his attention wandered over her body, accessing and appreciating.

So much better than he could have dreamed. Every bit of her was edible. Her curvy hips, her belly, her athletic thighs, and her breasts. Much better without the bra. They hung heavy, and he wanted to touch them, pinch her nipples, slap them until they swayed. But he would wait. At least until she had a shower.

He let his inspection move lower to the small patch of curls covering her mound. A perfect little patch, well groomed. She kept herself tidy.

"Do you have a boyfriend?" he asked absently. It wouldn't matter, but he wanted to know.

"No."

"Previous?"

"Previous what?"

"Boyfriends."

Rage simmered in her expression, her fists clenched and unclenched at her sides. If she thought this little display was indecent, she was about to have a very rough time of it.

"Yes."

He rolled his hand in the air. "How many? Fuck, this is like pulling teeth."

"Four. I dated four men during and since college. I had a boyfriend in high school, so I guess it's really five. Would you like their stats? Height, weight all that?"

He pointed a finger at her. "I like a little sass, but you're getting close to the line. And if I were you, I wouldn't cross it."

She shifted from one foot to the other, probably trying not to give him another smart remark.

"Sex?"

Her eyes flashed to his then moved away again quickly. "Yes. I've had sex, and the number of partners is none of your damn business."

He dropped his feet from the bed, letting his boots hit the

floor hard enough to startle her, and stood up. He towered over her, nearly two heads taller, but she didn't seem frightened, not even a bit. He gripped her face, pressing his fingers into her cheeks and pushing back until her eyes settled on him.

"You gave yourself to me. I didn't go searching for you. You showed up here. And I accepted your offer, which means, you're mine. Everything about you, everything you think, everything you do, what you wear, what you eat, is all my business." He'd used a lower voice. His control would affect her more than a raised voice or hand. And he did have the control. She just didn't understand it yet.

When the storm in her eyes simmered, he released her.

"How many partners?" he asked. He hadn't planned to, but since she had to go and have a little tirade, he'd have to push her further. "Did you fuck all of them? More, maybe? A few one-night stands?" He'd bet no. She didn't seem the type to do a one-nighter.

"Go. To. Hell. I said I'd work off my father's debt. I didn't say you owned me."

Her mind twisted the truth to make it easier on her. He couldn't allow it. Her reality would only be a hell of a lot more shocking if he permitted her to pull the cover over her eyes.

"You gave yourself in exchange for him. What I do with you is my decision, not yours." He inched a little closer to her, invading her space. "How many?"

It warred within her. The decision to tell him, or maybe she was considering lying. Too many men and he might think her a whore, too few and he'd condemn her a virgin.

"Three."

He smiled at her and patted her cheek. "See, not so hard. And did they make love to you or fuck you?"

Her brows knitted together.

"There's a difference. You know that, right?"

"What difference does it make?" Her question came softly.

He studied her expression. Darkness settled around her eyes. The maids had said the bed hadn't been touched. Had she slept at all since arriving the night before? He could order her to sleep as he did with eating her dinner. Though he doubted making it an order would aid her ability to obey.

"It makes a difference. But I'll let you answer another time." He stepped away from her, letting her breathe some relief at his absence. "Take a shower and go to bed. You need sleep."

"I'm not tired." A lie.

"I don't tolerate liars, Ellie. A fact you should memorize quickly." He stared at her for a solid moment then stalked toward to the door. "Shower and bed. If I find out you didn't obey me, there will be consequences."

"What are you going to do with me?" she asked in a rush as he opened the door.

He glanced over his shoulder at her standing in the middle of the room, naked, with only her arms covering her belly.

"Whatever the hell I want."

CHAPTER 3

*H*is room connected to hers.

Ellie woke just after the sun began to rise. She scooted off the massive bed and peeked through the blinds at it, watching until it chased away the shadows of the night.

She surveyed the room for the umpteenth time, still finding nothing out of the ordinary. Still exactly as it was when she'd arrived.

Arrived.

She'd been so naive to think Ash would give her more time. She didn't know much about him, but what she'd found online, and what Jason had warned her about appeared to be true. He didn't care about anyone or anything other than himself. And money.

Thinking about money made her start wondering again how would he make her repay her father's debt. Would he put her in a strip club? She had no rhythm; she'd only end up embarrassing herself. Perhaps he could use her as the court jester—comedic relief for the pervs lined up around the bar, waiting for the next gorgeous dancer to come out and shake their groove thing for them.

She needed to get out of the room. At least to take a breath. He couldn't keep her locked up forever. Just sitting around waiting to see if he would return, with more questions. And those eyes. Those piercing blue eyes that almost hurt to stand before.

Getting undressed in front of him had been humiliating. Having to stand there fully nude mortified her, and then his damn questions. She'd thought he wouldn't leave until he used her, at the very least touched her again. And then he would have noticed. He would have felt the wicked wetness between her legs. The more humbled he made her, the wetter she became. It was a huge relief when he simply ordered her to shower and sleep.

And a bit of a disappointment. But she wouldn't dwell.

When she had finished with her shower, she had found a nightgown on the remade bed, along with clothes folded on the table for her. The dishes were gone and the window had been shut. It had been locked, too, and she couldn't find a latch to open it.

Trying to escape had been a harebrained idea. Even if she'd made it to the ground without breaking her face open, she'd have had to get through the gates and hitch a ride. His estate, although not far from town, wasn't exactly within walking distance, either.

She needed to get out of the room. Dressed in the black leggings and sweater left for her, she eyed the door he had used the night before. She hadn't heard a lock click, but he could have done it after she'd gone into the shower.

Relief washed over her when the knob turned, and she pushed the door open. She rushed in and closed the door quietly behind her. When she turned around, she nearly groaned. Another bedroom.

His bedroom.

His jeans were thrown on the foot of the bed, and his boots lay on the floor as though he'd kicked them off on his way to the bathroom.

She took a step toward another door, assuming it led to the hallway, when the bathroom door swung open, and he stepped out into the room.

"Need something?" He gave her a cocky grin. His hair, wet and hanging loose, brushed across his shoulders, his very broad, very naked shoulders. The man wore only a towel tied around his waist. But it didn't hide very much. He was too tall. His muscular abs pointed the way for her gaze to travel his length. And tattoos, so many, and of varying sizes and shapes.

She wanted to soak it all in, to see each one, but she was already spending too much time gawking at him.

"Uh. No. I was—"

"Just trying to leave again?" he supplied for her. "I thought we talked about that last night."

"I wasn't leaving. I just wanted to walk around, to get outside for a bit." She averted her gaze when he started to unwrap the towel. "I'll just go back—"

"No, stay here," he ordered. She could see in her peripheral vision he was rubbing his hair with the towel.

"No, that's—"

"I wasn't fucking asking, Ellie." He dropped the towel and within a few strides was right in front of her. She raised her head, looking away, but he cupped her face and dragged her to him again. "I said to stay. You'll stay. If I say to sit, you sit. If I say jump—what do you do?"

Those eyes again. Blue and sharp, demanding she give him her full attention, her obedience.

"I ask how high?" She tried to force a smile, something to gentle his fierceness.

But he didn't smile. He didn't laugh.

"No. You just fucking jump." He released her and moved to the closet. She let herself get a peek at his ass. The thick muscles of his body tensing and gliding as he moved. More tattoos on his broad back. What was the purpose of so many?

When he came out of the closet, a pair of black boxers hugged his body. "Breakfast is probably ready. I'll take you downstairs. Then you can have your tour of the place with Peter." She inched her way to the door she suspected led out to the hall.

"Why did you put me in the room next to yours?" She blurted out the question while he stepped into jeans.

"Because it's where I wanted you." He yanked his zipper up and turned to her, his chest still void of a shirt. "The answer to any question you have starting with the word *why* is because I wanted to." He went over to the dresser and withdrew an undershirt, pulling it on and tucking it into his jeans. She stood in silence watching him work a thick, black, well-worn leather belt through the loops and buckle it. It took her a moment to realize he'd been staring at her while she spied on him.

Her cheeks heated.

He chuckled. "A belt girl, huh? Well, we'll see about that later."

"My phone is missing from my bag." She raised her chin. Letting him unsettle her wouldn't be a good way to start things. He couldn't get the impression she was some wallflower.

"I know." He nodded and worked the buttons on his shirt, still keeping his infuriating gaze on her. He was obviously trying to intimidate her. Scaring her would probably turn him on.

He really was a beast.

"I'd like it returned." She crossed her arms over her chest, giving the illusion she had a much sterner disposition than she actually had.

"You don't need it." He rolled the sleeves of the shirt to his elbows, plucked his own phone from the charger, and stuffed it in his back pocket. "C'mon. Breakfast." He moved past her to the door, but when she didn't immediately follow, he paused. "Are we going to do this again?" he asked on a sigh. "I can and will make you. Don't mistake the kindness I've shown you so far for weakness."

"Kindness?" she huffed. "Which kindness do you mean? Where you locked me in a room for almost two days? Where you took away my father without letting me say goodbye? Or maybe when you tried to humiliate me last night?"

His eyes narrowed as he squared off with her. She held her ground, not changing her stance. He wouldn't get to her; he wouldn't scare her. She repeated this mantra in her mind while he continued to stare at her.

"The kindness of not killing your father. The kindness of instead of throwing you naked to my men for a night of entertainment, I gave you a warm bed and shelter. Are those kind enough for you, or would you prefer I strip you and give you to my men? Because they'd love to get a naive ass like yours for a night of fun."

She swallowed the sob forming in her chest at the image he presented. No one would stop him if he wanted to do it. Not a single person would come to her aid if he had her held down while his men did whatever they wanted to do to her body.

"Now. Like I said. Breakfast, then you'll get to see the place. This is your new home; might as well see it." He opened the door and waited for her to get moving.

Ellie made herself walk, her elbow brushing him as she passed through the doorway. Not really sure which way to turn in the hallway, she had to wait for him. He placed his open hand on the small of her back and led her to the right, toward the winding staircase Peter had brought her up two nights prior.

Breakfast was ready when they arrived in the dining room. Two plates were set out, piled with scrambled eggs, toast, and fresh-cut fruit. Ash put her in a chair then took the one at the head of the long table.

The table could easily seat twenty, and the room could double as a ballroom. The architecture and the light décor, contrasted with the obscure man she sat with.

Ash cleared his throat, and she realized she hadn't picked up her fork yet. Most of his plate was already cleared.

"Have you decided what I'm going to do? Where I'll work?" She took a small bite of watermelon, enjoying the full burst of flavor and juices. She'd been starved, only having eaten the potatoes from the plate the night before. Her stomach had growled through most of the night.

"Well, stripping's out." He wiped his napkin across his face. "I saw you last night, remember?"

Her face heated. She may not have the body of a high-priced stripper, but she wasn't exactly chopped meat.

"Men like a little more sensuality in their stripteases," he clarified as though he knew she'd taken his words the wrong way.

She shifted in her chair and took another bite of fruit.

"I can waitress," she suggested between bites.

"I suppose you could," he agreed, pushing his plate away. "I think I want you here, though."

She finished the fruit and took a large bite of eggs before placing her fork across the plate. "Here?"

"Yes." He nodded and turned his attention to Peter walking into the room.

"Okay. I'm not a horrible cook, and I'm good at cleaning."

"No." He stood up. "Peter, show her around for me. I have a meeting this morning but will return for lunch."

"No? I don't understand. Then why would you want me here?" She rose as well, not liking him towering over her.

"Remember what the answer is to why?" He moved around the table, putting himself so close to her she could smell the musky soap he'd used in his shower.

"Because you want it," she parroted his earlier statement. "But I want to know why you want it, what is it I'm going to be doing. You can give me at least that, can't you?" The unknowing put her nerves on edge, and she'd had enough of uncertainty in the last few days.

His touch surprised her when he slid his hand beneath her hair and cupped her neck. He drew her to him, and his lips pressed over hers. Not hard, yet fully demanding. His tongue ran along her bottom lip and, before she could think to push him away, she parted her lips, accepting his presence. He deepened the kiss, pushing his body against hers while holding her against him. The tingles began at her lips but traveled with electric speed down her spine, through her core, and straight to her clit.

He left her breathless when he retreated, flashing her a cocky grin. The hard rod pressed against her told her he'd been at least affected a little by the kiss, if not as much as she had been.

"I want you here so I can do whatever I want, whenever I want, to you and this body." He fisted his hand in her hair, yanking her head back and exposing her neck. He dragged his tongue up her throat and dropped another kiss to her lips. "Because I own this body. I own you."

His eyes sparkled. His cocky grin remained while she tried to find words to reject him, to tell him no one owned her. Suddenly, he released her, leaving a chill to settle over the places he'd touched.

She heard him say something to Peter. The door to the dining room closed, and he was gone.

"Ellie." Peter's soft voice pulled her out of her stupor. "Let's go for a stroll."

ღ ღ ღ

THE GARDENS STOLE HER BREATH. Everything bloomed, lush and vibrant. Peter let her wander around without invading her thoughts with chatter, and she was grateful for it.

After she had her fill, she made to sit on a bench, but Peter stopped her.

"We have only a short time before you have to meet Ash for lunch." He waved toward the path leading to the house.

She sighed. Peter had given her a quick tour of the main house, nothing out of the ordinary, before taking her outside.

"I'd like to speak to my father."

"Not until Ash has given you permission."

"Permission." She stiffened. "Do I need permission for anything else?" She'd meant the question as a joke, but his serious expression told her there would be no laughing in her near future.

"Everything you do will need his okay," he answered and led her into the house.

"Of course." She noticed a doorway as they entered the mudroom. "What's that? There's another wing, isn't there?" She started toward the door, but Peter's hand on her shoulder stilled her.

"Yes, but you aren't to ever go there." He waved her into the main house.

"What's in there?" She took another step, but he gripped her elbow and kept her from reaching the handle.

"Not for you. Let's go." He towed her into the main hallway.

"Why?" she asked, yanking her elbow from Peter's grip. He wasn't as demanding as Ash, but she was learning they had similar qualities. Similar signs of dominance, and neither seemed to understand the word no, unless they were the ones using it.

"Ash will probably let you call your father in a few days. Once you're settled in. If I were you, I'd just relax and obey him." He arched a dark brow and smiled. "But you haven't listened to any advice I've given you so far."

"You were kidnapping my father," she argued as they made their way through a long corridor. "Why would I trust you? You're nothing but his hired goon."

He only laughed at her insult. The man didn't even know when to be offended!

Her entire life, she'd been responsible, in charge of making sure all the ends were neatly tied, but since getting off that bus two days ago, nothing had been neat. All the ends were frayed and misplaced. And trying to grasp control only resulted in being laughed at, or manhandled.

Though she could admit, just to herself, the manhandling hadn't been too bad.

"I'm a bit more than a hired goon, but I get why you'd be confused. Don't worry about it."

"Don't worry about it? Just obey him?" She stopped and faced off with him. "I don't know him other than he was going to kill my father. The man would as easily have me gang-raped as he would feed me lunch. He's a monster. A beast, and you aren't much better." After having her say, she marched off toward the staircase. Ash could have lunch alone. She wasn't going to go along with him. Fuck him. She wasn't going to act his sweet little captive any longer.

"He's been kind so far, Ellie. Don't push him," Peter called after her as she made her way up the steps.

"Yes, he's been a fucking gentleman," she responded over her shoulder. "He will either give me an actual job, or he'll leave me be. I'm sure he's got a line of women waiting somewhere to be whatever it is he wants them to be." She quickened her pace, fearing Peter might climb the steps and drag her back down.

She wouldn't be able to stop him, or Ash for that matter. They were both so much bigger than her, stronger than her, had so much more power.

The door to her room was locked, so she went to his room, saying a small prayer he wouldn't be inside when she entered. Empty. She quickly shut and locked the door and made her way to the adjoining one. A reflection from the mirror caught her eye, and she paused.

His room at first glance seemed just like her own. Sharp-edged furnishings gave it a more masculine feel than the room she'd been in, and the darker bedding gave it a more sinister one. As she let her gaze wander over the room, she found what had struck her. Black metal rings were mounted on the wall near the bed. Four—two up high and two toward the baseboards. She hadn't seen them before. She'd been trying to get out of the room with him marching around naked and all.

The closer nightstand had deeper drawers than its mate on the other side of the bed. Curiosity getting the best of her, she opened the top drawer and sucked in her breath. Paddles, hairbrushes, and several strips of leather bindings filled the drawer. As though simply seeing them would poison her, she shoved the drawer closed and stepped away.

Was that what he had in mind for her? Would he torture

her for his own pleasure? Was that what he meant by he'd do whatever he wanted to her body?

She had to get out, had to find a way to get away from him, away from this dark, scary place and keep her father safe at the same time.

Running into her room, she locked the adjoining door. She would find a way, but until then, she wouldn't go willingly to him, or allow him near her.

She would protect herself against everything he stood for.

CHAPTER 4

*S*illy girl actually thought a lock would keep him out of her room. He had the key; she couldn't think he didn't. Why would he allow any room in his house be locked without a way for him—the owner—to get inside?

His morning meeting hadn't gone as well as he'd hoped. The buyer wasn't listening to the rules, was trying to make new stipulations not in the best interests of him or the product. And the product was too precious to be sent off with such a careless buyer. No, he had to release him from further negotiations and would have to start a new search.

It turned Ash's stomach to let a million-dollar transaction float out the door, even if it was for the best.

The all-knowing smirk on Peter's face when he walked into the kitchen while Ash was telling the cook what to make for the evening meal didn't help ease his already-sour mood. Worse, Ash recognized the grin for what it was. The man yearned to scream "I told you so," but he wouldn't. Not with Maria, the cook, around, anyway. No. His cousin would wait to gloat until they were alone.

"Komisky's out. I'll find someone soon," Ash announced, deciding to get the gloating over with."

Maria's eyes darted between Peter and Ash before she picked up her pad of paper and left them alone in the kitchen. The cockier the smirk, the more Ash understood his cousin hadn't come in to gloat about the failed meeting.

"What did she do?" he asked, crossing his arms over his chest. He'd only been gone a few hours. How much trouble could she have caused?

"Nothing." Peter shrugged. "She asked about the auxiliary building, though."

Ash raised his brows. "'She would have found it eventually. You didn't bring her in there."

"Of course not." Peter went to the fridge and helped himself to a bottle of water. "It pissed her off, though."

"Is she waiting in the dining room?" Ash glanced toward the adjoining door, wondering if she was sitting primly in her seat.

"Uh. No." Peter twisted off the cap and took a long sip of water. "She went to her room. Said something about you either giving her an actual job or leaving her alone." He took another sip, the bottle only half masking his grin.

Ash rubbed his forehead. One minute she conceded, the next she fought him. It was dizzying.

"I guess it's time to let her know what her actual job here will be, then."

"You're keeping her for yourself. That's new for you." Peter put the water on the counter, giving him a serious look. Concerned. His cousin always watched out for him. It was why he kept him so close.

"I'm sure I'll tire of her soon enough." Once he had her, writhing and crying his name beneath him, he'd be able to push her from his mind. It was how he did things. He wanted them until he had them, and then they weren't so exciting anymore. The fun of the chase, he supposed. And Ellie would give such a beautiful chase.

"Hmm. Well, she's already tired of you. I don't think she plans on joining you, or allowing you to see her. She locked the door to your room, and I'm sure the door joining the two."

"You checked?"

"Of course, I did." Peter's eyes darkened. "She wants to talk with her father. Maybe if you—"

"No." Ash pushed away from the counter. "She's not going to get what she wants by demanding, or pouting. If she wants to lock herself away in her room, fine. I'll have food brought to her, and if she doesn't eat, I'll force her myself. Make sure you tell Maria to let her know if her fucking plate isn't clean when I see it, she's going to be punished."

"You want Maria to give that message?" Peter's eyebrows rose, humor dancing in his tone. "Those exact words?"

He had a point. Maria, although aware of his business dealings and his private preferences, had never been involved. He wouldn't make her party to it, now.

"You're right. You do it. And inform her, if she doesn't join me for her meals, then she won't be let out of her room. Lock her in."

"Ash—"

"Do it, Peter." Ash stalked off. He needed space. He needed to find a new buyer, and he needed to get control of the girl upstairs thinking she could bar him from his own fucking room.

☙ ☙ ☙

Remembering the door to her room was locked, Ash went to his nightstand to retrieve the key.

He had left her alone the rest of the day, spending his time working. Rejecting Komisky left him without a buyer, and waiting to find another would only decrease his return on the investment he'd made in the product. Less revenue made his head hurt.

When Maria informed him Ellie wouldn't be joining him for supper, he hadn't even batted an eye. He'd just told her to bring a tray up for Ellie.

But it was time to talk with her, to make her understand her place. Peter had said she was an innocent, but Ash could tell the difference between innocent and inexperienced. She was no innocent. Or at least she wouldn't be by the time the night was over.

The drawer of his nightstand wasn't closed all the way when he reached it. The top drawer of his toy chest was ajar. A smile tugged at his lips.

She'd been snooping.

He wondered if she had blanched when she saw the things inside the drawer. Or had her cheeks tinted in the pretty pink hue he had enjoyed the first time he'd seen it?

Grabbing the key, he stalked to her door. There'd been enough of her hiding and pretending she had any actual power in his house. Time for her to learn who made the rules and who obeyed them.

She sat on the bed, pushed up against the headboard with a book in her lap. He hadn't barged in, though the urge had been there, so she didn't lift her gaze until he said her name.

The book tumbled from her hands, landing on the mattress with the pages displayed. An art book. His mother had been passionate about artwork. A few of her books remained stashed in the bookcases of the adjoining master suite.

"Nosey, nosey," he said, making his way to the bed and reaching for the book. Baroque. He'd gotten his love of the period from his mother. He slammed the book shut and dropped it on the end of the bed.

"I ate." She pointed to the empty plates on the small table. Peter had delivered the message. *Good.*

"What else did you do, Ellie? While I was in my office working, what were you up here doing?"

"Reading." She thrust her chin upward, tucking her feet under her. She hadn't put on her nightgown yet, which worked for him, since after tonight she wouldn't be wearing one anymore.

"Get up." He grabbed her elbow and dragged her from the bed. She squirmed and pulled, but he maneuvered her into his room with little effort.

"Ash." She yanked, but still she couldn't get free.

He released her near the nightstand and pointed to his drawer.

"Did you find what you were looking for?" He raised an eyebrow, and cocked a grin at her. Her unease fueled him. "Maybe you wanted me to know you'd been naughty so you could have your first dose of the paddle in there?" He opened the drawer and fondled the leather paddle, but didn't pick it up.

"I-I'm sorry."

"An apology, so easily given? I'm a little disappointed, Ellie." He pointed to her shirt. "It's time for the rules. When you are in this room, no clothing."

"I'll go back—"

"Rule number two, you don't tell me what you're going to do, you *ask* me what you are allowed to do." The fire lit up in her expression, and his cock reacted immediately to it.

"May I go to my room?" she asked.

He wondered how much pressure it would take before a

tooth actually cracked when clenched together like she was doing.

"Take off your clothes, Ellie. Or I will." He closed the gap between them. "And if I do it, you won't like it." He winked at her. Or, maybe she would. Plenty of time to experiment later.

She huffed but finally followed his directions and pulled off the shirt and shimmied out of the leggings. She'd gone without any underwear, which probably had everything to do with the fact he'd told Peter not to give her any.

"Good." He swept the clothes up from the floor and went to his closet. After tossing the clothes down the laundry chute, he turned back to her and leaned against the closet doorframe.

"I didn't mean to go through your things," she murmured. "I'm sorry if it pissed you off. I won't touch anything else."

He remained quiet, taking in the gentle beauty of her natural state. Her hair fell loose over her body, almost long enough to cover her breasts. He'd have to keep it tied back if it grew much longer.

The creamy coloring of her skin ended at her neck. From there it took on a deep crimson. Embarrassed from being nude or from being found out?

Time to get to know his captive a little better.

He stalked across the floor to her, keeping his eyes focused on hers. She hated it, he could tell, but she wouldn't back down. No, she had more spunk than that. She may be well-mannered, easily embarrassed, but she was no shrinking violet.

"Tell me what you saw in the drawer." He trailed a finger down her arm when he reached her, delighting in the goose bumps littering her flesh.

She tried to turn away, but he tsked, and she managed to hold his gaze.

"Nothing."

He shook his head. "Liar, liar." He swatted her bare ass hard with an open palm. "Ass on fire."

The surprised yelp she gave him wasn't enough to appease the need bubbling inside him, but he would take his time.

"What did you see?"

She huffed. A few locks of auburn hair blew toward him with the heavy breath.

"Just stuff. The paddle, a strip of leather. It's none of my business," she quickly qualified.

He continued to study her. The quickening of her breath, the subtle dilation of her pupils. Peter was an idiot. This woman may not have experience, but she sure as fuck was no innocent.

"Are you—is that what you want me for, to do those things to me?" She kept her voice from shaking, but barely. Her body trembled, and it wasn't from any chill in the room.

"Two lessons tonight, I think." He nodded, decisive. "You'll learn your first and, if you do well, you'll learn the second."

"What are you talking about?"

"Have you ever had a spanking before, Ellie? Were you ever naughty enough to earn one?" He left her standing beside his bed and picked up the leather paddle. By far the most innocent toy in the room, it would make a great introduction for her future.

"N-no. My father—"

He let out a laugh. "I doubt your father was ever the real parent in your house. No, I mean with your five boyfriends. Maybe one of the three who fucked you? Did any of them get irritated enough with you to redden this luscious ass of yours?" He grabbed hold of her ass cheek, digging his nails into the generous flesh and inhaling when she gave him the delightful shriek he sought.

"No." She jerked her head to the side, looking away from him, but he saw the moisture on her lips. She'd licked them, and he'd missed it.

"Then this will be a first for you. Bend over the bed, stretch your arms over your head, and spread your feet shoulder-width apart."

Her eyes darkened and widened with her hitched breath. She tried to shake her head, but he stopped her easily enough by wrapping her hair around his fist and holding her steady.

"You were a naughty girl going through my things, not coming to dinner, and trying to lock me out of my own room. For all those things, you're being punished."

Her lips parted. An excuse? A plea? He didn't wait to find out. Shoving her hard, he pushed her face into the thick quilt of his bed and kicked her foot out until she was spread for him.

She tried to get up, but he splayed his hand across her shoulder blades and kept her pinned.

"Arms. Now." He pressed harder against her back, letting his nails dig into her flawless skin.

She cried out and still scrambled to get out of his grip, but he only dug deeper into her. He would not relent, and if it took drawing her blood, she would learn it.

"Now, Ellie." He leaned over her, bringing his mouth to her ear. Her hair covered her face, but it wouldn't be much of a barrier. "Do as your told, or you won't get to learn lesson two. And trust me, you'll like lesson two."

When she didn't respond, but didn't move her arms, he nudged her hair from her face with his nose and captured her earlobe between his teeth.

She yielded when he bit down, and slowly, with more

effort than it should take anyone to move their limbs, she positioned her arms over her head.

"One hand on top of the other," he instructed, still holding her earlobe hostage. With another huff, she slapped her right palm over her left hand.

The fight wasn't completely gone from her, and he would do everything in his power to make sure her bright light never died. But obedience was required, and when one of his girls was naughty, they were punished.

Simple. Just that simple.

He kept her pinned with his hand and shifted until he sat beside her on the bed.

"If you move it doesn't count, if you try to get up it doesn't count, and if you swear it doesn't count. Do you understand, Ellie?" She wouldn't face him, and he decided to let her hide, just this once.

"No. I don't understand any of this." Her protest came hard, but her ass clenched when he pressed the leather to her cheeks.

"I think you understand well enough. You were a bad girl, so you're getting a spanking. You can thank me later for being lenient and only giving you a little paddling."

Before she could start fighting him again, he brought the paddle back and swatted the upcurve of her ass. She yelped, but he was too fascinated with the bounce of her cheeks to care. Another swat, the other cheek, and then he returned to the original. He continued this way, one then the other, moving his swats all around her ass before repeating the strokes.

What started out as a little groan grew to soft pleas for him to stop. Her creamy complexion quickly morphed into hot crimson.

He listened to her breathing patterns, guarded her muscle

reactions to each swat to show him when she was reaching her limit.

Ellie, he found with great pleasure, had a higher threshold than he would have given her credit for.

She wiggled harder, and he had to move from restraining with just his hand, to using his forearm across her back while continuing to rain down the punishing strokes.

"Please! Oh! I'm sorry!" She pushed up onto her toes, which only gave him a better view. Her pussy, so plump and ready for him, was also coated in her juices.

Innocent, his ass.

"If you have questions, you ask me. If you want to see something, you ask permission. If you ever think of hiding away and locking me out, remember this." He brought the paddle down in a hard stroke, and she lifted one leg in the air with her cry.

"Okay! Okay!" she cried. Her fingers dug into the quilt, and her ass continued to bounce as her skin reddened beneath the punishing implement.

With one last swat to her thigh, he ended the spanking and rested the paddle on her back. Her shoulders shook with her soft sobs, but he could see it for what it was. Embarrassment. He'd spanked her hard, but not enough to elicit such tremors.

He reminded himself it was punishment, and he would not rub away the fire surely burning in her ass. Instead, he dragged his nails lightly over the tender flesh, smiling to himself over the hissing sound she made at the new sensation.

"Such a beautiful ass, Ellie." He slapped her once more and sat back, releasing her from his fetter. "But if I have to punish you again for locking me out, or you snoop, you'll have marks from my belt on it for days. Do you hear me? Do you understand?"

"Yes." She nodded, not moving her hands or her feet from their positions.

"Good." He patted her backside lightly and stood. "Then, on to lesson number two. Stand up, hands behind your head and legs spread wide."

He snagged the paddle and returned to his drawer of toys to gather up the second instrument of the night.

CHAPTER 5

Lesson two?
She barely had her breath under control from the first lesson, and her ass throbbed. Thinking he'd only give her a few swats, a little spanking as a symbol of his power over her, a chest-thumping ceremony, she hadn't fought enough to get out of the spanking.

She'd been wrong. When it came to Ash, it appeared everything she thought she knew was wrong.

The paddling had been relentless, and her swollen backside proved it. She just knew when she finally got in front of a mirror she'd find purple splotches, but she wasn't being freed just yet. He wanted to teach her another lesson.

But he had said she would like this one. Too many emotions and sensations ran through her to understand what he babbled on about as he walked around the room.

Even with the heat in her ass, the real fire, the one needing the most taming, raged between her legs. What the hell was happening to her? How could this man with his long hair, his fierce exterior, and his arrogant dominance draw so many emotions from her?

She didn't want to be spanked like a child, yet the wetness between her thighs suggested otherwise. And she could do without his arrogant grin, yet her nipples hardened when the little crease on his right cheek deepened when he did.

A loud growl worked its way through her chest, but she managed to swallow it. He was the animal here, not her. She wouldn't give in to her animalistic instincts. She would keep her wits and her head on straight. And once he finished with whatever humiliating thing he wanted to do to her next, she would demand he lay out how he planned for her to work off her father's debts.

The drawer shut, and she realized she hadn't moved yet. Quickly, she scrambled off the bed and stood up. Tossing her hair over her shoulder, she linked her fingers behind her neck, trying to ignore how high the position brought her breasts, or how hard her nipples became.

Ash sat on the bed where she had been draped, with a vibrator in his hands. He spread his knees and toyed with it while peering up at her.

Sinking into the floor would be too easy. He'd probably drag her out and put her right where he wanted her anyway.

"Do you know what this is, Ellie?" He held up the bulbous-shaped vibrator.

"It's a vibrator," she said without looking at him. If he wanted a reaction, it would take more than making her name sex toys.

"You've used one?" he asked, and she rolled her eyes.

He could wait all night; she wasn't answering him. What woman her age hadn't used a vibrator? And she wasn't going to enlighten him that she'd worn through so many battery-operated ones she'd she opted to purchase the higher-end plug-in vibes.

Now she just sounded sex crazed. She needed to get her mind clear, but how the hell could she do that with his silvery-blue eyes staring up at her, his brow creased, and his hair loose around her shoulders.

"Ellie, I asked a question, and don't forget the little problem I have with liars."

Seemed odd, given what she knew of his profession, that he would expect anything but lies from the people around him.

"Yes, I've used one," she answered, but chose to focus on his ear instead of his lips, because when she glanced at his mouth, the grin he showcased made her stomach flip. And the last thing she needed at the moment was to allow herself to have any level of attraction to him.

He was her captor, the man who would have killed her father if she hadn't stepped in. No. He wasn't attractive.

Except when his strong hands, covered in tattoos, twisted the knob on the bottom of the vibrator and held up the device, she couldn't stop the melt happening in her core.

"Look at me, Ellie." The command came softly but lost no power in the gentleness. "Do as I say and you'll learn what good girls who obey receive. Don't listen, and be naughty, and we'll have to restart lesson one."

Her ass twitched at the mention of the first round of the paddle. She definitely could go without repeating that lesson.

Ellie brought her gaze to meet his. A satisfied smirk rested on his lips, but she chose to ignore it. Focusing on getting through the next portion of her encounter with him took hold of her.

"When you're a good girl. When you do what you're told and you please me, you'll be rewarded." He scooted to the edge of the bed, trapping her between them, his mouth close enough to her body his breath warmed her skin.

The vibrator disappeared from her sight, but she wasn't left wondering where it went.

He pressed it directly onto her sex, making her jump.

"Shhh. Stand still." He gripped her hip with one hand while the other began to play. He ran the tip of the vibrator down her slit then up again, circling her needy clit before heading through her folds again.

He leaned forward, the bed creaking beneath his movements, his mouth wrapped around her nipple. The hot wetness of his tongue was the only foreplay before his teeth bit down.

"Ah!" She arched her back, trying to move her chest out of his reach while still keeping the vibrations on her pussy.

"Uh, uh. You don't move away from me, Ellie." He pulled her closer to him, and she stumbled in her step.

He held the tip of the vibrator to her entrance. The need to be filled overtook her, and she pushed her hips toward him.

His teeth scraped over her nipple again, and instead of the sharpness pushing her away from the pleasure of the vibrations, it pulled her closer to it.

"Your pussy was wet before I even touched you," he said against her breast. "You can say you didn't like it, but the spanking made you hungry for this." He bit hard on her breast, and she cried out but didn't try to pull away.

The bite mingled with the easy throb of her pussy. She found herself rocking her hips. She was fucking the vibrator. But he didn't make fun of her for it. Instead, he flicked his tongue over her nipple and moved to the other side, sucking it hard into his mouth.

She walked her feet as far apart as she could with his legs still trapping her.

"Do you want to come, Ellie?" he asked, slipping the tip of the vibrator into her pussy.

"Yes," she answered with a clipped response. Her body may react to his ministrations, but she would not become too willing a participant. Doing so would make him a part of what was happening, and he was a monster, he couldn't possibly be giving her the pleasure she felt.

"You have to ask. Everything you do comes with my permission or my denial. Ask me nicely if you can come."

Of course, there would be a fucking condition. She tried to glare down at him, but at that moment he moved the vibrator back to her clit and slipped two fingers inside her passage. Curling his fingers, she could feel him stretch her and drag her closer to the edge than any other man had ever been able to do with just his fingers.

Air became harder to collect, and she tensed. She propelled closer to a line she couldn't see but desperately wanted to jump over, leap over, crawl over, anything to get past it to the utopia she knew awaited her.

"Oh God." Her knuckles ached, but she wouldn't let go; she would hold her position. If he decided to punish her by taking his fingers away, she'd die.

"What do you need, Ellie?" he asked, flicking her nipple with the tip of his tongue.

"I have to come. Oh fuck. I have to. Please," she pleaded with him, her mouth dry, her heart hammering inside her chest.

His eyes, so clear and beautiful, watched her. His full lips curled up in a smile. She wanted to tug on his beard, drag him forward so he would give her the bite she wanted.

"Go ahead. You took your first spanking well enough. Come for me, Ellie. Do what I say and come for me." He observed her, not taking his eyes off her while his fingers worked inside her. Pumping in and out, curling and rubbing, while the vibrator titillated her clit, driving Ellie to the brink of insanity.

No longer able to stand the pain, the pleasure, the enormity of it, her body released. Breaking the dam and releasing the waves of intense pleasure.

She screamed. So help her, she screamed out with her orgasm. Every nerve ending in her body sprang to life with the pulsations, with his stare, with his fucking smile.

Her fingers never lost their grip, but she arched her back inward, and her thighs shook so badly he wrapped his arm around her waist to keep her standing. She felt the loss of his fingers immediately, but the vibrator continued, running up and down her slit until every last wave, every last little electric pulsation waned and left her standing, spent and exhausted.

She hunched over, her head resting on his shoulder, her long hair falling from her shoulders to curtain her face. The vibrator was gone. He pulled her into his lap and held her, tucking her head beneath his chin.

He'd been in the gardens. She could smell the lavender on him.

"That was good. You learned what bad girls get and what good girls get." His voice penetrated the safety net surrounding her mind, and she pushed away.

Satisfied. He seemed every bit pleased with himself.

"Is this how I'll pay the debt? Taking spankings and orgasms?" She hadn't meant to sound surly. Exhaustion spoke for her.

His arms tightened around her as he lifted her. He carried her in silence to her room, laid her on the bed, turned down the covers, and tucked her beneath the thick quilt.

"I'll have my men bring some of your things here tomorrow. But don't forget. If you come into my room, you do it naked." He towered over her, his hair falling from behind his ears and brushing over her cheeks. "I own you, Ellie. Every inch of your body and every fiber of your soul."

An argument formed in her mind, but she couldn't say the words. There would be time to fight him in the morning. After a solid night's sleep.

"I'll keep your door unlocked, but if you misbehave, you'll find I can be much stricter than a little paddling and grounding to your room. I expect you at breakfast."

She nodded, moving her gaze to his lips. But he didn't kiss her. He shoved off the bed, making her bounce with the give of the mattress.

"Good night."

She heard him just before the adjoining door clicked closed.

As she drifted off to sleep, replaying the immense scene in her mind again, a thought struck her. He'd taken no pleasure. No physical pleasure in what they'd done. She had noticed his cock pressing against his jeans, had felt it when she sat on his lap, but he had made no move to fuck her, or make her give him relief of any kind.

How could such a monster, a beast, give her the sort of pleasure she had received and not demand the same in return?

CHAPTER 6

Meeting assholes came with the job. Ash didn't bother questioning if any decency remained in the world; his own part in it answered him easily enough. If decency existed, it sure didn't come from him.

Peter joined him in the hallway leading to the annex.

"You didn't have to take this meeting."

"I know." Ash nodded.

"You don't have to honor the old oaths."

Ash glanced sideways at his cousin. "I'm aware." He didn't need a lesson in etiquette. What he needed was backup.

Komisky went crying to Daddy, and Daddy demanded a meeting. Ash may not be required to honor oaths uttered by old men, but his honor dictated he do so. He would not turn his back on old allegiances simply because the business changed when he stepped into power.

Peter pushed the door to the annex open and stepped aside to let Ash pass. He could feel her eyes on him, but he didn't turn around. The door to the second wing could be seen from the staircase if she stood in just the right spot, and with the hairs tingling behind his neck, he knew she had.

Perceptive imp.

"She's watching. Make sure you lock the door," Ash told Peter and pushed her from his mind. He already wasted enough of his morning at the breakfast table with her. Enjoying the light blush of her cheeks, and the hunger she finally had, he'd watched her fill herself with scrambled eggs and fresh fruit. After instructing her to stay out of trouble while he held his meeting, he directed Maria to get more watermelon and strawberries from the market for dinner.

"Ashland." Kristoff Komisky nodded and held out his hand when Ash and Peter entered his office.

Ash took the extended hand, noting the weakened grip. Kristoff had sat the head of his family for the past forty years, and even with his son starting to take over their businesses, he needed to step in often enough he couldn't quite claim retirement.

"Please sit." Ash pointed and rounded the desk to find his own seat. Peter stood off in the corner. "Marcus didn't come with you?" Ash didn't find it surprising.

"No, no. Business matters to see to." Kristoff waved a hand.

"Ah, then it's pleasure you seek here?" Ash smiled. Kristoff wouldn't find what he desired in his annex. But it was all a game. Everything was a game with these assholes. Say one thing, mean another. Time wasting.

"Marcus came to you for a purchase." Kristoff struggled to adjust his seating before he continued. "He had money ready to be transferred, had brought transportation, but he says you didn't honor the deal. I said, that's not like Ashland. Not the way his father did business. I'll go and see for myself."

Ash's neck tensed, and he clenched his fingers together beneath the desk. Old ties did not break easily.

"Your son did want to make a purchase, but he didn't

agree to the terms in the final agreement. I won't sell without all parties in full agreement. It's bad for business to allow anyone to leave the negotiations unhappy."

No fucking way Komisky was going to be buying anything from him anytime soon. A man who ran to Daddy to fix his problems wasn't much of a man.

Kristoff wiped his hand across his neck. The passage of time hadn't treated him kindly. Spots littered his skin, and just the stress of dealing with this problem left him sweaty and agitated.

"That's what I don't understand. Your father never bothered with the depth of these negotiations. He never allowed them so much say in the contract."

His father didn't do a lot of things Ash did. Not giving a shit about his product had not been a tradition Ash carried over when he took his father's businesses.

"My father and I saw things differently. He's not here, now, so I'm running things the way I see them. And I won't allow anyone who can't honor the limits of the contract to make the purchase. Marcus wouldn't adhere to the guidelines, so the sale didn't take place."

Men had little else if they did not have honor. Ash's mother had taught him that. It wasn't a lesson his father could have conceived of teaching, or being an example of.

"I see." Kristoff pinched his fat lips together. Perhaps thinking of a new tactic.

Ash couldn't see why Marcus wanted to make this deal so badly. Surely, he could find something else to meet his needs.

"I didn't say he couldn't make another offer, just not on that particular item. He's free to choose another, make another bid, and begin negotiations. He might find something better suited for his—uh—needs."

Doubtful, but Ash wouldn't let Kristoff leave thinking Ash didn't know how to strike a compromise. He may not have continued the traditions of his father, but he did not see the need to make enemies, either.

"Ah. That's the Ashland I know." Kristoff smiled after a moment. "Levelheaded. Not hot tempered like your father. That's good. Smart and even." He shook a finger at him. "Good. Then I'll tell Marcus to move on to something more —appealing to him."

Ash moved one hand to rest on his desk while the other remained fisted in his lap. Marcus would shop around, but he wouldn't find what he wanted. No one would agree to the terms he offered, and Ash would never force it.

"Good. I will make sure he's on the list for the next showing. I believe we have one in a few nights, is that right, Peter?" He could see the unease in his cousin's expression, but to Kristoff he probably just looked bored.

"Yes, two nights from tonight. I will personally be sure his name is on the list." Peter swallowed hard, and Ash knew the action for what it was. Peter wanted to remark on Marcus's tastes, but he had been raised smarter than that. He kept his mouth shut.

"Excellent. I knew something could be done. Marcus, you know, is just stubborn and hotheaded." Kristoff used the arms of the chair to wiggle himself out of the chair and stand up. "Since I'm here, do you think I could take a look around?"

Peter's jaw clenched, but Ash ignored it.

"Peter will give you the tour." The exact one he'd been given at least a dozen times over the past two years since Ash's father passed away and Ash took over the business.

"Of course, Right this way, Mr. Komisky." Peter pushed the office door open and waited for him.

Peter glanced over his shoulder as he exited the room, letting Ash know exactly what he thought of being sent on the errand. He would have to make it up to Peter later.

Dealing with these petty assholes left him on edge. He

wouldn't get away from his father's old associates; he had known that going into it. But when one of them made the comparison, it set his spine to stone. Reminded him he wasn't like his father wasn't an insult.

His thoughts drifted to the woman walking his upstairs halls. He needed to do something with her, figure what the hell his plan would be. He couldn't very well just let her wander the grounds for the rest of her life.

He grabbed his cell and sent out a text to have a car ready at nine and a dress brought up to his guest.

They were going out.

CHAPTER 7

*E*llie caught a glimpse of Ash's reflection in the car window. Sitting beside him in the backseat of the Cadillac put her on edge. They hadn't talked much other than over breakfast, after what happened between them the night before, and it seemed the stark silence would continue.

Aside from a maid informing her Ash required her attendance for the evening and laying a dress on her bed, she had no idea what they were doing. Ash hadn't even accompanied her to the car. Once she was settled, he slipped into the seat and gestured for the driver to pull out.

"Where are we going?" she finally asked when the traffic became thicker and their progress slowed to a crawl. The bright lights of downtown surrounded them.

"To one of my clubs," he answered, fingering his phone. He hadn't tied his hair back for the evening, and the unruly locks covered his features from her view.

Her hair twisted up into a braid and wound tightly showcased the earrings he'd sent up to her. She pretended it was all just a game of dress-up while she had gotten ready for him. It had occurred to her, she could refuse. Not go, or at least to wear something from her own wardrobe brought from her condo, but in the end, she'd done what he expected. At least she could spend the evening out of the house. As large and beautiful as the estate was, she couldn't help feeling the chill in the air everywhere she went.

Ash filled his home with beautiful artwork and architecture, but there was little warmth. The staff remained aloof and distant no matter how she tried to provoke a conversation, and if she dared ask a question about Ash, they quickly ended their chat and rushed off to a random chore.

"Which club?" she asked, yanking the short hem of her dress down. The thin black dress barely covered her thighs, tug as she might it wouldn't reach her knees.

He tucked his phone inside his back pocket and captured her hand in his, leaving it resting on her knee.

"Delilah." He ducked his head to see out the window. "We should be there in a few minutes."

She stared at their fingers entwined on her lap. He could easily hold both her hands in one of his.

"Why did you bring me?" she asked when the car pulled up in front of the club. A crowd milled around the entrance, being contained by a single man with an earpiece, letting them trickle in as people left.

Ash turned to her, tucked his hair behind his right ear, and grinned. "You're my escort. Why would I not bring you?"

"Can I ask how much each of these excursions will remove from the debt total?"

His grip tightened, but his grin didn't fade. "I suppose it depends on the quality of your work." He fondled the teardrop diamond dangling from her earlobe. "Before we go in, there are rules. You may not speak to anyone other than me, unless I give permission. I have business associates here, and they will mistake your intentions if you talk with them."

"So, only speak to you." She gritted her teeth against the

smart-ass comment simmering on her tongue. "Got it. Anything else?"

"Plenty, but it's all summed up easily enough with one rule. Obey me. Do that, and you'll be fine." He leaned over and brushed his lips across hers. "I don't like your hair up like this. Next time, leave it down."

He knocked on the window, and the door opened. Without letting go of her, he helped her out of the car and led her past the crowd and into the club. She tugged upward on her neckline, feeling the bouncers' eyes lingering on her while she followed the pull of Ash's possessive hand.

Once inside, he dropped her hand and moved his to the small of her back, leading her toward a set of stairs in the rear of the club. He paused at the bottom of the steps to speak with the man guarding them, and took the opportunity to survey her surroundings.

She wasn't so ignorant to not know what the inside of a strip club should look like, but this didn't fit the bill. Instead of seedy men drooling over a catwalk, or women flaunting every bit of flesh they possessed as they strutted around, there was a subtle stage. Men sat around cocktail tables, dressed in fine clothing. No drooling, but full appreciation for the women strolling around. Their outfits were a far cry from conservative, with the short petticoat skirts and black leather corsets, but they weren't half-naked, either. Graceful. The woman promenaded through the tables, carrying drinks and food with their heads held high.

The music started up again, and the deep-purple curtains parted, allowing two women to step on stage. Just as they began to dance, Ash gave her a little push, and she climbed the stairs.

She turned to keep her gaze on the two women while they walked, and Ash made no comment. They moved with skill and rhythm she would never possess, no matter the number of hours she practiced. Touching each other with well-crafted seduction, they moved with the beat of the music, fondling and rubbing.

"Enjoying the show?" Ash pressed his lips to her ear. She had stopped and stared at the stage, mesmerized by both the beauty of the women and their skill.

She pulled back from the railing she'd been leaning over and tried to give him a disgruntled look. Since he laughed in response, she counted it as a failure and followed him to a table where two glasses of red wine stood by an open bottle of cabernet.

He offered her the seat closest to the railing, and she considered it a favor. She would be able to observe the dancing without him in her line of vision.

The music changed to a faster tempo, and the women moved closer to each other, removing each other's lace jackets.

"That is how you undress." Ash's words bit at her. Of course, he'd remind her of the first time she'd removed her clothes in front of him.

"Maybe you should hire them to do it for you, then," she shot back, glaring at him over her shoulder.

He laughed. "I already did."

Oh. Right. It was his club.

Giving up on watching the duo peel off one another's clothing, she leaned back in her chair and took in the artwork around the club.

"All of the paintings depict Samson and Delilah," she commented.

She could feel him surveying her.

"Yes. The matching club, Samson, is a few miles away and is decorated in the same theme."

"Samson. Isn't that a male strip club?" A girl from her art class had told her about it and had asked her to go with her for a night out. To enjoy the priceless artwork supposedly decorating the walls.

"Women enjoy sex just as much as men," he commented. Brushing a finger across her jawline, he grinned. "As you demonstrated nicely last night."

She jerked away from him and tried to turn her attention to the new woman on the stage, but he wrapped his hand around her neck and drew her to him.

"Don't deny you loved it."

"Sir, my apologies, but Mr. Komisky is requesting a moment of your time."

Ash didn't let her go but turned a frustrated expression on the man standing at their table. She hadn't even heard him enter the private area or approach.

"Which Komisky?" Ash's voice held bitterness.

"Marcus, sir," the younger man answered, clearly trying to conceal his fear over having intruded.

Ash gave him a curt nod and waved him off.

"I have to talk with him. Stay here. Do not wander off." He gave her neck a little squeeze and stood.

Where exactly did he think she'd wander off to? He had a man stationed at the top of the stairs, preventing her from leaving the private area they were sitting in.

Ash didn't leave the area like she thought he would. Instead, he moved to the far corner of the room. A man stalked up the stairs, waving off the guard when he tried to speak with him, hiked over to Ash, and launched into a list of problems at the club, casting a quick glance in her direction. It was brief, but long enough to make the hairs on her neck stand up.

Ash never gave more than a raised brow in reaction while

the man waved his hands and smacked the tabletop. After a few minutes, the guard near the stairs headed their way, but stopped when Ash gave a brief head shake.

No matter the volume of the man's voice, Ash's remained so low, she couldn't make out a word.

She turned her attention to the dance floor to find it empty. Intermission? Did strip clubs have those?

"What about her?" She turned to see Marcus charging in her direction, his face tight with irritation.

"She's not on the menu, Marcus." Ash moved to stand behind Ellie. His hands rested on her shoulders.

What menu exactly were they talking about?

"I'll make an offer." A fat tongue darted out of his mouth and licked his red lips.

"Not on the menu. You have been put on the list for two nights from now. I suggest you wait until then to make your offer." Ash's thumb brushed along her neck. The touch eased her, letting her know the man blustering before her wasn't a threat to her.

Marcus's stare left a dirty sensation over her skin as he took her in, still licking his fat lips. "Fine. Two days." He winked at her and turned to leave. "If she's there, she's mine." He jerked a thumb in her direction before shoving the guard out of the way and descending the stairs.

Once they were alone again, Ash retook his seat and grabbed his glass of wine, gulping it in one swallow.

"What did he mean, two nights from now? What happens then?"

Ash regarded her for a moment, a shadow cascading over his features. "Nothing." He poured another glass of wine.

"Does it have something to do with the wing of the house Peter wouldn't let me see?" She sipped wine. The red blend warmed her as she drank more.

Ash took the glass from her when she'd drained it.

"Are you having some sort of party over there or something?" She tried to sound only mildly curious and didn't argue about him taking her wine glass. Giving him a reason to deny her answers wouldn't be the way to go.

"You aren't allowed in that wing." His eyes narrowed. "Let me be clear about this, Ellie. If you even turn the knob, I'll show you what those rings on my wall are for."

She swallowed, her throat constricting under his intense glare.

"I was only asking. Don't worry." She gave him her back while she feigned interest in the girls entering the stage.

His hands dug into her hair, plucking and pulling out the pins holding up her braid. She tried to stop him, but he smacked her hands away and went about undoing her updo and running his fingers through the strands until they all cascaded around her shoulders.

"Better." He tossed the pins onto the table. Ellie brushed her hair over her shoulder. The tension she'd witnessed in his jaw after Marcus left eased, and she wondered if Ash ever knew a moment where he didn't have complete control over his world.

She stood and moved a few paces away, leaning against the railing and observing the crowd below. The men below didn't shout out catcalls or whistles like she expected.

"If they can't behave like gentlemen and respect the women, they aren't allowed in," Ash stated from behind her as if he had read her mind. His body trapped her against the railing, one hand on either side of her.

She didn't understand this man. One moment he acted every bit the Neanderthal, promising her a punishment for not obeying him. The next, he demanded respect for the women of his club, to the point of not allowing patrons in if they couldn't give it.

Taking a deep breath, she took a chance he would be agreeable with her wishes. "I'd like to call my father. To let him know I'm okay." She found strength in not being able to see his face while she made her request.

"No." The answer came hard and with no further explanation.

When she tried to protest, she felt his hand on her leg, lifting the hem of her dress.

"Bend over a little, Ellie," he whispered in her ear.

She glanced over, but the guard had suddenly made himself scarce. Had Ash dismissed him so he could play with her?

A new song carried over the speakers, louder and with a quick tempo. The wicked beat of the music sank into her, giving her a sense of danger.

Ash's hand splayed out over her exposed ass. The thong she wore didn't cover much of her body from him, and she doubted would be able to keep him from what he wanted.

"Be a good girl for me." He swept her hair from her neck and kissed her, licking the sensitive flesh and nibbling. So many sensations, all at once.

A woman danced on the stage in next-to-no clothing. Her hips gyrated, her breasts swayed, and she was the most graceful thing Ellie had witnessed all night.

Ellie leaned forward, the railing biting into her stomach. If not for the heels she wore, she wouldn't have been able to take the position he wanted.

His hand left her ass and appeared in front of her mouth. "Lick my fingers, Ellie," he commanded, shoving his middle digit into her mouth before she could think to disobey.

Salty and thick, his finger moved in and out of her mouth, over her tongue, before he drew it out. She didn't have a chance to wonder what he was going to do next, because he was already doing it.

He pulled her ass cheek to the side, exposing her tight ring. His finger, moistened by her mouth, nudged against the muscle.

"No." She tried to stand up, but he was too strong, too large for her to buck against and win.

"I know you aren't telling me no." He pushed against her asshole. "Focus on the show, Ellie. Watch her tits as they bounce with her moves. See how her ass sways with the music."

Ellie couldn't take her eyes off the beauty of the woman dancing. The men were mesmerized. The few ladies in the crowd beheld the dancer with the same curiosity Ellie felt.

Ash penetrated her ring, just the tip of his finger, but she sucked in her breath at the burn of his intrusion. She gripped the banister with more fever.

"That's good, Ellie. Good. Girl." He thrust in and out, slowly, to the beat of the music. "Do you feel the stretch? How much your ass wants me inside?"

"No. I—oh." She rolled her head to the side, bumping his and sighing. Her body accommodated him, as though it recognized him as her complete owner. And from the way he worked her, the ease with which he seemed to break apart her guard, it would seem he was.

His finger pushed farther in, and the burn quickly gave way to pleasure. He continued to kiss her neck, nibble on her earlobe.

"You'll come for me like this. Right here." His command was impossible. But he quickened his thrusts, went deeper.

"Keep your hands on the banister, and watch the girls dance." He swept his free hand under her dress. Anyone gazing up at them, would see everything. They would see her lace thong being ignored and his fingers touching all her intimate areas.

He rubbed her clit through the fabric and bit her shoulder. The pain mingled perfectly with the pleasure in her clit. Another hard thrust of his finger in her ass had her moaning.

"That's it. Relax. Come for me. Give me what I want."

The coarseness of his beard ran along her shoulder while he spoke into her ear.

He bit her neck while rubbing her clit, and drove his entire finger into her ass. Too much to control, her body released beneath his command. She gripped the banister, trying to hold herself up as her knees gave way. Her mouth fell slack, and she cried out with the intensity of her orgasm, but the music swept the sound away.

Only after she had lost the energy to keep standing did he retreat from her ass and help right her dress.

He returned her to the table, filled her wine glass once more, and handed it to her.

"I'll have the car brought out front," he said softly.

"We're going home?" she asked, averting his gaze. Until she'd met him, she'd only had sex with a handful of men. And all of those experiences had been private and under the covers. Twice now, Ash had brought her to orgasm, and neither time did she have the comfort of a blanket covering her, and not once did she care about that while it occurred.

"Yes. Since my fingers have been inside every hole, I think it's time my cock did the same." He walked away before she could react.

She watched him go to the stairs and beckon someone. She couldn't quite make herself drink the last of her wine.

They'd been talking about the forbidden wing. How had she gotten to this point? Having her ass finger fucked in public, and now she was to go home with him and let him fuck her in his bed?

If he was trying to make a point as to what her position in his household was, he was doing a fine job.

She downed the wine, quickly refilled the glass, and

gulped the contents before he returned to the table and took the bottle from her.

If she was going to be served up to the beast, she would need all the courage she could find. Liquid or otherwise.

CHAPTER 8

Ellie could not have given him a more perfect evening. Short as it was, she'd shown him how responsive she was to his touch. Finger fucking her in the club hadn't been his original plan.

Originally, he'd wanted to spend the evening just letting her enjoy the dancers and gauging her reaction to it all while he let a bottle of good wine soothe his muscles. But then she'd started asking questions, probing into the purpose of the annex, and he needed to distract her.

Given the fact she lived with him, she'd eventually have questions. He didn't think she would never wonder about the wing she was forbidden to enter, but he would keep her from it for as long as he could—if forever was possible he'd do it.

Taking Ellie as payment for her father's debt should have been easy—if he'd done exactly as Peter suggested the first night, turned around and unloaded her on someone else for a tidy profit. Earned back what her father had borrowed and rid himself of the problem. But he hadn't, and he wouldn't.

He just needed to figure out what the fuck to do with her. And why the hell he couldn't seem to get her off his fucking mind. Thinking of her distracted him, and with a man like Komisky starting to cause trouble, he needed to remain focused. Too much remained at stake.

The car pulled up to the front steps, and Ash took the moment to focus on Ellie. She'd been quiet and reserved on the drive home from the club. Did the idea of fucking him repulse her or terrify her?

Didn't matter. The end result would be the same. He'd been kind enough letting it go this long before claiming her. And he didn't misjudge the situation—fucking her would make her completely his. It would wipe away any ideas of her working in the annex, or at any of his clubs. She would be his until he tired of her, and then he'd figure out what to do with her.

He helped her from the car, enjoying how the soft evening breeze blew her hair from her face, showcasing the light blush of her cheeks. She'd come hard at the club, but the flush wasn't from her orgasm. No. The knowledge she'd found the release while his finger was fucking her ass, and with a packed club beneath the balcony—that made his girl crimson.

As they climbed the steps to the door, he could feel her body tense. Each step brought them closer to his bedroom and one inch closer to having her naked, writhing beneath him with his cock buried inside her. His dick twitched at the very idea of it.

Daniel, one of his men, greeted them in the foyer.

"Sir, there's a matter needing your attention." He glanced over at Ellie before continuing. "In your office."

"I'll be right there." Ash waited until her large, unreadable eyes focused on him. "Go up to my room and wait for me, Ellie."

She pulled her hand free, as though she'd just been given a

reprieve from the electric chair. "You're busy, and it's late. I'll just head to bed."

He let her get halfway up the staircase before calling her name. It almost pained him to wipe the hope from her expression, but not enough to actually stop himself.

"Ellie. What did I say?"

"You're busy." She eyed Daniel, who remained at his side. Daniel wouldn't leave until he'd been dismissed, and if Ash were a gentleman he'd excuse him from the conversation. But, as she'd already mentioned, he was anything but.

"Repeat what I told you to do." He hardened his voice and firmed his jaw. No one in his employ or under his command told him no, and they sure as fuck didn't change his dictates because they thought better.

The blush faded from her cheeks, and her fingers tightened on the handrail.

"You said to go up to your room and wait for you." If he hadn't been watching her lips move while she spoke, he probably wouldn't have understood her, she spoke so softly.

"Which means you're going to do what?" He slipped his hands into his pockets. He could stand there all night until she got it through her head she no longer owned her movements. She would go where he said, when he said, and how he said. No fucking questions or comments required.

She swept her gaze over to Daniel once more, her jaw tightening. Daniel wasn't going anywhere. She could feel as embarrassed or as stubborn as she wanted, Ash would keep control of this moment.

"I'll go to your room." Her eyes locked on his own when she gritted out the response. The little-lost-lamb look from a few moments ago was replaced by a fierce lioness. She wasn't accustomed to being told what to do.

She'd get used to it.

Or, she'd have a very sorry ass.

"And do you remember the rule about being in my room? Or do you need me to remind you?" He could've just let her walk up the stairs, but the temptation to savor the sweet moment won over.

Her lids narrowed, but the blush returned. He loved the light-pink hue to her cheeks when she wasn't quite embarrassed, but wasn't full of indignation, either. Just the right mixture of humility and anger.

Fuck. She was delicious.

"I remember." She turned and rushed up the stairs. The little dress he'd given her to wear for the club exposed her back, and he admired every muscle as she made her way up the long staircase. Tensing and relaxing. Carrying herself as regal as any queen, she didn't hesitate at the top of the stairs. She simply turned the corner and was gone.

Daniel had an odd expression when Ash finally faced him. Grinning. Clearing his throat, Ash put his mind to the task at hand.

There was a problem. And it was in his office.

"Which one?" he asked and stalked toward the office he kept in the main house.

"Amber. Komisky's commission." Daniel kept up in stride. "She's freaking out because he contacted her on her cell."

Ash's jaw tightened, along with his fists.

"He shouldn't even have her fucking number. Did she give it to him?"

"She said no."

Ash nodded and pushed through his office door.

Amber, a short, thin woman paced the floor, wringing her hands. Her long blonde hair, usually braided and pinned up, hung loose and wild around her shoulders.

"Amber." Ash shut the door, leaving Daniel on the other side. He didn't need to scare her further by having an audience.

"Ash. He texted me, and when I didn't answer, he called." She yanked her phone from his desk and thrust it at him.

Keeping his gaze steady on her, he took the phone. "You need to calm down. You know you're safe here."

Ash flipped through the brief messages from Komisky. Nothing threatening, but not words of devotion, either.

"What did he say when he called?"

"I didn't talk to him. I let it go to voice mail." She folded one arm over her midsection while shoving her other hand into her mouth and biting her nails. A nasty habit, but one he couldn't break her of, no matter the consequences.

He went to the voice mail program, and put the phone to his ear while removing her fingers from her mouth and shaking his head.

"Sorry," she said softly and sat on the couch, tucking her hands between her knees.

Just answer the phone, babygirl. I know if you'd let me explain my conditions it would be fine. You wouldn't be so stubborn.

"How did he get your number?" Ash turned the phone over to her.

"I don't know." She cast her eyes down. He sighed.

"You aren't allowed to give your number out—you know this."

"I know, Ash. I didn't. Not really." She went back to biting her nail.

"How did you not really give him your number?" Ash folded his arms over his chest. He needed to finish this so he could get upstairs. Ellie would be in his room by now, naked and waiting. Daniel could have handled this little mess for the night and told him about it in the morning. His presence wasn't necessary.

"He's opening a restaurant. On the other side of town, by the river. He said they're hiring for waitresses and stuff. Told me I should apply."

Ash took a deep breath.

"He brought you an application, or did you go down there?"

"He brought it to me."

Ash shook his head. Komisky owned three restaurants along the river, and as far as Ash knew, a fourth wasn't in the works. And Ash made it his business to know what men like Komisky were up to at all times.

A lesson from his father he heeded with loyalty.

"You realize your error."

She nodded and swiped a tear from her cheek. "There's no restaurant. He just wanted my information."

"This is why we have rules, Amber. This is why Peter is to know any time you're asked for your contact information."

"I thought he really wanted to hire me at his restaurant."

"Do you want to waitress? Is that what you're looking for? You know you're free to work and live wherever you want. You don't need to remain in my employ." Ash went to his desk, giving the girl some space.

"It's not that I don't want to work for you, it's just he…he promised a lot of money with the tips and such, and I figured I could still work the parties. But that was before he offered those terms. It's not that I think he's wrong to want that sort of play, but I just can't."

Ash let silence spread between them. He wouldn't push her or anyone to stay in his ranks. He wasn't his father; he didn't rule with fear.

"Amber, I will keep Marcus from reaching out to you again. You won't be working the party tomorrow night."

She shot up from the couch, her mouth open, ready to argue.

"You aren't sure what you want exactly, and until you do, you're pulled. In the morning, you'll meet with Peter to discuss breaking the confidentiality rule and receive your new offer. If you chose not to take the offer, the usual unemployment benefit will be given."

"Ash. No. I didn't want that. I don't want to leave the Annex."

"You aren't sure, though. The promise of a waitressing job had you breaking our rules. Rules there to protect you, keep you hidden from men like Marcus who will just take what he wants when given the opportunity."

"I am sure. I promise." She nodded, her eyes filling with tears.

"Speak with Peter in the morning. See what the offer is."

"I came to you for help, not to be thrown out." Anger shook her voice. She was scared, he knew, but he wasn't about to have her raising her tone to him. He already had one unruly woman in his house who felt she could defy him at will.

"You aren't being thrown out. You'll speak with Peter, you'll take what he gives you, and you can decide your future then."

"You're not being fair," she whined when he reached the door.

"I never promised fair." He left her to stew.

"That didn't really require me. You could have gotten Peter to handle it." Ash glared at Daniel.

"Yes, but Peter has been out all night as well, and she wouldn't stop pestering."

"If you can't control little situations like this, I'm not sure you should be in charge when Peter's not around." Ash didn't wait for a response. "Take her back and tell Peter to see me in the morning before he meets with her."

"Yes, sir. Of course." Daniel didn't follow him down the hall.

When Ash got to his room, he paused a moment. Amber

had irritated him, but he wouldn't carry it into the room with Ellie.

Ellie would be able to irritate him all on her own. She didn't need the residual effect of a staff member to help her.

He wondered if she was sitting on the bed, maybe lying beneath his covers, having caught a chill from waiting for him. Maybe she would be even more intuitive than he could hope for, and she knelt beside the bed, her head bowed, her hands resting on her spread knees, waiting to service him.

The image of her auburn hair covering her face, her breasts peeking out of the strands, and her pussy on display with her open knees thickened his cock.

Pushing the door open, he set his jaw and readied himself for what he found.

An empty room.

Damn her.

He let loose a low growl and marched toward her room. His bathroom door opened just as he palmed the knob, and there she stood. Completely naked, beautiful curves for him to see, a bright-eyed, freshly washed face staring at him from the bathroom doorway.

Something similar to relief coursed through him. She had obeyed. Ellie hadn't gone to hide in her bedroom.

Ash stepped to the bed, keeping his eyes on her while he moved, willing her to make her way to him. But she remained planted in the doorway. Her hair, he noticed, hung loose around her shoulders, but it didn't cover her breasts. Such beautiful long auburn hair. He wanted to run his fingers through it, brush it, and tug on it. All before he wrapped it around his fist.

"Come here, Ellie." He crooked his finger at her.

She opened and closed her hands, but he didn't have to tell her a second time. Taking shaky steps, she approached him at the foot of the bed. The scent of his soap from the bathroom hung between them. What little makeup she'd put on for their night at the club had been removed.

She didn't need the fucking paint anyway.

"I'm not pleased you tried to use the presence of one of my men to get your way." He couldn't blame her for trying, though. She was a resilient, resourceful woman. It would be disappointing if she didn't use what tools she had before her to get what she wanted.

"Are you going to spank me again?" If her tone had been cheeky, he could have laughed the presumptuous question away. But apprehension and desire entwined her words.

Ash brushed away her hair from her shoulders, placing all of it behind her and exposing her voluptuous body.

"I should." He nodded. "I should take my belt to your ass and remind you of your place." His eyes flicked to hers. "But I won't fault you for trying. This time." He trailed his fingertips along her collarbone, feeling the warmth of her skin and delighting in the little goose pimples rising in his wake.

"I am going to show you how to wait for me properly." He removed his hand and stepped away from her. "Get on your knees, Ellie."

She swallowed what would have most likely been a smart-ass retort and licked her lips. It didn't take her long to decide it was probably in her best interest to obey him and slide to her knees. She sat her ass on her heels and bent her head back to keep looking up at him.

Fuck. No woman existed anywhere as beautiful and vulnerable as her in that moment. His dick ached to be inside her.

"Good, now spread your knees." He wiggled his booted foot between them. "Shoulder-width apart. I want to see your pussy when you're kneeling for me."

She huffed but didn't resist him as he went about positioning her. Squatting, he grabbed one arm then the next, placing her hands on her knees. "If I've instructed you to wait for me in my room, this is how I expect to find you. Legs open, palms down, and head bowed."

"Like some toy waiting to be played with?" she asked with more bark than bite. He could smell her arousal already, and if he touched her pussy, he had no doubt he'd find her wet for him.

"Not exactly. But I suppose that's what it seems like." He patted her head and stood.

He left her kneeling at the foot of his bed and went about undressing. Her gaze burned him as he moved around the room, removing his shirt, his boots, his jeans. Her breathing picked up, too, but he doubted she even realized it.

Stripped to his boxers, he returned to her and lifted her chin. "Very good." He smiled at her and found the hard edge of her stare softening with his approval.

Fuck. If she understood her own reactions, she'd be pissed as hell. The thought made him chuckle.

"Get up on the bed." He watched her scramble up to her feet and take the few steps to the bed. "Lie down, Ellie." He sighed. Like a lamb waiting to be slaughtered, she eyed him. "I'm not going to eat you," he promised, immediately knowing he would in fact devour the delicious woman lying on his bed.

He climbed up to lie beside her. His cock pressed against her hip, no way around her feeling it, and he didn't give a shit if she felt it anyway.

"Close your eyes," he said, waiting until she obeyed before continuing.

He ran his fingers over her skin, such soft, smooth skin. No tan tinted her creamy coloring. Her nipples stood erect for him, and he hadn't even touched them yet.

Oh, she had no idea how her reactions pleased him.

Leaning over her, he took one nipple into his mouth,

flicking his tongue over the peak. He held back his growl of pleasure at her moan.

"Arms at your sides, stay out of my way," he ordered when one hand moved to rest on her stomach.

He moved his attentions to her other breast, and did groan when her pleasure-filled moan reached his ears. He ran his tongue through the valley of her breasts, down her trembling stomach, until he reached the small patch of auburn hair.

Ash brought one leg toward him, giving him better access to the pussy before him. He checked to be sure her eyes were still closed, and grinned at her when he found her staring at him.

"Such a naughty girl. I said to keep your eyes closed."

CHAPTER 9

*E*llie sucked in a breath with his words. She had been naughty. He'd ordered her to keep her eyes closed, but when his tongue reached her mons, she couldn't anymore. She needed to see him.

His devious glare didn't do much in the way of comforting her at the moment. When he pulled her legs farther apart, she had to forcibly tell herself not to arch her damn hips at him.

The tickle of his beard mingled with the warm wetness of his tongue awoke her need for him.

"What should I do with you?" His lips spread into a calculating grin. He moved onto the bed, kneeling between her legs and peering up the length of her.

His gaze wandered over her, scathing her skin as he made his way up to her breasts and back down to her wanting sex. She could easily make out his erection pressing against the black cotton of his boxers. Her tongue ran along her lip while thinking about the long, thick cock she'd seen the morning before when he changed his clothes in front of her.

Her hunger matched his.

"I didn't mean to peek." Argh, she sounded pathetic. She tried to clear her throat, to wiggle out from beneath his stare. It took only his hand flattening on her thigh for her to completely still.

"That doesn't really change the fact you did."

His fingers curled into her flesh. She winced, and a small sound escaped her.

"Fuck. Yes," he said in a low growl. He closed his eyes and dug his nails harder into her thigh. When she gasped with the pain, he released her, opening his eyes to showcase his aroused state. It wasn't just his cock ready for her; his entire body emitted sexuality.

He moved from her thigh, leaving little crescent moon marks behind.

It shouldn't excite her, the small bite of pain he introduced to her. She should shove him away with her feet and run for her room. Instead, she lay beneath him as his hand covered her pussy.

"I think I know how to teach you." He spread her lips wide, exposing her clit. Sliding to his belly, he lowered his head and sucked her swollen nub between his teeth.

"Ah!" She started to sit, but his arms wrapped around her pelvis kept her from getting away.

He bit down, scraping his teeth against the oversensitive part.

"Ash!" she cried out, arching her hips up at him. His hot tongue lashed at her before he dragged his teeth along her again.

She gripped the quilt in her fists and threw her head back. The pain blended with the pressure building in her belly. She wouldn't last much longer. She was going to explode again.

Leaving her at the cusp of another orgasm, he pulled away, licking his lips and grinning at her again.

"Oh, not yet, Ellie. You won't get another one until you've learned who controls this body."

He unraveled one arm from her waist and thrust two fingers into her aching passage.

She sucked in her breath, not wanting to give him the reaction he seemed to want. He could wait for it. Except, he knew her body. He could read her in an unacceptable manner. When he curled his fingers, she groaned and felt the edge of heaven barreling down on her again.

"Uh, uh." He raised his eyebrows, the damn smile still lingering on his lips. He stopped stroking and just stared at her.

"Ash. Please." She moved up on her elbows. He still had her pinned, so she couldn't get away from him.

"Oh, begging. I like begging." He winked and curled his fingers again.

"Fuck. Yes. Like that." She nodded, tossing her head back and gritting her teeth. If he would just keep it up, the pressure on the exact spot, she'd be done for.

A third digit joined in, but he stopped moving.

"Fuck my fingers," he ordered.

She darted her gaze to his. He had to be kidding. If she was going to fuck anything, it was going to be his cock. How she wanted his thick cock inside her.

"Go on. Show me how you'll fuck my cock." He readjusted his position, letting go of her waist.

She glimpsed at her body, where he stroked her with such demanding heat. Small movements at first, but she began to wiggle, until her body obeyed his command.

He never took his eyes off of his fingers disappearing into her pussy and reappearing.

She'd never witnessed the act before. Even on nights when she took matters into her own hands, she never watched herself. Just seeing him lick his lips, seeing his nostrils flare with lust made her pussy wetter and hungrier for him. For his cock, not his damn fingers.

She'd had enough of the inferior substitution.

"Good. So fucking good." He removed them and locked eyes with her while he sucked the juices from his digits.

She swallowed.

"Ash, please." She gave a pointed look at the straight-edge tent of his boxers.

He laughed, obviously not ready to give her what she wanted. Grabbing her hand, he brought her toward him, pushing her palm against his hardness.

Warm and so thick. She wrapped her hand around his shaft, gauging his reactions to see if she went too far. If she overstepped, he might pull away, not give her what she needed.

He closed his eyes with a growl when she began to stroke him through his boxers.

"Fuck, woman." He yanked her hand away and shoved off his boxers. She bit her lower lip and made to grab him again, but he brushed her off. "Back. Get on your fucking back," he demanded, and shoved her shoulders until she fell flat to the mattress.

In a swift movement, he was on top of her, his cock pressed against her entrance.

"I'm going to fuck you senseless, Ellie. And you are going to be a good girl and take it."

"Yes, Ash. Yes." She touched his shoulders. The head of his cock eased into her pussy, stretching and filling her as he slipped into her. She tried to arch up, to take him in faster, but he chuckled and stilled.

"Still don't understand, do you?" he said, pinning her hands over her head. "It's okay. I love teaching you." With a pained expression, he gingerly pushed into her cunt.

Nowhere near the amount of force she expected or wanted from him.

She moaned and bent her knees, pulling them up toward her chest.

He rolled his head back. "Fuck. Ellie." His control slipped, and he thrust hard into her, until his balls slapped her ass.

She gasped at the sudden fullness.

Her wrists ached beneath the pressure of his grip, but it could not compare to the ache in her cunt when he stopped moving again.

"Ash," she groaned. She wanted to fight him, to scratch and kick at him. How could he get her body to respond to him so fucking easily and with such wanton lust, and not help her through it.

"There's my girl." He bent and kissed her. A fierce, possessive kiss. He nipped at her lip until she opened for him. His tongue swept in just as he pulled back and thrust his cock into her again.

It went on like this. A nip, a kiss, a nuzzle, and a thrust. Over and over again until her mind felt likely to unravel with desire.

"Ash, please."

"Please, what, Ellie?"

If she had to say it, she might break from the embarrassment. She wasn't supposed to be enjoying his torture, his fucking. Her plan to be tolerant of his touch had fallen out the window the moment his eyes landed on her when she stepped out of the bathroom.

He'd seemed relieved, almost happy to see her.

Damn him. He confused her.

"Ash, please," she repeated her plea. She searched his expression for a crack in his resolve, revealing a spark of kindness.

"Ask me, ask me and I'll decide." He pulled almost

completely out of her and remained there. Just the round head of his cock remained seated in her. The emptiness grew to unbearable heights.

"Please, Ash. Will you please fuck me? Hard?" Approval spread across his eyes.

His hair fell over his face, brushing her cheeks, and his nose pressed against hers.

"Say pretty please." His low voice came at her in a growl.

Moving slightly forward, she moaned again. She needed him, needed to feel every inch of him.

His silvery-blue eyes pierced her. She'd never win this battle, and she wanted the spoils more than the victory.

"Pretty please," she whispered. "Sir," she added.

Ash kissed her hard, pressing her lips into her teeth and sucking the breath from her before coming up for air.

"Fuck, Ellie. Come hard for me, baby. Come hard." He released her hands and gripped her hips, taking away any gentleness he'd bestowed upon her.

The bed creaked, their moans mingled, and the sounds of his body slapping against hers filled the room. She drew her legs up, flanking his sides while he plowed into her.

"Fuck. Fuck. Fuck," she chanted as his body slammed into hers.

"Come, Ellie. Be a good girl and come." He reached between them, brushing her clit lightly then pinching it.

"Oh Fuck! Ash!" she screamed, her release tensing every fiber of her body. Waves of pleasure smashed inside her while he continued to fuck her hard.

"That's it. Come for me, my girl." Two hard strokes, and he stilled.

As her orgasm ebbed slowly, the throbbing of his cock replaced the waves of pleasure. His heavy breaths washed over her face as he took a moment to compose himself.

He kissed the tip of her nose then slid out of her body, her pussy already missing and wanting him to come back to her. Rolling to her side, he snaked his arm beneath her and pulled her to his chest.

His cum leaked from her body, smearing across her thighs, but she made no move to get up to clean herself, finding comfort in the deep movements of his chest as he breathed.

After several long moments passed, he patted her shoulder and gestured for her to get up.

"Off to bed, Ellie." He threw his legs over the side of the bed and snatched his boxers.

She sat up, covering her breasts with her arm, and frowned as he pulled up the briefs. He tucked his hair behind his ears and raised his eyebrows, as though questioning her.

"Bed, Ellie," he said, jerking a thumb at the adjoining door.

He was kicking her out of his room? After he'd just fucked her three ways from Sunday?

If he was hoping for a reaction, a fight, he could just hold his damn breath. She would be damned if she gave him one ounce of emotion. It was a fuck. Nothing else.

She'd just given herself to the man who wanted her father dead. Sure, she was fulfilling her part of the deal. Her life for his. Her body for her father's. But she wasn't supposed to fucking enjoy it. She shouldn't have come so damn hard. Seeing stars, barely able to breathe, wanting it never to end. She'd acted like a fucking whore.

As she gathered up the clothes she'd left piled on the ottoman and padded to her room, she realized exactly what her place was.

She was a whore. His whore.

CHAPTER 10

*A*sh found Ellie standing at the front door, arguing with Daniel. He hadn't been looking for her; he was just walking through the house, trying to find a moment of peace.

The morning meetings with staff and financial advisors left him with a dull ache behind his eyes. Numbers had never been his friends, and staring at ledgers and balance sheets for over an hour only reminded him of that fact. Maybe if he hadn't ditched out on all the math classes in high school, he may not emerge from those meetings ready to drive an ice pick through his eye.

"I'm sorry, but you can't go anywhere unless you have permission from Ash, and he hasn't given it." Daniel held his hands out, warding her off from the front door.

As Ellie dodged around him for the doorknob, the few books she held in her arms slipped out of her grasp.

"I know, but I don't know where your lord and master is, and since I can't go into the secret building, I can't find him," she argued, bending to get the spilled books.

Ash stopped a few steps behind her, enjoying the view of

her muscular legs and ass when she bent to gather her things. He'd had most of her things brought from her apartment, but when he observed the condition of her clothing up close, irritation bloomed.

Fashion didn't mean a damn thing to him. Which worked well, considering the majority of those in his employ worked with their clothes off. But he knew outdated and over-worn fabric when he saw it. The flimsy romper she wore with her brown strappy sandals reminded him of something dusted off in a bargain bin five years ago.

"Dammit. Don't you have a walkie-talkie or something? I just want to go to class, not escape. I'll come back." She threw her free hand in the air and juggled the books in her other arm to keep them from toppling again.

"Class?" Ash's curiosity was caught. Peter had told him she took at least one class a semester at the university on the other side of town, but he'd assumed she wouldn't continue after the change in her lifestyle.

Ellie's body tensed, both arms wrapped around her books. Did she think he would steal them from her?

When she turned around, he expected to see a bit of annoyance at being stopped at the door. What flashed before him was hurt. When her eyes met his, he could see it. It didn't last; she masked it immediately, but he witnessed it.

A pang struck his chest, but he shook it off.

"What class?" He pointed to the books in her hands. She could grip them as tightly as she wanted. They both knew if he wanted them—he would just take them.

She didn't answer him, but eased the books away from her chest to show him the cover of one.

"*Italian Baroque Art. Edition one*," he read out loud. "This is what you're studying? Art?" He gave Daniel a subtle nod to dismiss him, and folded his arms. She seemed to give him straight answers when he towered.

"This semester, yes." She pressed the books close to her chest.

For a brief moment, his mind flashed the image of her lying on her back on his bed, her arms pulled over her head and her tits pressing against his chest while he thrust into her. Just a brief moment of weakness before he shoved the memory away, but it was enough wake his cock.

"Do you have a declared major, or are you just winging it?" He'd never gone to college; his father dunked him right into the business after high school. Completely against his mother's wishes, but her opinion rarely counted when it came to Ash's upbringing. He supposed he was lucky his father let him graduate high school before bringing him to his first business meeting.

"Art is my major. Well, it's not really a major. I mean it is, but the degree doesn't really mean anything. When my father retires, I'll take over—" Her words dropped heavy between them, and she averted his gaze. "I would have taken over the coffee shop," she added.

Sidestepping the blatant land mine, he observed, "One class a semester will take you almost a lifetime to finish."

She picked at the edge of the book, still not looking at him.

"Yeah, well, classes are expensive, and tips only get you so far, and most of what I had saved up went—" She shook her head, as though she just remembered his position. "To people like you. Are you going to let me go to class, or am I truly a prisoner here?"

He moved to put himself between her and the exit, bending his knee and resting his foot against the door.

"What if I need you while you're gone?" he asked with a smile. Her attention darted to him at his question, and her cheeks heated. Good. The fire was still there.

"I think you have plenty of girls at your clubs who can see to whatever you need for the two hours I'm away."

Completely true, but he didn't want any of them. Not like he wanted her at that moment. The romper clung a little too tightly to her breasts. Other men would see it, and he hated them for it.

He could let her stew, but something in the way she glanced at him before returning to her books made him change his mind.

"You'll have to miss class today. I don't have a driver for you right now. Get your class schedule to Peter, and he'll make sure to have someone ready for you."

Her eyes lit up, and a gentle smile tugged the corners of her rosy lips upward. "Oh. I don't need a driver. I'll get a cab, or the bus. I can take the bus."

"No," he said and pushed off the door.

"But—"

"I said no, Ellie. Would you rather I said no to school altogether?" He didn't wait for her answer, but instead walked toward the main hallway.

She hadn't moved from the spot he'd found her.

"Come here, Ellie." He beckoned her with a crook of his finger. The exasperation in her expression stiffened his cock to the brink of pain. One eye roll and he'd have no choice but to throw her ass over his knee for a solid spanking and a harder fucking.

He led her down the hallway way to his office. The place he had put his eyes on her the first time. The spot his fingers had penetrated her sweet pussy.

Once inside the room, he took the books from her and put them on his desk. She stood at the door, staring at him, quietly demanding to know what he wanted.

He wanted her. Naked and on her knees.

"I wanted to show you the artwork in here. I keep most of

it in this office and some is in the dining room." He pointed to the oil paintings on the walls.

Her gaze flittered over to the framed pieces, and she moved closer to one in particular. His favorite of the collection.

A scene depicting Samson and Delilah.

Tension eased away from her body as she took in the brushstrokes and the darkened coloring. Her lips softened, and her gaze wandered over the scene. She lightly touched the frame but didn't go near the canvas. Oils from her skin could damage the piece, a fact she would already know.

"This is beautiful. Samson and Delilah, right? Just like your clubs?" She continued her inspection of the piece.

After moving on to appreciate the other paintings on the same wall, depicting similar scenes, she pointed to the name scribbled on the bottom. "These are all by Janet Debouis? Do you know her?" She glanced over her shoulder at him.

"She was my mother." He clenched his fists and released. Willing his body to ease off the tension. The throbbing the accountants started would blast into a migraine if he didn't get control of himself.

"Your mother?" She read the name again.

"My father never married her," he qualified for her. His father never did many things he should have, but not marrying his mother had been probably the most generous things he did for her.

"Oh."

Most reactions he'd received upon sharing that bit of his history usually held more weight. She just brushed it off like he'd told her he had cereal for breakfast.

"She's very talented. These are stunning." She tilted her head, admiring the work.

"Yes, she was." He emphasized the past tense, eliciting a glance from her. "She passed away five years ago." Two years before his father had had the decency to keel over and give her the freedom she never had with him. Freedom to live her own life without his cruelty and disregard.

Sort of like the disregard he'd showed Ellie the night before when he tossed her from his room, but he wouldn't think about those actions. This situation didn't compare to his mother's. His mother hadn't offered herself to his father. She'd been forced, and continually forced throughout her life. Ellie had made her choice on her own.

Ellie's expression softened. She didn't pity him. She had lost her mother years, ago, too, from what Peter told him. Understanding. For a brief moment, maybe she understood him.

She couldn't, of course. He'd been an adult when his mother died. So, if she thought his mother's death helped to make him the man standing in his office, she had it all wrong.

"The paintings in your club last night, were those painted by her as well?" she asked facing him again.

"Most of them. Others were purchased. Samson and Delilah was one of her favorite stories." He hadn't told anyone that little fact, ever. Shifting his weight to the other foot, he cleared his throat. "Anyway. I just thought you'd enjoy them. There are others throughout the house."

"And in the secret wing?" she asked, perching herself on the arm of the love seat, far enough away from him he couldn't reach out and touch her, but close enough he could smell the apricot conditioner she'd used.

"You heard what happened to the cat with all that curiosity, right?" He pushed away from the desk.

"You have something hidden in there, something horrible and terrifying." She cocked her head to her right and smiled. "Or, do you run a children's hospital from the wing and don't want anyone to know what a Good Samaritan you are?"

Ash picked up a file folder from his desk and opened it, needing to keep his eyes off her. She was being cute. And she looked sexy as hell when she acted cute. And if he kept watching her be cute, he'd bend her over and make her show him how fucking sexy she really was.

"Get your schedule to Peter so you don't miss any more classes. And the next time you're on campus, get yourself registered for a few more. You'll have the funds now to actually finish your degree."

"Oh?" She straightened, her body stiffening before him. "You'll just add it to my tab?" He could do without her damn snark when he was trying to do something decent. He could understand her suspicion. Being kind didn't exactly sit easily with him, either, but she could be graceful enough to hide her distaste for him.

"Exactly how much is my tab, anyway?" She advanced, stalking his desk, her eyes narrowed and her hands fisted. "After last night? How much did that little roll in your sheets deduct from the two hundred and fifty thousand?"

He ground his teeth, tossing the file folder onto the desk and leaning back in his chair. Fine. She wanted to be mad. She wanted to get herself all worked up. He could play the game. He would oblige her. Why not?

"How much do you think it was worth?" he asked.

She frowned at him.

"Maybe we should put a menu together," he suggested, standing again and moving at her, coming to stand right beside her.

Her gaze focused forward, at the bookshelves behind his desk.

"What do you think?" He brushed her hair over her shoulder, exposing the sensitive bit of her neck. If he kissed her there, bit down a little, would she moan for him?

"A thousand," she announced spinning to meet his eyes.

Fire burned in her features. The rose was back in her cheeks, her pupils large and round.

He grunted. "For one short fuck? You think mighty highly of yourself." He would have paid ten times that much to relive the experience of thrusting his cock into her for the first time once more.

"Fine. Just tell me, then." Her shoulders slumped, triggering his irritation.

"Oh, well. Let's see." He ran this thumb over the vein in her neck pulsating with each beat of her heart. "There's a lot of things. A thousand for a decent fuck seems fair. A few hundred for a good face fuck. Another hundred or so for a session with some of those toys in my drawer. More for some of the really dirty shit I want to do to you."

He moved his caresses to her collarbone, trailing down to her breasts. Her chest expanded beneath his touch, but he wouldn't fool himself into thinking it was lust. At least not entirely.

"What do you mean? Dirty?"

Of all the questions, he didn't expect that one. Few people surprised him these days, yet Ellie seemed to find a way to do it every day.

"You want me to show you? Right now? In my office?"

She sighed. "It was just a question."

First, he needed to get her out of the damn romper. And have it burned.

A knock on his door grated on him. When it opened before he'd answered, he got pissed.

"I'm busy," he barked, ready to throw a fist in the face of whoever barged in on him.

Except it was Peter.

"Sorry." But he didn't appear sorry. He looked downright entertained. "One last thing to deal with for tomorrow night."

Parties made the Annex one of the most sought-after business opportunities. Without it, potential buyers would have to thumb through a catalogue. And the day before and day of the party were the busiest. He didn't always get deeply involved, leaving Peter to handle most of the work, but given Komisky's little fuckup, Ash would have to get his hands dirty for this one.

"Fine. I'll be there in a minute." He glared at his cousin until he laughed and left them alone.

"There's a party tomorrow? Here?" Ellie asked softly. Almost as if she had a good sense she wasn't invited, but hadn't really been expecting to be anyway. He wondered how many times she'd been overlooked for a party or a date because she worked harder to unbury her father from his debts.

"It's business. You don't have to go."

She crossed her arms over her chest, covering the beautiful swell he had just started getting ready to thrust himself into.

"I don't really have anything else to do. Maybe I could help with serving drinks or something?" She smiled, but the lightness did nothing to reach her eyes. She still stared him down with expectations and hurt. He could handle the first, but the second was new for him.

Even if he bothered to notice the emotion in one of his girls, it never weighed on him. An easy brush-off. But Ellie wasn't going anywhere. He'd already seen to that with his fucking plan to keep her. And now he'd given her a list of ways to pay off her father's fuckup, all of which shrank her to basically being his whore.

Well, wasn't that what he'd decided to make her when he agreed to her offer?

He raked his hands through his hair. He needed to get the hell away from her.

"No. You'll stay in your room tomorrow night. I don't want you even downstairs. You stay up there." He walked to the door and flung it open. "There's a laptop in my room, on the dresser. It's for you, I meant to give it to you this morning after breakfast. Stream a video or something for now."

Her hint of a smile dropped, as did her hands.

"I don't mean to be such a fucking bother, Ash." She snatched her books from the desk. "If you'd let me go to class today, I wouldn't be in your hair to begin with."

She marched past him, the scent of her body wash lingering in her wake.

He shouldn't let her talk to him like that. He should squash her attitude and be done with it, but all he could do was grin at the sway of her ass as she stalked off. Even pissed, she moved perfectly.

She could have the afternoon. But, after dinner, he'd go into her room and show her again who ruled her. And she'd start ticking off some of the items on their list.

Right after dinner.

CHAPTER 11

Ellie found a bench in the back of the gardens, well hidden behind a rosebush, where she could be alone but still see the comings and goings of the secret wing. She couldn't get anyone in the household to even hint at what went on behind the forbidden door. Though she could hardly be surprised. Everyone was Ash's employee, and surely to defy him would mean getting fired—or worse.

Yet, still she couldn't help but keep wondering what went on in there. The window blinds were closed, but she could make out shadows moving behind them on the upper floor and a small handful of times on the first floor.

She easily made out Ash's shadow and figured it was his room, since he remained in it for a long duration. No one had the physique he had. She could peg him from blocks away, with his broad shoulders, and strong back.

His strength should frighten her, and the fierceness of his scowl shouldn't make her hungry with need the way it did. But he didn't scare her, and when he pinned her with a glare, she wanted to touch him, to trace the lines in his forehead and wipe them away.

None of it made any sense to her. And things needed to make sense if she was going to find a way to repay what her father owed so she could return to her life. She had offered her life for her fathers, but the money was what Ash wanted. Once she could get hold of that, she could return to The Café, back to school, and back to the few friends she had in her life.

"You look awfully serious for a woman sitting in a rose garden on such a beautiful night." Peter's voice startled her, and she dropped the pencil she'd been holding over her pad of paper.

"You scared me." She picked up the pencil and frowned up at him.

Peter had a build similar to Ash's, just as hard everywhere, but he didn't quite meet Ash's height. Standing over her in the rose garden, though, he was just as menacing.

"I doubt many things scare you," he remarked. "What are you up to out here?" He leaned over her to peer at the pad of paper. She hadn't gotten much accomplished once she noticed all the movement in Ash's office, she'd been staring at the secret wing, contemplating all the evil things going on behind those windows.

"Just playing around." She snapped the pad shut and held it close to her chest.

"Hmm." Peter glanced over his shoulder at the house. "Good view here, I suppose."

Did every man in this damn place have the capability to read her thoughts?

"Did you want something?"

"No, not really." He shrugged. "The rest of your things were brought over, and I was wondering if we missed anything."

"Did you go to get my stuff? You were in my apartment?"

She quickly thought back to the state of the room before she'd left it last, but couldn't recall. Had she folded the last load of laundry, or were her panties and bras still strewn across her bed?

"I went with my men." He nodded. "Small place."

It was home, and damn him for commenting.

"Well, we can't all be loan sharks and thieves."

"No, some of us need to be the idiots who take loans from the sharks and thieves," he flung at her.

Her father was one of those idiots. She wouldn't deny it.

She toyed with the edges of her sketch pad. "Was my father there when you went?"

Peter stared at her with a blank expression for a long moment before he answered. "Yes."

"You didn't hurt him, did you?" She shot up from her seat. He father wouldn't have let them in to go through the apartment; in his stubbornness, he would have tried to stop them.

"No one got hurt," he assured her. "He's fine, Ellie. I promise you." If so much sympathy hadn't played on his features, she might have been able to just forget it.

"Did you talk with him? Is he really okay? Who's helping him with the café?"

Peter's eyebrows rose. "I didn't talk with him other than to assure him you were safe and wouldn't be harmed."

Harmed. No. Just whored out. She could feel the heat build on her face. Her father had witnessed Ash touch her the first night. He'd been forced to see the Ash fondle her in a way no father should have to see.

"Do yourself a favor. The faster you obey Ash, the faster you give over to him, the quicker he'll let you talk with your father, maybe even see him."

Ellie backed up a step. Give over? Submit to him?

"He's not the monster you think he is, but he is determined to have your obedience. Give him what he wants, and you'll be rewarded."

"Rewarded? Like some little girl who gets a gold star for doing well at school?" Everyone around her was insane.

"Fight him if you want. He'll win, either way." Peter glanced back at the house. "He never loses."

She didn't doubt that. Bullies rarely lost. Not because they were stronger, but because they were willing to do horrible things in order to get what they wanted. Even if it meant hurting someone else.

"What's in the wing? He called it the Annex. What is it?" She'd googled it with the laptop Ash gave her, but found nothing.

Peter frowned. "Like a dog with a bone, you are. Leave it be, Ellie."

Ellie was taking a breath, getting ready to ask more questions, when Ash stepped into the garden. And he wasn't alone.

A woman, nearly his own height, her body manufactured by Mattel strode at his side. Her long, flowing blonde hair covered her shoulders with perfect curls and highlights. Even from where Ellie stood she could see the shimmering lipstick on her full lips.

Ash's arm was linked with hers. His eyes searched the gardens and stilled when he found Ellie's. His stare tore the breath from her.

Peter followed her gaze and mumbled a curse.

Ash had smelled of lavender the night before. Had he been in the gardens with Barbie before coming up to fuck her?

"Stay right here, Ellie." Peter pointed to the bench she'd vacated and made his way over to Ash.

Ash's eyes narrowed in on Peter as he approached. He

couldn't be upset they had been talking. Not when he had that woman on his arm.

Ellie couldn't take her eyes off Ash as he spoke with Peter. If she did, she would take stock of the blonde. And doing so would only tighten her chest even more. The dull ache annoyed her enough as it was.

She reminded herself of her position. How could she have forgotten? Why did her mind continue to find some good in all this mess she was in. Ash wasn't her boyfriend, or even a friend. He was her owner. He owned her until she could repay him or worked off the money.

Ash and Peter finished their discussion, the blonde not giving Ellie a second of notice while hanging on Ash's arm. With one last glance at Ellie, Ash handed the blonde off to Peter. Together they strolled into the Annex.

Ellie stood in the rose garden, scrutinizing Ash. His hair hung loose around his shoulders again, and he'd replaced his suit with a casual button-down shirt and jeans.

On instinct, she took a small step back when he moved in her direction. Fire built in his glare as he approached her.

She hadn't done anything wrong. Why should she shrink away?

Thrusting a determined chin upward, she set her jaw, readying for him.

"I'm going out for the night," he announced when he reached her.

Ellie's gaze flicked from the door the blonde had disappeared through to him. She didn't appreciate his arrogant grin and considered giving his beard a good yank to show him.

"Well. Have fun." She forced a smile. If he wanted to go out, that was his business. Not hers. She didn't care where he went, what he did, or who he did—shit—who he spent time with.

"I'll be home at midnight, and I'll expect you to be waiting for me in my room."

He'd spend the night flirting with blondie and get himself good and riled then come home to fuck her? No way.

"Sorry. My bedtime is ten." She tried to step around him, but he caught her arm and pulled her against his side.

"Your bedtime is when I say it is. Midnight, or I'll come get you, and punish you first." He lowered his voice so much, if she hadn't been completely focused on him, she wouldn't have heard him.

"Can't your date take care of you?" She bit her tongue. Dammit. That question should have stayed in her head.

He chuckled and loosened his grip on her arm, maneuvering her until she faced him again. Cupping her chin, he drew her mouth up to meet his.

What started out as a warm brush of lips, quickly deepened to another possessive mark on her skin. When he pulled away, her toes tingled and her lungs decided to take some time off.

He brushed the tip of his nose against hers.

"You're jealous."

"I am not. You can fuck whoever you want." She had to admit her outburst lacked conviction. Could the tension in her chest actually be jealousy?

No.

He was wrong.

He had to be.

He tugged her earlobe. "I don't like when you use that word unless my cock is buried in your tight pussy."

She swallowed hard. His words shouldn't be making her react. Repulsive. His crudeness should be repulsive.

So why the hell did she find her pussy starting to dampen beneath his gaze?

"Your date is waiting." She retreated from his touch.

His smile grew when he looked back at the house. "Midnight, Ellie."

She watched him saunter inside, promising herself it would rain dollar bills before she cheapened herself any further by kneeling in his room and waiting for him like some damn puppy.

CHAPTER 12

The house was dark when Ash returned home. He removed his jacket, tossed it on an armchair in the foyer, and stood at the foot of the stairs, looking up.

Five minutes until midnight. Was Ellie already in position, or was she pacing around the room, trying to convince herself not to obey him?

When he had walked into the garden with Arabella on his arm, he had expected to have a quick word with Peter. He didn't see Ellie until Peter shifted his position. And then, there she stood, relaxed and casual, talking with his cousin.

No stress lines wrinkled her forehead. No tension visible in her body.

Ash hadn't meant for Ellie to see Arabella, but it was too late. She had, and the little hellcat had become jealous. That idea made the rest of the evening go by much easier. Even listening to mindless prattle meant to kiss ass and lube the sale had been more tolerable.

Ellie had been jealous.

But would she be obedient was the more pertinent question.

He made his way up the stairs to his room. The house never felt very warm growing up; his father didn't allow anyone other than immediate family to stay inside. Luckily for Ash, he'd allowed his mother to remain in the house. When he needed her, he didn't have to go into the Annex to find her.

Since his father died, and he took over, Ash had offered a set of rooms to Peter and a few other men who spent more time on the grounds than at their own homes. Only Peter took him up on the offer, and he moved into the suite of rooms on the third floor. If he was home, Ash wouldn't know. The house had been built sturdy, and very little could be heard from room to room.

Which would work beautifully tonight. He doubted Ellie would want anyone to hear what he had planned for her.

He entered his room.

Ellie sat on the edge of his bed, not in position, but she was in the room. He'd give her some credit for that. But not much.

The click of the door closing sounded louder than usual. Maybe because she was staring at him with those doe eyes of hers. The same expression as the night she arrived. A mingling of fear and furiousness.

"You aren't in the correct position," he stated with a firm voice.

"I'm here."

"Might as well not be if you aren't going to follow your directions. I'm going to take a shower. When I get out, either be in the correct position or bend over the bed and be ready for your ass to be lit up with my belt."

Her eyes widened, and she stood, fists clenched, all the softness she'd had with Peter, nowhere to be seen.

"Is that your solution to everything? Someone doesn't pay

you, so you beat them? Someone doesn't obey completely so you beat them, too?"

Ash took a deep breath and ran his tongue over his teeth. She had a way of crawling under his skin and bringing his temper to the surface with so little effort.

"Why are you here, Ellie?" he asked.

"You told me—"

"No. Why are you here in my house? Why are your things in the next room, and why are you living here now?"

He would take responsibility for every act he took, but he would not allow her to continue blaming him for her presence or her fucking position in his life. He had enough evil deeds to pile against him, but that wasn't one of them.

Color drained from her cheeks, and her hands loosened at her sides. She wasn't even naked. She still wore the damn romper he'd seen her in earlier.

"Because you were going to hurt my father." She raised her chin.

"Go on." He gestured. "Then why are you here and not him?"

Her throat, begging him to wrap his hand around the gentle area, constricted with a swallow.

"I offered to work off his debt. To take his place." If words could actually choke a person, he would have to worry for her safety. But he wasn't letting the victim card be used anymore.

"And when you came to me, begging me to take his place... Did I make it seem like you'd be washing dishes for the next few years?" He remembered vividly shoving his fingers into her hot, wet pussy in his office. No. He'd been clear.

Her eyes flittered away. "N-no. You didn't."

"You showed up uninvited, and I took you up on your offer. Isn't that right?"

She bit her lips and nodded.

"I don't hear so good when you don't use your damn words, Ellie. Speak."

"Yes." If she could have yelled it, he figured she would have, but having to realize her situation was completely her own doing probably took the wind right out of her sails.

"Then why the fuck are you standing here in my room, still clothed, and not on your damn knees like you were told to be?" He could have gentled his voice, but the little spark of fear his tone evoked in her expression couldn't be passed up.

Her graceful fingers moved up to the row of buttons on her romper, but she didn't meet his gaze.

Not moving a muscle, he watched her disrobe. She hadn't worn a bra under the romper, so as soon as she peeled away the top portion, her breasts bounced free. So soft and supple, he had to force himself not to go to her and hold them, cup them in his hand, and kiss them until his cock forgave him for not coming home earlier.

She hooked her thumbs into the rolled fabric and pushed it over her hips, letting it pool at her feet before stepping out. She picked up the one piece and draped it on the bed before bringing her hair from behind her. The length almost covered her breasts, but not quite.

Although, naked, she still hadn't moved into position.

"You realize I have to punish you, now," he said, enjoying her little jump when his voice sliced through the silence.

"Yeah," she whispered, her hands moving behind her and rubbing her ass. Undoubtedly an act done from the memory of her previous spanking. But a spanking would be too easy, too childish for her degree of defiance.

He walked past her, making sure he brushed her bare arm as he went for his toy chest. Grabbing the leather restraints from the top drawer, he stepped behind her.

Her emotions boiled near the surface, and he was glad she'd never had reason to learn how to hide them.

Wrapping the leather bindings around each of her wrists came natural to him. It should have been like any other woman's wrist. Curl the leather around the delicate skin, slip the strip through the buckle, and secure it. Yet, when his fingers touched her wrist, a tingling shot through his body.

He stared at the back of her once she was secured; she wiggled her wrists, testing the endurance of her bonds. They'd hold. They held stronger women than her, during more intense scenes, but she couldn't know that. She didn't know what was coming and had no idea what she had really signed up for when she made her offering that first night.

He wouldn't think about it right now. Right now, he had to get her on her knees.

"Down." He pressed on her shoulder until she moved to the floor, her feet having to slide under the bed since he hadn't let her move from where she stood.

He rounded her and squatted until they were eye to eye.

"I wanted to come up here and fuck you senseless. Let you come hard and wear you out with it, but instead you were defiant. Tried to take away my pleasure. So, that's what's going to happen to you."

She scraped her teeth over her bottom lip and remained silent.

"I'm going to take your pleasure away from you. And every time you beg me for it, every time you feel like you're going to die without it, I want you to remember all you had to do to get it was to be obedient."

Her expression flattened. She could try to hide from what they were going to do all she wanted, but he wouldn't let her. And she couldn't. She may never have had a paddle put to her ass, or been told to kneel before her boyfriend, but she craved it. He could sense it inside her. The joy shining in her eyes when he smiled with approval, the tinge of fear when she tried to be defiant; she couldn't hide the natural reactions.

He stood to his full height and unbuttoned his shirt, peeling it off and tossing it to the floor. When his hands came to his buckle, her eyes widened and her lips pinched together. Maybe she thought he was still going to spank her.

"Open your mouth, Ellie." He finished unbuckling the thick leather belt and unzipped his jeans, pulling out his hard-as-stone cock and letting it wobble in front of her lips.

She stared at it, hungry and determined. He gathered her hair, holding it in a ponytail in his fist.

"Open your mouth wide." He yanked, and she parted her lips with a resounding yelp. "There. Now. Your mouth is going to act as a pussy, and how do I fuck a pussy?"

He dragged her back until her eyes met his, her neck elongated from her position. Fuck, he wanted to squeeze her throat, just enough to get that stripe of fear again, just enough for her to look at him with longing and concern.

But he held back.

"H-hard?" she asked.

"Real hard. Keep your mouth open, swallow when my cock hits your throat, and make sure your tongue is sticking out. You'll choke a little less."

He didn't wait for her agreement or for her to understand his directions before thrusting all the way into her mouth. When the head of his dick hit the back of her throat, she gagged, coughed, but he didn't pull out. He relented just enough for her to take a breath before plowing forward again.

"Swallow." He ground out the order. His cock inched down her throat. And when he felt the muscles there constrict around him, he almost lost his load right then.

"Good girl." He grinned at her. She peered up at him; a tear slipped down her cheek. Fucking beautiful.

He pulled back and let her take a deep breath. "Again," he ordered and pushed forward until he was in her throat. "Stick your tongue out." He tugged on her hair.

She moved her tongue, pushing it out and licking the underside of his cock.

"Good fucking girl," he cheered her on and pulled out again.

"I'm going to fuck you hard now, and I'm not going to stop until I spill every drop of my cum into your throat. Swallow all of it, or you'll be licking it up. Got it?" He held her face with his free hand, wiping another runaway tear away with his thumb.

"Yes, sir," she answered.

His knees buckled beneath the weight of her words. Sir. Could a sound really stroke a man's cock?

He gripped her hair harder and jerked her back until her head was pushed against the edge of the bed. Bracing himself with a hand on the mattress, he forced his cock past her tongue and down her throat again.

She swallowed and sputtered as he began to move into her throat.

"Oh fuck," he growled, letting go of her hair and using both hands to steady himself on the bed. Effectively pinned between him and the furniture, she had nowhere to go while he fucked her throat.

She gagged, but he didn't release her. Drool leaked out, running down his balls and dripping to the floor. He'd make her lick that up. The mental visual pushed him right over the brink.

Her tongue lashed out beneath his shaft. She swallowed and coughed.

"Fuck. Here it comes, Ellie. Oh. Fuck." He grabbed her

head, cradling her face with his hands, and thrust forward one last time. His balls tightened just before his orgasm ripped through him. He spurt his cum into her mouth, down her throat. She stilled, not coughing anymore, only swallowing several times in succession, trying to take every ounce of his seed.

"Fuck," he sighed. As he gazed down at her, his cock nearly filled again for her. Tears streaked her cheeks, her eyes glistened with the unshed tears, and his cock still perched in her mouth.

He slid his dick out free, and saliva spilled from her lips. With her hands bound behind her, she couldn't wipe off the spit; he wouldn't have let her anyway.

Holding his cock up, out of the way, he pointed to the mess she'd made on his balls. "Lick this up," he ordered.

Something close to rage flashed in her eyes, but she obeyed anyway. She leaned in and ran her tongue over his balls until she'd wiped away the slobber.

When she leaned back on her heels, he picked up her romper from the bed and used it to clean the mess off her chin and her chest. She'd made a proper mess of herself while taking her face fucking.

He couldn't have asked for anything more perfect.

She'd been so good for him. But her punishment was far from over.

CHAPTER 13

⚜

Ellie sucked in a breath, taking in as much air as she could while Ash stepped away from her.

If his intention was to humiliate her, he hadn't succeeded. She supposed she should have been at least embarrassed, having him fuck her throat with such force. But the harder he thrust, the harder her clit pulsed.

She needed his touch, or his cock, anything to take away the ache and the hunger he created with his "punishment." Maybe he didn't understand the way punishments were supposed to work? Or maybe he used the word to make the moment more erotic but wouldn't really deliver it.

After all, he'd spanked her hard but made her come right afterward. And now all he'd done was make her hungry for more, more of his cock, more of his tongue, more of his touch. He'd made her horny, not sorry.

"Get on the bed, naughty girl." Ash undid the clasp between her wrist restraints. The leather cuffs were heavy on her arms. The grip comforted her, though. Strange that being tied would center her focus.

She climbed up on the bed and lay flat when he motioned

her to do so. He retrieved the vibrator from his drawer and sat on the bed beside her.

"Spread your thighs. Show me your soaking wet pussy." His words sank hard into her psyche. Such crass talk, yet she found herself obeying without hesitation. Obedience would get her what she wanted; that's what Peter had told her. And, at the moment, she wanted the vibrator to kiss her clit.

With a small twist of the base, the vibrator sprang to life. He brought it close to her pussy, but not touching, not even close enough for her to inch down and make it touch.

"You may not come without permission," he announced with raised eyebrows.

She nodded, keeping her gaze glued to the humming toy held just out of reach.

Yes. Yes. Fine. She'd wait for him to give his almighty approval, just so long as he touched her.

He grinned at her, a cross between angelic and evil, and brought the vibrator to her entrance. She wiggled her hips, but he slapped her thigh.

"No, you just enjoy. If you want something, you beg." He didn't look at her while he gave his instructions, though. He was too busy sliding the bullet-shaped toy through her folds. When the vibrations licked her clit, she moaned.

"Please. Do that again." She fisted her hands at her sides, wanting to throw her hips up at him and make him give her what she wanted.

"I will, but first you have to pull your lips apart for me. Spread yourself and show me your little clit."

She let out a frustrated sigh but did what he wanted. What choice did she really have? If she refused, he'd stop, and he'd probably get the damn paddle out again.

"Well, I guess it's not so little." He flicked her swollen nub with his finger, and she moaned again. With a chuckle, he rolled the tip of the vibrator around her clit. Never touching full-on, but still delivering satisfying sensations.

He continued rubbing the vibrator over her clit, and, at some point, she had starting humping it. She realized she was pushing her hips at him, trying to get more of the vibrations, but she was too close to the edge to care. And he didn't chastise her again, so she assumed it was what he wanted.

"Oh God," she moaned, planting her feet on the bed, arching her back, and pushing her hips at him. Just a few more passes, and she would come unglued. A tiny bit more pressure. There. Just like that. Almost.

"Not yet." He removed all sensations from her body just as she was about to topple over the edge.

She growled at him.

He laughed.

After a long moment of silence, he flicked the vibrator on, stronger this time, and brought it back to her pussy. Immediately, she arched up, taking all the sensations and craving more.

The edge came faster, almost surprising her, and she clenched her lips shut. Not giving him a clue she was about to dive over into paradise.

This obviously wasn't his first torture session. Just as the first wave started, it stopped. He removed the vibrator, and she slammed her fists into the bed.

He turned her into a tantrum-throwing toddler.

"Fuck yourself, Ellie. Show me how good you can make yourself feel." He handed her the vibe, and she grabbed it, flicking it to life, and going straight for what she wanted.

She slipped two fingers into her passage and rubbed the bullet over her clit. He faded into the background. Her need too great to be tampered with by his presence.

Moving the vibrator around her clit, she found the sweet spot. Nothing could stop her.

Except his demanding tone.

"Stop."

She ceased her movements, but she didn't let go of the vibrator. He couldn't mean it. No, too bad. She wouldn't. She started to move the vibrator again, but he snatched it from her hands, and brushed away her fingers from her pussy.

"No!" she cried out, wishing she had the courage to slap him.

"Yes." He tossed the vibrator beside her and positioned himself between her thighs.

Oh. She licked her lips as he licked his.

"Do you want something?"

"Yes. I want you to let me come," she demanded.

He chuckled.

"I wanted you to be in the correct position when I arrived home." His counter remark only irritated her.

How could she do that? How could she strip down and wait for him like some damn lap dog?

His tongue touched her pussy, and she cried out with the soft wetness of it. Spreading her lips farther apart, he sucked in her clit, nibbling and licking.

She gasped, clenched the quilt in her hands, anything to keep him from understanding how close to the brink she teetered. But he knew.

Why did he know her body so well?

"Please, Ash. Please. I promise. Next time, I'll be waiting the right way. I promise," she begged when he let go of her clit and hovered just over her sex. Her starving, desperate sex.

"I know you will." He nodded with a grin.

He dragged his tongue from her entrance to her clit while keeping his eyes focused on hers. Her jaw dropped; her throat dried from the heavy breaths. She probably looked like a desperate slut, but she didn't care. She was desperate.

"Please." She reached for him when he pulled away, but he shook his head.

"No." He dragged the back of his hand across his mouth and slid off the bed.

He grabbed his jeans off the floor.

"What are you doing?" she demanded. He couldn't leave her like this.

"Getting ready for bed," he announced and stalked off toward the bathroom. "If you touch yourself, I'll know. I can keep you all tied up and continue this lesson for even longer, so I'd start being a good girl again."

She swallowed hard, clenching her fist until her nails dug into her palm.

He was just going to get ready for bed? Her pussy leaked onto his quilt, the throbbing relentless in annoyance. She had to do something.

Snapping her legs closed, she tried to let the pressure bring her to some satisfaction. Only more friction to build the dam but not release it.

Irritated and beyond aroused, she leapt off the bed. If she had just done what he asked, just knelt for him, she probably would have been fucked hard. She could be exhausted from release, not tense with frustration.

She'd done it to herself. And he had been quick to show her the error of her actions.

She would rather have the paddle than this.

Which is why he did it.

She wanted to growl but took a calming breath instead. She had made her bed, and now she had to lie in it. Completely aroused and alone, but she had to do it.

He emerged from the bathroom and disappeared into his closet. When he returned, he would probably dismiss her again. Another night of using her body and tossing her aside.

At least she could control that much. She yanked on the

buckles of the restraints and tossed the cuffs onto the bed before snatching her romper and going to her room.

Once snuggled under the warm quilt of her own bed, she touched her lips, remembering how thick his cock had been in her mouth. How she'd struggled for air. All of the fear and the excitement coated her pussy, ready for him to plow into her. Lying in her bed, just thinking about it again, made her arousal painful.

She needed to touch herself, to relieve the pressure. He said he would know. Could he have cameras in her room?

Deciding not to test his threat of performing the same punishment for even longer, she flopped onto her side and hugged a pillow to her.

The next time he told her to wait for him in his room, she would do it exactly as he'd taught her. No. Even fucking better. Because she couldn't survive going to bed this hungry again.

Ever.

CHAPTER 14

"Look. I'll have it. I swear, Ash. I just need more time."

How many times did he have to hear the same plea in his lifetime? Everyone needed more time, but there was never enough time. Gambling to pay off a debt was just that—a gamble. And it never worked. Only more debt, more promises, and more lies.

Ash could be accommodating to a point. But there was a time to cut your losses and be done with it. And that moment had arrived.

"Jacob, you've told me that twice already. And didn't I give you more time?" Ash scratched beneath his beard.

"Well, yeah, but then you increased the interest, so now I owe more." Jacob, a semiprofessional poker player, leaned forward in his chair.

"I see. So, this is my fault?" Ash motioned for his two men standing at the door to come closer. He'd wasted enough time with Jacob.

"What? No." Jacob looked over his shoulder at Marc and Steven stalking toward him, smiling wider with prey in their sights.

"It's my fault. Totally my fault. I just need a little more time. A month. All I need is a month. I swear." Jacob begged as Mark and Steven flanked him, yanking him out of his chair.

"Please. I swear it." Wild eyes flicked around the room, trying to find an escape or someone who gave a damn about him. He wouldn't find either.

"You know…" Ash stood from his chair and moved to where Jacob struggled against his men. "Every week I get one of you fuckers coming in here and begging for more time. Like some fucking goose is going to lay a golden egg on your front step."

Ash grabbed Jacob's face, pinching his cheeks until his mouth opened.

"If you were a real man, you wouldn't be in here sniveling, asking for loans and more fucking time to pay your debts. You'd get a real fucking job and pay your god damn bills." Anger simmered in his chest. He'd seen too many men destroy their families, their lives, for a game of chance. It sickened him.

"I gave you money. You were supposed to pay me back with a small interest fee for my trouble. But you missed your payment then another and another. So, yeah, you owe a shit ton more now. Do you think I'm running a fucking charity here?"

Jacob stared at him with wide eyes. A bead of sweat formed on his forehead. Ash could smell the fear on him. If the man pissed himself, he'd feel less compassion and would have to beat the fuck out of him.

"I asked a question." Ash squeezed until his fingernails turned white, and he knew bruises would mark the asshole's face.

"No," Jacob said, but it came out warped. Hard to talk, Ash supposed, when you couldn't move your damn mouth.

"You're out of time, Jacob." Ash pushed his head back, releasing his grip enough to open his mouth more. His eyes narrowed. "Open your fucking mouth, Jacob." Ash patted his cheek.

Jacob's eyes flew to the gun seated on Ash's hip.

"As much as blowing off your pathetic head would make my day, I don't want your brains all over my fucking rug. Open your mouth."

Jacob swallowed hard and opened his mouth, showing off exactly what Ash had suspected he'd seen.

Ash laughed. "Well. There you go."

He hooked his thumb over Jacob's bottom jaw and tilted his head some more. "Are these just plated, or the real thing?" Ash tapped a finger on one of the golden teeth inside his mouth.

"Real," Jacob said, again muffled by his position.

Ash tilted his head to the side, counting. Five solid gold teeth nestled in this fucker's mouth, but he couldn't pay his debt?

Ash patted his cheek and stepped away.

"We'll consider that this month's payment." Ash nodded to his men who didn't need to be given any more instruction.

"What? No! Wait, you can't! They're my teeth!" Jacob struggled, but his men easily dragged him from the room and out the back door. Unpleasant business wasn't taken care of in the main house.

Ash ignored Jacob's cries for reconsideration fading off down the hallway and went back to his desk. One more order of business to take care of and then he could check on the progress for the party.

Picking up the phone, he dialed the Annex extension and sent for Daniel.

With a grin, he pressed the intercom button that would open a line between him and Ellie's room.

"Ellie," he called. "Come to my office." He let go of the button. She couldn't call him. She didn't know the code to turn on the two-way talk. A design of his father's he'd never corrected when he took over the house. He'd never seen the usefulness of such a device, but now he almost chuckled, imagining how frustrated she'd be when she couldn't respond.

He'd beckoned her.

But would she come?

"You needed me?" Daniel entered the room after a quick knock.

"Yes. But I need Ellie, too. Give her a second."

Daniel grinned. "I saw her coming down the stairs, mumbling to herself."

Ash almost regretted not being witness to it. Her cheeks were probably flushed with irritation.

"You called, my lord?" Ellie barged into the room, stopping short when she noticed Daniel's presence.

"My lord? Hmm. I like it, but I prefer Sir." Ash kept his eyes pinned on her. The little flush of pink deepened, and his cock hardened along with it.

Again, she was dressed in her old clothes. He'd had Peter send her some things from the Annex. Nothing like the employees wore, but newer, better-made things that didn't look like she'd just knocked over Goodwill.

"Did you want something?" Ellie asked in a softer tone. Not submissive by any means, just delicate. She probably remembered the last time she'd tried to argue with him in front of Daniel.

He ignored her and turned to Daniel. "Take her to school. She needs to register for two more classes and get her schedule printed up and over to Peter. He'll organize her transportation from there. After you're done on campus, take her to the boutique on Fifth. She needs some new clothes."

"What? Wait. No." Ellie stepped between them. Her head reaching only his chin, she had to tilt it to give him her glare.

Ash raised his eyebrows in response.

"I mean, I don't need new clothes, and I can get myself to school."

"Go get your purse, or jacket, or whatever and meet Daniel in the front room in ten minutes," Ash dictated.

She chewed on her lower lip. She wanted to argue with him so badly, he could taste her desire. But to do so would go badly for her, and good girl for realizing it. She was finally learning.

"Why do you care about school? I'll be done with all this in a few months." She waved a hand through the air. "Considering the menu you gave—"

He lowered his face to hers until he could feel her breath on his skin.

"Forget the menu. I humored you with that. You're not done here in a few months. Maybe not ever. You gave yourself for your father's spot. A life for a life."

Her eyes widened along with her gasp. He wouldn't give her false hope; it wouldn't serve anyone. Realizing her situation depended solely on him would get her a lot further along with accepting her place.

"You never said—"

"Get your sweater or whatever you want to take with you. Daniel is also going to buy you a new phone while you're out."

"You can't really mean what you're saying." She whispered the words, unbelieving he would and could keep her to himself forever? She didn't know him well enough. He had been playing nice so far.

"And, Daniel"—he kept his gaze fixated on Ellie as he spoke—"if she disobeys, if she gives you any fucking trouble, do not hesitate to take your belt to her ass."

He waited for the words to sink in, for her cheeks to flame, and her lips to pinch together in anger, before continuing.

"And if he has to spank you while you're out, you'll be sucking his cock tonight as his reward for having to deal with you."

"You're an asshole."

He didn't care for the sign of defeat in her eyes, like she'd expected something else from him and gotten gypped. Well, didn't everyone get screwed out of what they really wanted? This wasn't different. This was business.

He reminded himself of that little fact over and over again when it came to her.

"Do you understand me, Ellie? You're going to be a good girl and do exactly what I say, right?"

The glistening of her eyes squeezed his chest. If a tear dropped down her cheek, he might lose his resolve.

"Go." He pointed a finger at the door.

Her jaw tightened. "Fine." She spun around, long tresses of auburn hair brushing his chest, and stalked out of the room, slamming the door behind her.

He'd let her have that.

"Wouldn't just putting her in the Annex make more sense? I mean, she's tying you all up," Daniel said.

Peter bounded in. "What did you do to Ellie?" he asked, jerking a thumb at the door.

"He reminded her what she is, that's all." Daniel shrugged.

Ash turned to Daniel. "And what is she?"

Daniel's complexion paled, and he looked to Peter to save him.

"What is she, Daniel?" Ash asked again.

"Man, I don't even know. You took her as payment, but you keep her in the room next to yours. You haven't let anyone even talk to her other than the staff." The hole grew bigger beneath Daniel, but Ash let him keep digging.

"That's right, she's payment to me. Since when is this a corporation where you think you can have a share? What's owed to me is owed to me. You get your fucking paycheck like everyone else, and you don't worry about how I get my payments."

Daniel was one of his top men. He trusted him with his life, but if he thought that meant he could start questioning him, he had another fucking think coming.

"I get it." Daniel retreated a step. "I get it, boss. I didn't mean to offend. Of course, she's yours. All yours."

"Take her to school and to the shop. Get the phone and get back here. No pit stops, do not lose her, and if she runs into anyone she knows at school, you stick close to her. Got me?"

"Yeah. Yeah, of course." Daniel couldn't get to the door fast enough.

"And, Daniel? If you touch her, I'll kill you myself," Ash warned.

"But you said—"

"That was for her ears. This isn't. If you touch a single hair on her head, hold her hand, even breathe the same air she does, I'll break your head in two."

He knew he sounded like a man obsessed, but he didn't give a shit. No one would touch what was his, and Ellie was his.

"Got it." Daniel nodded and left.

"You've been less possessive about your cash," Peter said. He went to the bar and poured himself a drink.

"I don't need him or any of the other men thinking they can go around taking what's mine, or even thinking to touch it," Ash countered. "Pour me one."

Peter brought him a glass of bourbon and gestured to the back door of the office.

"Jacob?"

"Mark and Steven have him. Extracting payment as we speak. You'll need to have it melted down."

Peter raised an eyebrow but didn't ask any further questions.

"How are things in the Annex? I need to get over there this afternoon, but I wanted to get a run in first." He hadn't gone for a long run in weeks, and his body craved the burn.

"It's all going like it always does. You don't need to oversee every detail, you know. That's what you pay these assholes a shit ton of money to do."

Ash downed his drink. "Yeah. I know. Did you want something?"

"Are you bringing Ellie tonight?"

"To the party? Fuck no. I told you, she stays with me." Of course, his men had reasons for their questions. He'd never not shared. Not once had he hidden away a treasure not to be at least admired by his men.

But Ellie was different.

A rarity. Pure. And as much as he would fuck up her world, turn it all upside down and inside out, he would not let that dirty world touch her.

"Don't worry about her. She's really pissed at me right now, and an angry Ellie is a hiding Ellie. She won't come out of her room tonight. Just make sure the kitchen knows to bring her dinner upstairs for her. Text Daniel and tell him to stop at an art store and let her get some books or a new sketch pad. Hers are mostly full."

Ash had checked on her the night before, after he came out of the closet and found the leather cuffs on the bed but no Ellie in sight. She'd been sound asleep in her bed, her hands tucked under her chin. Her sketch pad had been on the dresser he walked past, opened to a drawing of the rosebush and the window behind it.

She'd been sketching in the gardens earlier. When he picked up the pad and examined more closely, he made out his own figure in the window. She had been studying him.

He left the pad on the dresser and her to sleep in her own bed. She acted before he could. Run from the room before he could banish her from it. Protect and save. So predictable.

"Got it." Peter finished tapping out his message and put his phone away. "Anything else?"

Ash waved him off. "No. I'm going for a run. I'll meet you in the Annex in a few hours."

"You can run as many miles as you want; the thing you're running from will be right here when you get back," Peter said with a knowing grin then left him in peace.

But could he really ever have peace?

Or did he want it?

CHAPTER 15

For over an hour, Ellie stood at the window in her bedroom overlooking the gardens. People had trickled in at first, but now they strode through the gardens in one thick line. Men in suits, mostly, but a few women sprinkled throughout the mob as well.

"What are they all doing here?" She pressed her face into the chilled glass to see better.

She couldn't make out many faces with the dimness of the evening, but when they passed an overhead light, she studied their features. Several of the men were familiar from newspaper articles and magazine photos. She couldn't recall any of their names, but remembered a few were on the city council. Others appeared as menacing as Ash.

And where exactly was Ash?

She hadn't seen him since Daniel, the overgrown baby who'd been assigned to babysit her, brought her home. Daniel had kept his mouth shut for the most part, only using words when he needed her to make a turn or pass her something. And when he didn't, he kept his hand far enough way to be sure they didn't touch. Did Ash tell his men she had cooties?

Checking the time, she sighed. Only ten o'clock. She could climb under the covers, but the likelihood of her falling asleep knowing some secret party was taking place didn't exist.

Ash had told her he'd never let her go. She lived there full-time. Forever. So, what stopped her from exploring? He might strap her again? She could handle it. Well worth the spanking to find out what the hell went on in that wing of the house.

Ellie dug through the bags of clothes Daniel made her buy at the little boutique to find the little dress. She'd only picked it out as a way to torment him at the time. She tried on the slinky number and modeled it for him, asking his opinion. It was the first time she smiled all afternoon, seeing his cheeks flush. Well, he could get pissed at his boss for making him go in the first place.

But, now, the dress would serve another purpose.

Dressing quickly and finding some pins in the bathroom, she managed to pull most of her hair up to expose her neckline. She couldn't very well wear one of her cotton dresses; she wouldn't fit in.

The quiet of the house made her slow her steps. Any sound coming from her might alert one of his men she figured he had posted throughout the house.

Keeping her away from the party had been a big deal to Ash.

And she was going to find out why.

Finding her way to the door leading to the west wing hadn't been hard at all. The staff had already gone home for the night to bed, leaving no one around to stop her.

Someone laughed in the garden. Ellie could make out

shadows through the garden door, and she crouched down. Another laugh—a woman's, full of flirt and seduction.

"C'mon, let's get inside before they come looking for us. We're not supposed to be paired up yet. You know the rules," a deep voice chastised but didn't sound anything like Ash when he wanted to take her to task.

"Such games. But you know Ash. By the book." The handle shook, and Ellie jumped to her feet, flattening herself against the wall.

The couple entered the mudroom and paused at seeing her. The man looked her up and down, sizing her up, while the woman glanced at the mysterious sealed entrance with apprehension.

"What are you doing?" the man asked, stepping inside and pushing the garden door closed quietly. The woman pressed herself into his back. They weren't supposed to be there any more than she was, Ellie guessed.

"I was…I mean, I'm supposed to be at the party, but I'm late." Ellie tried to give her most desperate smile, but threw a little seductive pout in as well.

From the odd expression the man gave her, she figured she had a lot of work to do in the seduction department. She'd never had to seduce anyone before. Nor did she ever want to.

"John, she's Ash's girl."

John's complexion grayed.

"I am not—well, I mean we aren't together. Not really." Ellie finally recognized the girl behind him. The blonde who had been on Ash's arm in the garden.

"We have to get in there, John. They are going to start with the announcements," she whispered and shoved at his shoulder.

"If I'm not there…" Ellie hoped they'd fill in the blank and feel partially sorry for her. Seeking out pity made her stomach ache, but the ends would have to justify the means in this circumstance. Having them help her and giving her some cover when she entered would make it easier than trying to slip by any guards she came across.

John blew out a long breath and groaned. "Fine. Fuck. Fine." He pulled a keycard from his pocket and passed it over the knob. After a soft click, the door opened.

Ellie stared at the knob for a solid moment before grabbing the closing door and following them. She'd seen key cards used, but not in such a way. No wonder she couldn't figure out how to get in on her own.

Once inside, Ellie sucked in a breath. She quickly caught up to her unwilling escorts and stayed a few steps behind them while they navigated the hallway.

It didn't look much different from the rest of the house, other than the darker, sexual appeal of the décor. The paintings depicted sexual acts. Some sensual, and some downright dirty. She couldn't help but stare at the more explicit of them.

Get a grip, dammit.

The couple led her to a ballroom that mirrored the dining room she'd eaten several of her meals in, except candles—real candles, not the electric sort in Ash's office—flickered in the chandeliers.

She saw no trace of delicate china or golden candlesticks. Instead, she found leather and black wrought iron. Along one wall, across from where she stood taking everything in, hung various implements. A few like those she'd seen in Ash's drawer, though these paddles and floggers were larger, heavier, made of leather instead of the wood he'd used against her bottom.

"We missed the announcements." The blonde cursed and surveyed the room, letting go of John's arm. "Peter is going to have my ass."

"Don't worry about him," John reassured her. "We've gone through this before. We know what to do. Let's mingle for a bit then I'll put in the contract. It will be fine." He grabbed hold of her hand and walked off into the room, leaving Ellie alone and exposed in the doorway.

Unsure of where exactly she could hide, she sidestepped and pushed herself into the background. Her black dress would blend into the darkened furniture and the deep coloring of the walls. The dim lighting would help her as well.

Slinking along the edges of the room, she took in the woman sauntering around. No one went unescorted, but all seemed to be mingling as though they were on their own. The man walking each of them, brought them to a single man standing, drinking whiskey, or seated at a table, sipping some other dark drink and leave her there for a few moments. She would smile and chat, and make no move to stop him even when he pinched her hip or boldly cupped her breasts through her corset.

"I think three thousand is plenty." A deep voice caught Ellie's attention as she wandered closer to a corner. Another man she'd seen in the house during her stay was speaking to Peter. A short redhead stood at the man's side, her arm curled around his, leaning her head against his shoulder.

"Three thousand for a week? No. Five thousand." Peter waved at the young woman.

The man, tall but stout, studied the woman.

"Five thousand a week?" He tilted her head and trailed a finger over her plump painted lips. "I want to test her first. See if this mouth is as fuckable as she says."

Peter gave a nod. "There are some rooms available in the back."

"No. Here." The man shoved the redhead to her knees, and she immediately clasped her hands behind her.

Peter took on a supervisory role as the redhead opened her mouth, took the man's stubby cock between her lips, and began to suck.

What the hell was going on? The "party," she realized foolishly late, was nothing more than a brothel. Ash was a pimp.

She retreated a step, shrinking into the corner, as the purchaser gripped the redhead's face and forced his cock down her throat. At first the girl seemed to manage it fine, but soon he thrust faster than she could handle, and she sputtered. He relented momentarily, letting her take a breath then shoved right back in.

The scene reminded her of her own face fucking with Ash. He had taken her mouth in much the same manner, but he hadn't been cruel. He hadn't been so cold. This man was using the woman's mouth as he would any vessel. It meant nothing to him. Or to her.

A loud grunt, and he stilled, seemingly dumping his cum down her throat.

"Well?" Peter asked, sounding irritated at having to wait.

"Fine. Five thousand." The crude man zipped up his trousers. The redhead started to stand, but he shoved her to her knees. "No. You stay there until I need you again. I'll sign these and have a drink. Then maybe I'll let you suck off one of my friends before we head home." He winked and gestured to Peter for a pen.

Ellie's hands fisted as the disgusting man signed a piece of paper and dropped the pen on the clipboard. The man had no decency about his actions.

"Have her sign, and I'll be back." He didn't even acknowledge the redhead before stalking off toward the bar. A thanks might have been in order, seeing as she just sucked him off with such grace and precision.

Peter bent over and whispered into the girl's ear. He

BEAST

showed her the papers before he acquired her signature. After a gentle smile and a pat to her shoulder, he left her, signaling to another man standing behind her to stay with her. Maybe he was her handler. Just as the other women in the room seemed to have one as well.

"Did you enjoy the little show, poppet?"

The familiar voice chilled Ellie's skin. She wet her lips and took a calming breath before turning to see Marcus standing too close to her. She remembered him from the nightclub with Ash, and she remembered what he had said.

"Ash must have changed his mind, huh?" He ran a finger down her jaw. "Where's your handler?" he asked, he searched around them before settling his sights on her. She could practically smell the scum on him.

"I'm not, I mean, I didn't—"

"Every woman in this room is for sale. Either for an hour, a few weeks, or forever. Which I want to buy you for is really up to me, though." His finger slid beneath the neckline of her dress.

Yanking away from him, she knocked into another man holding a drink. The girl beside him hissed as the amber-colored liquor poured down her dress.

"Shit. I'm so sorry." Ellie searched for a napkin or anything to help clean up the mess she'd made, but was waved off.

"It's fine. Go away." The man gave her a little shove. "I was about to strip her, anyway." He shot a glare at Marcus. "You usually handle your girls better than this."

Marcus, whose cheeks burned a deep red, grabbed her arm and jerked her to him. "She's not broken in yet. But she'll learn her manners." He spun her around and shoved her into the wall.

Ellie tried to call out, but he pressed her face flat, and

before she could free herself from his grip, his hand landed on her ass.

She kicked out, but he only smacked her ass harder.

"Get your fucking hands off her." Ash's voice penetrated her own yells. Without raising his voice, he pierced the situation.

Marcus didn't release her but stopped spanking her long enough to move to her left and face him.

"I said get your hands off her, Marcus. You overstep."

With Marcus distracted, Ellie was able to maneuver her head around and see Ash.

She shouldn't have looked.

A calm settled over Ash. If she hadn't seen him upset with her already, she wouldn't recognize the signs of it standing before her. The bored expression only slightly hid his tense jaw and dark eyes.

"I told you, Ashland. If she was here, she'd be mine." Marcus shoved her harder, flattening her breasts. Ellie pushed her hands against the wall, trying to leverage herself against his strength, but got nowhere.

Ash's pulse pumped at the side of his neck. Couldn't Marcus see it? Was he stupid enough to antagonize Ash when he was so angry?

"And I told you, she wasn't on the menu."

"Every woman here is on the menu," Marcus sneered. The sweat of his palm saturated Ellie's dress. Fine time to wear something so flimsy.

"Not her." Ash took a step toward them, his hands still at his sides, the calmness no longer evident. Patience waned, and the tic in his jaw strengthened.

"She's not marked, and she's strolling around here like a free bird. Well, she's going to be caged now."

"Not by you." Ash's voice hardened, but he still didn't

glance at Ellie. If he did, she feared what she would see. She struggled more against Marcus's hold.

"This girl is unattended. Didn't your precious announcements just say any girl left unattended would be dealt with. Isn't that what you said? She has no handler. She has no contract, and now you're telling me she's not on the menu." Marcus's voice rose, grabbing the attention of several other men in the immediate vicinity.

A small crowd formed.

"She is mine, and I will deal with her. I will tell you once more to get your hand off of her before I remove it myself. And when I say remove, I mean in the literal sense."

Marcus dug his fingers into her back.

Peter moved in closer. "Marcus, you are a guest tonight but can be easily removed from the list. I would suggest you find yourself another toy to play with." Tension boiled.

With a heavy shove, Marcus let her go. Ellie spun around, taking deep breaths she'd been denied by her position. Marcus wiped a fat hand over his sweaty mouth.

"This is the second time you didn't deliver what you promised. I'm not in the mood for any of your product tonight. My father will be disappointed."

Not a blink or twitch to Ash's composure over the blatant threat.

Marcus shrugged off Peter's touch when it landed on his shoulder. Marcus gave a nod to his two men standing behind Ash, and they stomped off.

Once they were gone, Peter gave Ellie a knowing grin. "You really know how to poke the beast, don't you?"

Before she could respond, he moved away, and Ash stood in front of her. No. Loomed. Over her. Standing at his full height and so close she had to crane her neck to look up at him. If she wanted to see his face. And, at the moment, she did not.

"What are you doing in here?" he asked with a clipped tone.

If her knees hadn't started shaking, she would have pointed out that obviously she had been curious.

She stepped forward. "I...just...I was passing through—"

Ash covered her mouth, pinching her nose closed and marched her back to the wall. He pressed her against it, pulling her face upward so he could glare at her, while he cut off her oxygen.

Tears burned her eyes, and she slapped at his hand, but he didn't budge.

"Now, you try to lie to me?" It was a growl, more than a question.

Her chest heaved; her throat burned. No matter how hard she struggled, he didn't let up. Her hand smacked against his then his chest.

Finally, just as the edges of her vision blurred, he uncovered her mouth.

She sucked in big gulps of air. Tears fell from her eyes. Space, she needed space, but he denied her still by pressing his hard body against hers.

"Do you have any fucking idea what you just caused?"

Shaking her head, she continued to catch her breath. "I didn't mean to, I was just—"

"Doing exactly what you weren't supposed to be doing." Ash pinned her to the wall by her shoulders then stepped away. "For once, you dress in something other than some Goodwill scrap, and it's so you can sneak in here?"

Scrap? She didn't dress in rags. There was nothing wrong with her clothing. Finally having acquired some common sense, she chose not to correct him.

"Peter." Ash's voice shook through to her core, and the intensity of his glare while he spoke kicked her heart into a gallop. "Take this naughty girl up to my room. Have her strip, and put her on my wall."

"Wall? What?" Ellie's arm was grabbed and yanked before she got an answer. "Wait? What? Ash!" She tried to scramble toward him, but Peter had already dragged her several feet away.

"Peter," Ash called, and Ellie almost smiled with relief. Good. He'd come to his senses. He'd calm down then he could yell at her in private.

"Ass out." Ash's words struck her, and she started to struggle again.

"I'd stop if I were you, but then again, you don't seem to listen to reason." Peter tightened his grip and dragged her from the room, away from the secret wing, to put her alone so she could wait.

Alone.

CHAPTER 16

"I'm sorry, man. She was up in her room." Daniel stood in front of Ash, wringing his hands. Though Ash suspected he wanted to have Ellie's neck between his fingers as he twisted them.

"And you figured she'd just go to sleep when she knew the party was tonight? You thought she would just tuck herself in and forget all about what the fuck was going on down here?" Ash paced behind his desk.

The party hadn't died down since Marcus's departure and wouldn't for a few hours yet. But he had to deal with Ellie. He had to deal with Danny for letting her get into the wing, and he had to fucking figure out how to deal with Marcus and his father.

"She didn't even ask about it, Ash. She just said she was going to bed." Danny's eyes flicked to Peter who stood at the door, observing. Peter wouldn't interfere. Even if he wanted to, he knew better than to try.

"I told you to watch her. I told you to fucking make sure she didn't come near this place. Now, not only did she fucking get in here, Marcus had his filthy hands on her." Ash rarely raised his voice, but the image of that fat hand on her delicate body brought his voice up a peg.

"Where were you, Danny? If not where you could see her slip out of her room, or anywhere in the path between the second floor and the west wing?" Peter asked in an emotionless tone.

"I was with one of the girls." Danny looked away. "I thought I was done for the night. Amber couldn't go to the party, so I was with her."

Ash fisted his hand but took a step back. He didn't strike his men. He wouldn't, but fuck it would feel good at that moment to do it. To hear the crack of Danny's fucking jaw when Ash's hand planted in his face.

Peter stepped forward, coming to Ash's aid. "Amber's off-limits for the time being. You knew that."

"It wasn't like that. We were just together, not fucking or anything like that." Danny looked between Ash and Peter, probably unsure who presented a greater threat at the moment.

"Get the fuck out of here. I don't want to see your face until I call for you." Ash turned away. Punching him would have been kinder.

"Ash, wait, man, I—"

"Go, Danny." Peter opened the door, letting the music from the party into the room.

Danny huffed, but, in the end, he stalked out, the tension from his own irritation lingering behind him.

Once the door closed, Ash threw his fist into the wall. His knuckles split, and plaster cracked beneath the wallpaper, but it only fueled his anger instead of alleviating it.

"Yeah, you're not going upstairs until that shit is done with." Peter pointed to the break in the paper.

Ash rubbed his knuckles and took a deep breath. "That fucker touched her. He touched her, Peter. He knows damn well she's mine, and he fucking touched her. Right in front of me, he held her against the fucking wall. Right in fucking front of me."

Peter nodded. "I was there, Ash. I saw. I also saw you keep your cool, so the damage should be minimal."

"Damage? I don't give a fuck about his prick of a father. I don't deal with those families anymore. I'm out of that shit. That was my father's era, his bullshit game. Not mine. Everything I do stays away from them."

"Except you've sold to Marcus. You've honored two contracts in as many years,"

"It had nothing to do with the Annex. Nothing."

"Well, now what?" Peter didn't argue. There wasn't a point, and they knew it.

"Now? Now his father comes back to try and piss me off some more. He'll spout some shit about old ties and old promises. And I'll have to disappoint the fucker. Which means he's going to get even more pissed."

"How do you want to handle Marcus?"

"He's done here. That crap he was pulling with Amber should have been enough to blacklist him, but now…" Ash tore his hands through his hair, trying to block out the image of the fright in Ellie's eyes at being shoved against the wall by that dirtbag.

"He doesn't set foot on the grounds. Not past the front gates."

Peter nodded. "Do you think he's going to retaliate in some way? He'll see this as an insult."

Ash stopped pacing. "He touched what's mine. If I see him again, he loses his hands. If he makes one fucking move against me, he loses his life."

"That's a lot for one girl." Peter didn't back down. He never would, the bastard.

"It's not about that."

"It sure as hell is, cousin." Peter pointed to him. "You've had men give attention to a girl before. You never started a fucking war over it."

Ash clenched his teeth.

"No one has ever put hands on one of my girls," Ash countered.

"Well I guess it depends on what you mean by *your girls*. 'Cause plenty have tried to lure away one of the girls of the Annex. But, yeah, no one has dared to touch one of your personal girls. Is that what Ellie is? Is she more than repayment? Is she yours, really yours?"

Flipping the desk over and tossing his cousin across the room seemed an appropriate response. But Ash took a deep breath and steadied himself.

"She's just a girl under my protection," he stated, though he could hear the uncertainty in his own voice. He didn't do uncertain. Every decision, every choice he made came after calculating the pros and cons.

Peter frowned. "You can lie to me, and the guys all you want, Ash. But you don't believe that."

"Don't make more out of this than there is." Ash grabbed the whiskey bottle from his bar and poured three fingers of reassurance.

"You shouldn't have kept her, Ash. If she was just a repayment, you should have done exactly what she came here for. She offered. It was her choice."

Ash kept his eyes on his cousin while he swallowed his drink, embracing the heat as it rolled down his throat.

"I'm not discussing this. How I choose to take payment isn't for you or any of the fucking men to question. She's mine until I release her and, until I do, she will do what I say. And the men I put in charge of watching her will do what the fuck I say. Now, I have to go deal with her."

Peter blocked the door but didn't speak. Ash took the

moment to let his heart stop pounding. The anger boiling only a minute before lowered to a soft simmer.

"Don't take it out on her because you're pissed at Danny, or me, or Marcus."

Ash met Peter's gaze. "I wouldn't do that, and you fucking know it. But I will take it out on her that she disobeyed. And because she disobeyed, we most likely will have a fucking war on our hands."

Peter shook his head again, either from disappointment that Ash didn't just let the matter drop or because he realized Ash was right and something had to be done about Ellie's actions.

"Did you not do what I asked, is that it? Am I going to find her tucked into her bed with a cup of fucking hot cocoa?"

Peter grinned. The image of him tucking anyone into bed with hot chocolate would make anyone laugh.

"She's exactly where you want her."

"Good." Ash yanked the door open and stalked off to his room. He had a very naughty girl to deal with.

CHAPTER 17

The door creaked when it opened. Ellie's head snapped back, and she turned, trying to see him. It had to be Ash.

So much time had passed. But maybe it was Peter. Maybe Peter came to release her, to let her free of this nightmare.

"Ellie." Ash's deep voice carried across the room.

She lowered her head, pressing her forehead against the wall. Her shoulders ached, her body chilled, and her heart raced again. It had taken so long for her to calm down, to convince herself that when Ash came up he could be reasoned with. Hearing the darkness in his voice, her confidence slipped.

She tried to push the blindfold Peter had put over her eyes to the side with her arm, but she couldn't get the right leverage. Her hands were bound outward, stretched to each side of her, and her legs in much the same position. Completely displayed to him. Her ass facing him as he stood in the doorway.

Heavy steps fell behind her, but still she sucked her breath in surprise when the feather touch of his fingertips brushed across her back. He gathered her long hair and split it in half before tossing it over her shoulders, exposing her back to him.

"Do you remember what I said would happen if you started snooping around the other wing?" His nails dug into her flesh as he dragged them from her neck to her ass.

She hissed and moved up on tiptoe, but there would be no escape. The leather straps binding her to the iron rings bolted into the wall had no give and would be relentless in her captivity.

"I asked a question." His lips moved against her right ear. Warm breath brushed along her naked skin; the roughness of his beard scratched her shoulder. The scent of bourbon on his breath was intoxicating, though his firm control of his movements told her he hadn't overindulged.

No. Ash remained clearheaded. Stubborn and unrelenting, but his thoughts wouldn't be persuaded from too much drink.

"You said I wouldn't sit for a week." She had thought the boast an exaggeration, a mere threat. From his stony tone, she doubted she had been correct.

"That's right." He bit her earlobe, chuckling when she yelped. "Fuck, you're beautiful like this."

She swallowed her sarcastic retort. She was already strung up like a damn marionette doll; no need to add to the problem.

Although the lighting in the room was dimmed, it hurt her eyes when he pushed the blindfold away. She blinked a few times before he came into focus.

He still wore his black button-down and his trousers. He wore his hair loose, and it made him more menacing than she wanted to handle.

"My shoulders hurt, Ash," she said twisting to keep him

within her eyesight when he moved. She had to turn to the other side to see him walk to his bedside table.

"Don't worry. In a few minutes, your ass will hurt more, and your shoulders won't even be a thought." He opened the top drawer and pushed things away.

"Ash, please. I'm sorry. Can't you just lock me in my room?" She tugged on the leather straps again, not surprised when nothing happened.

"Oh, that's happening, too. Well, in a way." He gave her a wink and took out a leather band with a thick black ball in the center of it.

She clamped her lips shut and shook her head furiously. She would not allow him to gag her.

But what made her think she had any say in what Ash did? By now, she should have known he would have his way. He would do what he promised.

He pressed the front of his body against the back of hers, flattening her against the wall. Her breasts ached from the pressure.

The ball appeared in front of her mouth when she twisted her head away to keep from shoving her nose against the wall.

"Open your mouth, Ellie." He pushed the ball against her closed lips.

She made a noise, telling him no way in hell.

"Open it, or I'll force you, and if I have to force you, then you'll take five extra licks." His lips moved against her ear again. "And you don't want any extra of these licks, I promise you."

With a whimper, she parted her lips. Before she had fully complied, the ball shoved past her lips, painfully stretching her jaw and filling her mouth. Her head jostled as he clasped the buckle behind her.

"There." He patted her bare ass softly.

Cool air hit her back when he stepped away.

"Peter normally handles discipline for the girls. But you're mine, and I don't let anyone touch my things. I'll still use the strap the other girls get. They're used to it, doesn't really hurt them, but you..." He walked to her right side. "You haven't had a taste of the thick leather before. So this is going to hurt a lot."

He held up the strap. A short leather belt type of implement. Much thicker than any belt she'd seen before. She swallowed, trying to suck in the saliva pooled at the edges of her mouth.

"You'll get fifteen licks. Cry out as much as you want." He moved over to her left flank, running his hand over her ass. "You're still a tiny bit pink from where Marcus smacked you. That wasn't okay, and he'll be punished for it. But we're here to deal with your disobedience."

She tried to call to him, to make him understand, but he ignored her pleas.

The first fire-laden stripe landed across both cheeks, and she screamed with it. She'd never felt anything so heavy and painful before. He didn't give her time to finish processing the hurt of the first lash before giving her the second.

She yanked on her bonds. Still no give. Wiggling from one side to the other did nothing if she couldn't move her feet. The third stripe caught her on the upcurve of her ass.

Another and another barreled down on her ass and thighs. Heat like she'd never experienced spread across her backside.

"Halfway, Ellie," he said while he ran his fingertips across her throbbing cheeks.

She tried to suck in air. Containing her saliva failed, and it spilled over her chin. Pressing her forehead against the wall, she took a deep breath through her nose. Tears spilled over her eyelids, streaking her cheeks. The throbbing in her backside already consumed her thoughts. How could she take the rest of the lashes?

"Ready to finish?" he asked, a softer tone than when he'd started.

She shivered.

"Seven more, Ellie. You can do it." He squeezed her cheeks, and she squealed.

Once he regained his position, she sensed the backswing and clenched hard with his upswing. It didn't help. The pain radiated up her body. Her shoulders ached from straining against the bonds, her back hurt from tensing, her ass throbbed from the harsh strokes. Even while he kept the strap focused on her punished globes and thighs, every part of her hurt.

Sobs began, and she couldn't stop them as the next four licks landed meticulously, making their way down from the top of her ass to her thighs, leaving no flesh unburned.

Every bit of her felt swollen and sore. Pressing her face into the cool wallpaper, she let the tears flow, sniffling to keep from making an even larger mess of her face. Drool spilled from her gagged mouth while tears streaked her face, and her heart beat hard in her chest.

Ten strokes.

Fifteen hadn't sounded like a hard sentence. It had sounded manageable.

She groaned with his touch.

"Now for the last part of your punishment," he whispered.

She lifted her head to try and catch his eyes, but he had moved out of sight already.

"The girls at the party are to have their handler with them the entire evening," he explained as he moved around behind her. "It's for their safety, so anyone who doesn't have their handler with them, is punished."

A door opened and closed, but she couldn't crane her neck enough to find him.

She tried to tell him he had just punished her, but the gag muffled all sound.

He appeared next to her, smiling at her like they'd just enjoyed a fun game instead of the whipping he'd just dished out. With a finger, he pushed the hair from her face; some strands stuck to the wet tracks her tears had left behind.

Leaning his head against the wall, he eyed her silently. The moment stretched on, and she searched his features. She expected to see anger, satisfaction at making her cry the way he had. But he seemed to be studying her as well, with curiosity.

"The punishment for walking without a handler is ten with the cane." She assumed he would be pleased with her whimper, but he didn't show any reaction to it.

She tried to tell him she didn't know. How could she have known? But wasn't that the point? She wasn't supposed to have been there. How could she know rules for a place she had been forbidden from entering?

"Technically, Peter should be delivering these, but I won't let him touch you. Any more than I would let that fucker Marcus touch you. No one touches what's mine, Ellie. And, make no mistake, you are mine."

The possession and harshness of his words should have made her shiver with dread. After all, she was bound to the wall, her ass throbbing and swollen, and the promise of more pain hung over her. How could she find comfort in his words? Comfort in him?

"The punishment is ten, but like I said, you're mine, and I decide your punishment. You'll take five." He raised the cane level with her face and tapped her nose with the tip. "Five strikes of the cane, and your punishment is over. Have you learned, Ellie? Have you finally seen that I mean what I say?

And do you understand I make the rules, not you? Do you get I am the one who allows and forbids?"

She focused on what she could make out of the cane. With the pain starting to ebb enough for her to breathe easier, the idea of it starting again brought more tears to her eyes. This was her life, now.

His rules. His dominance.

She'd given herself over to him to save her father. She couldn't even find the energy to be angry at him. This was her doing. He'd told her to stay out of the Annex. He warned her what would happen. She had gone in with her eyes open wide to the consequences. And now she had to bear them.

She nodded.

This was her own fault. And she would take the next five licks with as much grace as she could muster. Maybe he would answer her questions afterward. Maybe they could find a moment of peace.

"Five." He moved away from her, and she turned forward, studying the swirled designs of the wallpaper with much less interest than she had during her wait.

He gave no further warning.

Fire ignited in a thin line across her ass, driving her up to her toes.

Another lash landed, and she cried out much louder than with the strap. She sank her teeth into the ball gag and squealed with the third strike.

Taking deep breaths through her nose didn't help with the fourth strike, and when the fifth landed across the back of her thighs, she screamed and rose as high on her toes as the bonds would allow.

Hard sobs racked her body. It was done. The pain seared her skin—the throbbing, the burning, all of it consumed her mind.

She barely heard his whisper in her ear.

"You did good, Ellie. You did really good." He wiped more hair from her face. She closed her eyes, unable to look at him while she continued to cry. Cry from the pain, the embarrassment, the arousal.

Her ankles were unlatched and then he unhooked her wrists. The weight of her body was too much for her legs, and she stumbled, only to be caught by him. He lifted her in his arms and took her to his bed.

Of course. He probably wanted to have a solid fuck before tossing her into her room.

He laid her on her belly and unhooked the gag, wiping her mouth with his hand after the ball fell out. Rolling to her side, she pressed her head to the pillow, the feathery soft pillow, and tucked her knees up to her chest.

He dragged the covers from the foot of the bed over her naked body.

"Rest a few minutes, Ellie." He gently placed the quilt over her shivering body. But it wasn't the cold making her insides quake. It was the desire, the longing she now had that he wouldn't do anything about. He was punishing her. She wouldn't get to feel his touch. Not in the way that would make this new ache go away.

She wiped her face with the back of her wrist and sniffled. Finally, the sobs slowed, and she could breathe evenly again. The lights went out, and the bed gave behind her just before his warm body pressed up to hers.

His erection pushed against her ass, making her wince. But he didn't say anything. She let him drape his arm over her and pull her to him, taking the comfort he seemed willing to give her.

"That was the harshest punishment I ever want to give you. Never disobey me again, Ellie. Not when it comes to your safety. Because I don't want to do that again," he whispered from behind her in the dark.

The sincerity lingered between them. Not sure how to respond, she kept quiet, letting the tears dry and her ass adjust to the ache.

"You didn't have to do that, Ash," she finally whispered into the silence.

His hand moved, cupping her sore cheek and squeezing.

"Yes, I did."

She wanted to argue, but she knew he was right. He did have to punish her. She'd broken his rule, she'd disobeyed, and, in his own way, he put things back together.

There was no anger now, no raw rage like she'd seen when he approached her at the party. Just her breathing settling down to match his own, and her body softening into his.

As time ticked by, she waited for him to release her, to scoot her back to her own room. But his arm anchored her to him, and his warm breath brushed over her neck.

"Ash?" she chanced.

He grunted.

"What do you want from me?" she asked softly, sure he was already half-asleep and the question would go unanswered. Besides, was she prepared to know? If he really did see her as his little plaything for the moment, could she handle it?

And, more to the point, why the hell did she care? The man had just whipped her, caned her. She'd have marks for a day if not longer on her skin from the whippy implement. Yet she lay with him, comforted by his warmth, feeling safer in his bed than she had in her own her entire life. None of it made sense.

His answer came out gentle, but held the low growl she'd come used to hearing in his voice. "I want everything, Ellie. And you're going to give it to me."

CHAPTER 18

*E*llie barely ate her breakfast, Ash noted as he finished his last bite. The fresh fruit he had made sure accompanied every meal, since she seemed to enjoy it so much, went untouched, and the eggs had long gotten cold on her plate. The only item she'd touched was her toast, and only two small bites.

She barely spared him a glance as well, finding the pattern on the tablecloth most interesting. Peter had joined them at first, but, after watching them silently for several moments, he'd made an excuse and abandoned the dining room.

"If you are having a lot of pain, I'll get you some ibuprofen." He sat back in his chair and enjoyed watching the fresh blush take over her cheeks.

She shook her head, thrusting her chin upward in the act of defiance he'd come to admire. No matter what he threw at her, no matter how deeply he made her submit, she would not break. And he didn't want her to. Ellie would bend to him, but he would not see her cracked.

"I'm fine," she lied.

He couldn't help but smile. "You know how I feel about lying, Ellie." He tapped his fingers on the table.

Her throat constricted with her swallow, and the heat turned up on her cheeks.

"I'm sore, but fine," she amended.

"I meant what I said, I don't want to repeat that lesson."

"Don't you have a meeting you need to get to? Time to shake the coins out of someone's pockets or something? Maybe put more helpless women in your harem?"

Ah. There it was.

"The Annex isn't a harem," he said. "If you have questions, ask."

She blinked at him. After she'd breached the Annex, keeping it hidden from her didn't need to be a priority anymore.

She toyed with the ends of her hair. "Okay." She straightened in her seat. "What is the Annex? I couldn't find any information on it when I searched."

Of course, she would try to find it on the Internet when his staff wouldn't divulge any information. He had known she would search when he gave her the laptop, but since the Annex was a well-kept secret among powerful elite, he had no worries she'd actually find anything.

"The Annex is a members-only club that provides services other clubs and dating services don't."

"That tells me nothing." She folded her arms over her chest. "Why did the women last night have to have babysitters? And what was the contract I saw being signed? Are you selling women? The rumors of sex trafficking are true?"

Anger built in her tone as she threw questions at him. He wouldn't react to the emotion in her accusations.

"No. I do not work in sex trafficking or human trafficking or any of that bullshit." And his father probably rolled over in his grave daily because of his decision.

"Okay." She softened her voice. "Then what?"

"Last night was a catalogue party. You know how women get together and have those purse parties or whatever? Well, this was similar to that."

"If you aren't going to tell me, then forget the conversation."

"I am telling you." He fisted his hand on the table.

"You're being vague," she shot at him.

"Well, we wouldn't be having this damn conversation at all if you hadn't snuck into a place you weren't supposed to be." He leaned over the table.

"I wouldn't have had to sneak anywhere if you hadn't been so secretive about it." She matched his irritation.

He blinked a few times and laughed. "So, it's my fault because I didn't want you to know? Do you need another demonstration of who is in charge here?"

Her cheeks blanched, and she sat back in her chair, shoulders slumping. "No." She turned her gaze away.

"Did it occur to you at all that my keeping you from the Annex was to protect you?"

She rolled her eyes. "I just thought you were doing something illegal back there and didn't want me to know. Are you? Is what you're doing something horrible?"

He didn't like the doubt in her expression. His father always showed his disappointment for his decisions. The men his father worked with had given him no doubt of the amount of dissatisfaction they felt at his actions, but none of that had caused the ache the expression of doubt in her eyes did.

"Not a single woman you saw last night was there against her will. Every one of them is free to leave when they wish. They come and go as they please. Well, mostly."

"Just start at the beginning, Ash. I want to understand." The softness in her voice drew him. The bitterness she'd shown him in the past waned. Could the spanking last night have gotten through to her? Or was it the way he'd held her all night?

He should have put her in her own bed. His mind told him it would be safer, but the rest of him demanded she be near him. She needed him. After such a harsh punishment, abandoning her to her own bed would have been cruel. Being cruel to Ellie, when she was so vulnerable, so open to hurt, wasn't an option. He wouldn't hurt her, not after seeing the hurt in her eyes after sending her away before.

"My father started a business before I was born. He sold women to other men who wanted sex slaves or house slaves, or whatever they wanted. The women didn't have a say. They didn't choose the men, and a lot of times they didn't choose to be sold at all. After my father died, and the business became mine, I made changes. The Annex is more of a service of pairing up women who want to find men to own them."

"They choose slavery?"

"In a way. Think of it as a kinky dating service. The women always have final say in a contract, they agree to terms, they agree to pricing, and they agree to time. If they don't agree to any of it, the deal doesn't take place."

"So how do you make any money?"

"A broker's fee." Explaining it all made it sound simpler than it really was. "I bring in the clientele, I make the deals, and I give the girls housing until they find the contract they want."

"So, they aren't prostitutes?"

"Some of them do work the parties like last night for one night of servitude, and men come to the Annex for similar dates."

He waited for disgust to show up in her expression. So far, only curiosity.

"Come with me." He pushed away from the table and took her hand, leading her out of the dining room.

She didn't say a word as they walked through the house to the Annex. And she held his hand tighter when he opened the door leading to the wing she'd snuck into the night before.

He would never get over the surprise and anger he'd felt when he saw her pressed against the wall by Marcus. It had taken immense strength not to kill him where he stood. Only focusing on Ellie made that possible.

Taking her down a corridor away from the main ballroom of the wing, he pointed out the doors.

"These are apartments. Most of the girls live in groups of two or three, but some do live alone. Each suite has three bedrooms, a kitchen, and living space. The doors are all locked, and they have keys, just like any other apartment building."

"You don't have a key?"

He smiled. "Only Peter and I have access to the keys to these apartments. They don't lock from the outside. See?" He pointed out the door to show he couldn't lock the girls in.

"But my room is lockable from the outside." She shot him a surprised look.

"Your room is different." He brushed off the subject for another time.

He led her toward his office.

"So, they can come and go as they please?"

"Well, mostly. If they leave the estate, they need to let Peter or whoever is in charge of security for the day know. It's for their safety, Ellie."

She remained silent as he brought her to his office.

"The contract I saw last night. The guy, he used the woman right there in front of Peter. He didn't stop him."

"It's part of the deal, Ellie. She's a product, and he was testing her out."

Ellie's pupils grew, and she averted his gaze again. She found the entire ordeal arousing, not distasteful. His cock found her arousal more appealing than his pants were comfortable with.

"She was aware of the contract. She agreed to the terms. Peter never would have allowed it if that weren't the case."

"And the handlers?" she asked while moving around the room, pretending to look at the books on the shelves. Mostly for décor; he hadn't read any of them.

"Security. The party has a lot of men vying for the same woman, so they are given a handler to keep away any unwanted attention or aggressions. I can't keep them safe if the women wander around on their own. Someone like Marcus is always present."

She stilled at the name but ran her finger over the spine of a book as if to distract herself.

"And if the woman doesn't want to be sold?"

"Well, if that was the case, they wouldn't be here to begin with. I never take a woman into the Annex who doesn't want to be there. They aren't allowed at the party if they aren't sure they want to be on contract."

She peeked over her shoulder at him.

"And me? I offered myself for my father's debt. Wouldn't you make back the money you lost on my father faster if you put me in the Annex?"

He felt the knot in his chest he felt every time Peter asked the same question, or Daniel chanced making a comment. Thinking to have her in the Annex made his skin tighten, his head ache, and his chest clench.

"Probably," he agreed, not giving her any indication the idea repulsed him as it did.

"Then, why am I in your house instead of your stable?"

she asked with more curiosity than bitterness. She didn't seem to have any issue with the concept of the Annex, but the fact she wasn't in it piqued her interest.

"Not sure you'd get a buyer for me?" she teased and turned back to the books.

He'd have a buyer within an hour, of that he had no question. Not just her body, or her obvious beauty, but her quick wit and intelligence would draw attention to her within moments of meeting the clients. He would probably earn every penny, plus more of what her father borrowed, on the first contract.

So, why not allow it?

"Would you want to be contracted out?" he asked more out of curiosity than giving the thought any actual weight. The only place Ellie would be going was back to his bed.

Ellie's delicate hand paused over the books and dropped to her side. She turned around, those large eyes of hers searing into him from across the room.

"What sort of things do the men buy these women for?" she asked with a tilt to her head.

He tightened his fists; could she even think he'd let her go with some other man? Someone who wouldn't put her needs or wants first, but only treat her as a piece of ass?

"Sexual servitude, always. Some want specific roles like Master slave or a house maid as well as sex slave. Some have specific tastes like blood play, forced sex, caging, humiliation, scat play."

Her eyes widened, and he had his answer. His little Ellie knew much more than she let on.

"But the women set limits? They can say no?"

"They can take things out of contracts or suggest things, but once they sign, the only way out is to void the contract and lose the money they were paid."

Ellie sighed.

"Is it so horrible?" he asked, leaning against his desk. "Many of the women here have done these things outside of the Annex, for less pay, with less security, and had no say. None of them are forced, and a lot of them are looking to find someone long-term."

Her eyes snapped to his. "What does that mean?"

"It means a client can put in an offer to buy the woman outright. Not a termed contract—they would be his until the two of them dissolved the relationship."

"So, you sell them like a prize horse?"

"I suppose you can see it that way. Just like any other transaction, the woman gets her share, I get mine, and the deal is done."

Ellie sank into the leather seat before him, folding her hands in her lap.

"Is that why you showed the Annex to me, now? I'll go in the catalogue?"

He would swear on his life he heard deep sorrow in her voice with her question. She actually thought she was worth so little to him he could just put her in line with the other girls? That over the past week, they hadn't made any headway?

But, why would she think otherwise? He'd kept her at arm's length, had all but called her and treated her as a whore. Of course she thought so little of herself. He'd taught her to.

That ended. Now.

"You're not for sale. To Marcus or anyone else." A shiver ran through her body. His tone remained hard. He managed to keep the rage over her thinking away from his voice, but it still sat in his chest. Nagging at him over the way he allowed her to feel, the way he'd treated her.

"What if I wanted to? I mean, with a few months'

contract, I should be able to make back what my father owed."

"I already told you. The debt amount doesn't matter. It was paid the moment you became mine. There's nothing left to work off."

Her lips parted, and he thought she would argue more. He could sense the relief in her. Why fight more?

"Come with me. There's something else I want to show you before I have to leave for a meeting." He gripped her arm and pulled her from the chair. The kindness he'd afforded by being gentle so far that morning was coming to an abrupt end.

She seemed confused by his roughness, but her body responded immediately.

"Last night, after I punished you, your pussy ached for me to fuck you, didn't it?" he asked as he led her outside the double doors to one of the three playrooms in the Annex.

"What?" She turned her head away. "No."

Lying didn't come easy to her, and he never failed to know when she performed the act.

"Hmmm. That's the second time this morning you've tried lying to me. I'm going to give you another chance." He pressed his back to the door, folding his arms over his chest, and glared at her. With his short sleeves, his tattooed arms looked menacing, and he'd left his hair down again. She seemed to respond better to him when he did. "How badly did you want me to ram my cock into you after I whipped you and caned you?"

When she tried to turn away again, he grabbed her chin and held her firmly in his hand. She blinked a few times but couldn't hide her dilated pupils, or control the quickness of her breathing.

"I did," she said, as though confessing the greatest sin a woman could commit. "It made no sense. You hurt me so bad, my bottom burned and stung and felt swollen, but I did. I wanted you to—I wanted you."

A smile grew over his lips. Such a beauty, this girl of his. So open and honest, even when she wanted to hide her reactions, her body listened to him.

"I'm not sorry I hurt you. You deserved your punishment, and I think you know that."

"I did. I'm sorry I barged into your party. Will Marcus cause you trouble, now?"

After everything that happened, she worried about Marcus stirring up problems for him.

He released her chin, smoothing her hair over her shoulder.

"Nothing I can't handle."

"What were you going to show?"

He grinned again and twisted the door handle behind his back. "I'm going to show you why these women look for long-term contracts. Why these women are here at the Annex willingly."

The door opened, and he took a step inside, gesturing for her to follow him.

"I'm going to show you not all pain is for punishment."

CHAPTER 19

Ellie stepped inside. Not having any expectations, she shouldn't have been shocked. And she wasn't, not really. More surprised at what surrounded her.

The dark décor matched the rest of Ash's estate. But the furniture made this room different. A spanking bench, a cross, and a leather-upholstered table.

Her heart jackhammered as she took in the room. Her pussy already began to respond. The ambiance chanted sex. The fading soreness of her ass was long forgotten as she approached the spanking bench and ran her fingers over the fine black leather.

"Take your clothes off, Ellie." Ash's dark voice shook her from her own fanciful thoughts. He shut the door and locked it before peeling off his T-shirt.

The man had too many tattoos to count, and his muscular build only cemented her arousal. He left his jeans and boots on and met her at the table.

"I didn't stutter, did I?" The demand hung there, right in front of her face. If she didn't comply, he'd make her, and if he made her, there wouldn't be as much fun for her. And she had no doubt he wanted her to have fun.

Unwilling to deny herself after having waited all night for his touch, she quickly pushed the straps of her dress over her shoulders and shoved it down, stepping out and plucking it from the floor. She'd worn one of the items he'd made her buy the day before. A simple dress, brand new and carrying a major label, that cost him more money than she made in a week at the coffeehouse.

"No bra or panties this morning?" he asked with a grin and raised brow.

Her face flamed. He made her do that too often.

"The panties hurt," she answered honestly. The fabric rubbing against her bottom had been irritating.

"Come here and bend over the edge of the table. I want to check the cane markings from last night." He stepped to the side and patted the spot he wanted her.

She'd seen them herself after her shower. Long welts crossed her ass, but none had broken skin. She wondered how many women he had to practice on before he could deliver such a sweltering caning without producing any scars.

The leather of the table cooled her heated skin when she laid her chest against it. She pillowed her hands beneath her head and held her breath, feeling his eyes on her.

Feather touches across her ass and a soft tsking of his tongue.

"Such a naughty girl, you were," he whispered, lightly touching one of the welts. "I won't spank you today, then. There are still raised marks from the cane. It has to be more than a little sore." He pressed down on the stripe, and she hissed, rising onto her toes.

He chuckled.

"Reach back and pull your ass cheeks apart for me." He

removed his hand from her and waited. She froze. She couldn't do that. He asked too much. Spread her ass cheeks apart so he could see her most intimate, private parts?

It was all fine for him to touch her, and fuck her, but to stare at her, to examine those parts of her asked too much.

But to deny him, to disobey again, would be asking for more punishment. And she didn't want any more of those. The choice didn't seem to be any choice at all.

She reached back, burying her face into the leather to hide herself from her own actions, and gripped her cheeks.

"Wider, Ellie," he chastised when she made only a small amount of progress. "Remember, I'm teaching you a lesson here. And it's a good lesson, so I would suggest you obey my commands."

Moaning, she moved her hands, feeling the cool air brush over her pucker and her pussy.

"Good girl." He placed a hand on her hip.

She started when his tongue touched her pussy entrance.

"Fuck, you taste good." He kissed her ass cheek. "You are already so wet for me, and all I did was take away your clothes and make you show me your asshole."

His crudeness only amplified her embarrassment.

"Did you get wet while we were talking about the girls? Does the idea of a woman being so powerful in her own sexuality she would sell herself to a man in order to get what she wanted make you burn? Or was it the idea she would be subjected to his whims, have to follow his rules, have to submit to his will?"

A thick finger slowly worked its way into her pussy, and she moaned with the pleasure of it. It wasn't enough, though. She wanted more.

"Answer me, Ellie."

Oh. He wanted her to respond? How the hell could she do that? She couldn't actually admit that the idea of submitting, of obeying someone turned her on. Not after how much she'd resisted him.

"Or did you want the lesson to end?"

Another finger slid in, and he scissored them, stretching her with each thrust.

"Both," she called out when he started to retreat. "They both excite me." She groaned after giving her confession.

"Good girl." His tongue swiped across her clit, and he thrust his fingers in harder. "Okay, now up and on your back." He tapped her hip.

She didn't want to get on her back. She wanted him to keep licking her, and fuck her just like she was. But he made the rules, and he handed out the consequences.

Once she lay on the table, he spread her legs and wrapped his arms around her thighs, yanking her to the edge. She winced against the pain of the leather rubbing her ass, but he didn't seem to care.

He wouldn't apologize for the punishment, and she doubted he would take it much easier on her today because of the soreness. Though he did say he wouldn't spank her until the welts healed.

Drawers opened below her, and she could hear him rummaging around. When he popped back up, he cradled a coil of hemp rope. He undid the tie and let the end of the rope fall.

She lay mute as he positioned her arms over her head, securing them with cuffs and the rope to D-rings on the table. Her legs were parted, almost painfully so, to a split formation, and the rope wound around her thighs. He tethered the end to the table behind her head.

She was completely bound, unable to move, and spread out so he could do whatever he wished to any part of her chest, her belly, or her pussy.

"Beautiful," he breathed as he stood between her legs.

He bent over and brought his face to her pussy, pulling her lips far apart and exposing her wanting clit. His silvery eyes level with hers, he flicked the swollen nub with his tongue.

Ellie closed her eyes at the pleasure coursing through her with the simple touch, and wanted to cry when he let her go and stepped away. Unsure of his next intensions, she opened her eyes and found him searching through the implements.

When he returned, she noticed he held a heavy flogger. She tensed when he laid the thick falls over her chest and ran them across her breasts.

"This isn't going to hurt you, but it's not going to be very pleasant at first." He raised it up and brought it crashing over her chest. She yelped but recognized it was more from shock than pain.

Again, it came down across her breasts, and she let out a low groan. Heat spread over her chest as the flogger landed a third and fourth time. She wiggled a bit, but the bonds didn't give her much room, and she found she wasn't trying to get away from the implement so much as needing to find a place to put her energy.

"Your nipples are so hard, Ellie." He paused in the flogging to tweak the beaded nubs.

He ran his nails over both breasts and whipped the flogger harder over her breasts. She sucked in a breath and arched her back, presenting him with her tits for another stroke.

She stopped trying to anticipate where the next lash would land and instead focused on the aftereffects of each. Heat spread to her core.

He brought the falls down over her chest again. His lips, those full lips surrounded by his beard, quirked up in a grin with each of her grunts. She could make out the outline of his cock against his jeans and licked her lips at the memory of having it in her mouth.

A hard lash dragged her attention back to the burn in her flesh. He'd moved away from her breasts and had delivered a hard crack to her belly.

Moving around her, he began to assault her entire body with the flogger. Her breasts then her hip, her stomach again, and then he stood between her legs.

"Ash." She wiggled beneath his mischievous gaze. He had his sights on her pussy. And although she desperately wanted his touch, she did not want those leather strips anywhere near her clit.

"Hold still, Ellie." He kept his hungry eyes on her pussy as he brought his hand back.

"Ash... Argh!" she screamed out when the flogger landed directly over her pussy.

"Like fucking music." He smiled and delivered another blow. She tried to close her legs, but the ropes held her open to him.

She cried out again when the flogger landed, and again when he moved to the inside of her thighs.

"Being bound open and helpless makes your pussy drip." He dragged a finger through her folds and presented the evidence glistening on his fingertips.

She turned her face, thinking to ignore the truth, but when his fingers entered her, she moaned with satisfaction.

Moving her hips as best she could, she tried to take more of his fingers into her. So focused on the pleasure between her legs, she didn't notice him move his other arm.

The flogger landed again, right over her peaked nipples, and she cried out, yanking on her bonds.

"Fuck, baby. Your pussy grips me when you scream like that." He repeated the lash, and she arched her body, letting a cry loose.

The pain morphed into something else, something warm and soothing. When the next lash came, she welcomed it.

"There you go. There's my girl." He sounded farther away. Was he whispering?

"Fuck," she groaned when the lash came down between her breasts and his fingers thrust hard into her pussy.

Ash draped the flogger over her belly and removed all touch from her body. She sought him out, desperate for more, not ready for him to leave her just yet.

He removed his pants and his boxers and came to stand between her thighs, gripping his cock in his right hand.

"I'm right here. I wouldn't leave you. Not like this." He ran his nails over her thigh, making her wince and sigh at the same time. How did this happen? How did pain meld with pleasure to the point she couldn't separate the two? Which did she need more? Which did she want more?

He pushed his cock through her folds, eliciting more sounds from her. Up and down, he ran his cock, and she tried to inch closer, to force him to her entrance. But it was Ash, and Ash only did what Ash wanted to do. And if he wanted to make her squirm and beg, then that's what would happen.

And she was at the point where begging wouldn't be beneath her.

He grinned at her, the hunger evident in his eyes even as he seemed to control his own need. Jaw tensed, he moved his cock lower, positioned it at her pussy.

"Please, Ash," she murmured. She'd wanted him inside too long to be denied another moment.

"Such a good girl when my cock is touching you." He pushed forward, only giving her the tip of what she craved most at that moment.

"Ash! Please." She could feel tears welling up, the frustration too great to contain.

In one hard thrust, he was inside her, buried to the hilt.

"Fuck." She drew out the word in a breathy sigh. Such fullness, such utter, beautiful fullness.

He stilled in his movements, and she brought her gaze up to meet his. Strands of dirty-blond hair curtained his features, but his eyes were easy to make out. Wild with passion, bright silvery-blue eyes pinned her where the bonds did not.

With calculated movements, he pulled back, nearly leaving her entirely, only to thrust hard into her. She closed her eyes to the pleasure as he did so again and again, until he gripped her hips and plowed into her repeatedly.

"Ash." She called his name over and over again, matching each time his cock plowed into her, filling her completely and making her want him even more.

"Ellie, don't you come yet." His harsh words struck her. He had to be insane.

"I have to. I have to." She fisted her hands, feeling the pressure building. The sounds of their bodies slamming into each other surrounded them. How could she stop the freight train when it was already at full speed?

"Not yet," he ordered, shifting his body in a way that left her clit completely exposed and untouched.

"Oh fuck." She shook her feet, wanting more, needing more, completely abandoned.

She tried to glare up at him, but the fierceness staring at her only drove her closer to the brink.

"Tell me who you belong to, Ellie. Who do you belong to?"

"You, Ash, I belong to you." She nodded, feeling more than just the words.

"Who owns this body, this pussy, these tits, and this ass. Who owns it?" He smacked her hip, eliciting another electric current through her body.

"You do. Please, Ash, Please." She tugged and writhed as best she could, trying to get the pressure off.

He stopped fucking her and leaned over her, his cock still lodged inside her, throbbing against her wanting cunt.

"And who do you obey?" His chest heaved as much as hers. She could see him trying to keep his body in control. He wanted to thrust as much as she needed him to.

Ellie lined up her gaze with his as she gave her answer. "You, Ash. I obey you."

He closed his eyes and thrust again. "Fuck yeah, you do." His fingers dug into her flesh. "Come for me, Ellie. You can come, now."

Maybe she should have been appalled at his arrogance, but it was too late. Her body had already submitted to him, had already accepted everything he'd been saying. He did own her. He could command her body better than she ever could. And this was no different.

His thumb rubbed her clit, alternating between hard and soft circles. Her orgasm ripped through her body, making her scream with each intense wave as it took over every fiber in her body.

As she slowly floated back to him, she opened her eyes, finding his steady expression.

"Fuck, oh fuck, that was gorgeous," he said, pumping two more times then pulling his cock back out. Running his dick up and down her pussy, he grunted and wrapped his hand around his shaft, jerking three times before streams of cum began to shoot out against her pussy and her stomach. Warm strings of his load crisscrossed her stomach, and she bit her lip, wishing she'd been able to take him in her mouth before he came.

He stroked one more time, gathering the small bead of cum from his head, and leaned over her body, offering his finger to her mouth.

She darted out her tongue and wiped it clean, smiling up at him afterward.

"Such a good girl," he said again in a coarse whisper.

He kissed her, pressing against the mess he'd left on hers. The tingling in her body had more to do with the taste of his kiss than the ropes binding her limbs.

After breaking the kiss, he stood to full height. "You'll need another shower."

The drawers opened again, and he pulled out two towels. He also grabbed a bottle of water she hadn't noticed on the small table beside the bondage equipment and wet one of the towels. He tenderly wiped down her stomach and her pussy, cleaning her of his semen.

Only after his shirt and pants were back on did he unbind and help her off the table.

"Give yourself a second," he ordered when her legs wobbled beneath her. "You can't just run off after a session like that."

She regarded him with curiosity. His tone held less irritation than she was used to, and more care.

He helped her dress then lifted her into his arms.

"I can walk, Ash," she protested when he reached the door leading to the main house.

"I'm aware." He held her tighter.

"Where are you taking me?"

"To our room. You need a nap, and I need to get to a meeting." He climbed the stairs, and she rested her head against his neck, inhaling the salty smell of him.

"What about my room?" she asked when he laid her on his bed.

"Unless I tell you to use it, it's off-limits. You'll sleep with me from now on." The gruff answer was softened only by the hint of a smile tinting his eyes.

"You aren't as much of an asshole as I thought." She snuggled into the pillows.

He pinched her ear to get her attention.

The chill returned to his expression. "Don't make me anything that I'm not. I'm not your Prince Charming."

She swallowed, feeling the sternness in him.

"I know." She nodded.

He stared at her for a long moment then left, closing the door quietly behind him.

She looked at the door, hoping he'd come back, leaving his hard exterior outside and showing her the warmth, she'd seen downstairs.

The flogging had left her breasts tender, and her body warm, but it didn't hurt as much as being shoved away from him. He would keep her at arm's length, no matter what she saw in him. She needed to remember beneath the kindness he'd shown her lived a beast.

No, he wasn't her Prince Charming.

He was more.

And she hated it.

CHAPTER 20

Delilah, Ash's first all-male strip club, stood across town from Samson. His mother's infatuation with their love story underlined his undertaking the two clubs. The others clubs he owned catered to both sexes, whereas these two were exclusive in membership defined by the gender of the patron. Maybe watching his mother treated like just another female by his father had more impact on him than he would admit.

Although his mother had been a woman of the Annex, she had been allowed to move into the main house when she became pregnant. Ash would give his father at least that much credit. He'd always thought there had to be something there, something his father felt for his mother. She wasn't the first girl his cock impregnated, but she was the first, and only, one he didn't force into an abortion. He may have ignored her existence for the most part after Ash was born, but he didn't put her back into the Annex. He didn't force her to spread her legs for money anymore. She had a comfortable, but loveless, life.

Seeing her pretend to be content as he grew up, Ash realized love could only bring pain. It wasn't that his mother loved Samuel Titon. She hardly mentioned him, or even looked at him should he enter a room they were in. But she wanted love, and not just the kind her doting son could give. She wanted to be held and cherished, and it never happened. Samuel didn't want her, but he wasn't about to let some other man have her, either. She was the mother of his son, after all, and how would that look?

To business associates, they were a typical family. Sure, they didn't marry, but his mother had been dragged to business dinners when required. No one said anything, at least to his face, about the oddity that a man in his position didn't take a wife.

But Ash knew the circumstances, knew what went on behind the closed doors of the massive estate overlooking the city. Maybe Samuel was too chickenshit to think about love. Maybe he thought it made him weak, or he figured loving her would make her have value. And from what he witnessed from his father, he placed no value on anyone, aside from monetary. And women were a product that made him limitless sales.

He didn't care if they didn't like the buyer. They were product, and product didn't choose who made the bids. The only line Ash ever saw his father draw was kidnapping, but even that wasn't completely believed. His father put on a big show in front of him about not dealing with traffickers, but Ash never quite believed him. The women in the Annex weren't always there by their choice. His father may have explained it away, saying they were like prostitutes,coming from bad circumstances, but the girls' expressions often told another story.

When Ash took over the Annex and the rest of the businesses, he made sure every woman was there at her own request and of her own will. Anyone who wanted to leave would be given a healthy severance and help to set themselves up outside the estate. A dozen women took him up on the offer, but he figured it was the new management policies that kept the other twenty or so girls from fleeing.

Letting Ellie see the Annex for what it was, giving her the tour and the truth, lifted a weight from his chest. Now she could see him for what he really was, and she could stop needling her way into his every thought.

Except, from the time he tucked her into his bed until the moment he stepped into the back room of Delilah, she had captivated every passing thought.

He'd have to spank her for it when he got home.

"Ashland." Kristoff extended his hand in greeting as he was escorted into the room. Ash took his hand and after a brief grip dropped it.

Ignoring Kristoff's irritated expression, he turned to the two men who had accompanied him.

"Mr. Jansen. Mr. Bertucci." Ash kept his curiosity to himself for the moment. "I assumed it would just be Kristoff and myself."

"He's brought us into the fold. I was sure you wouldn't mind. We did a lot of work with your father." Jansen, the oldest of the three, gave him a crooked grin that pushed the deep wrinkles of his cheeks back.

Which was exactly why he didn't do business with them. Everything his father touched had been tainted, and none of the men from that circle would play nice after they knew the new rules of the game.

"I still haven't changed my mind about the offer you made after my father passed. I'm doing well enough following my own direction." Ash took his seat at the table and gestured for everyone else to do the same.

"As much as I know it would hurt your father that you haven't followed in his footsteps, I understand. You're your own man, and have your own aspirations. This is a new deal, a new offer. Nothing unsavory, I assure you," Bertucci said.

Ash rested his hands on the table. Keeping a level expression trained on the three men staring at him, he nodded. "What's the deal?"

They weren't used to a straightforward question only moments after exchanging their greetings. They were used to the old-school way. Long-winded fake interest in each other's wives, or mistresses, or kids, anything to try and make the others believe they saw each other as something more than business associates one scandal away from being enemies.

After shifting in his seat, Kristoff cleared his throat. "Your father once offered us shares of the Annex. At the time, we didn't see the value. However, we've watched it grow under your management. Even my son seems infatuated with it. Imagine if you were to expand."

Ash curled his toes inside his boots, unable to make a fist without them seeing or commenting on it.

"I have no need to expand," he responded and motioned to one of his men to get him a drink.

"If we each were to have a piece, we could have multiple houses. We could offer women internationally," Jansen chimed in accepting the glass of whiskey offered to him.

"My father offered you a piece of the Annex?" Ash sipped his drink. Samuel Titon didn't share. No way he wanted to bring these assholes into the business with him.

"Yes. And we should have grabbed the chance." Bertucci looked over at his partners.

"My father's business with you went as far as the garbage contracts, the underground gambling bullshit, but the Annex was his prize project. His to control. Why would he want partners?"

Jensen narrowed his eyes. "Are you calling us liars, boy?"

Ah, and there it was. No matter how much of the city Ash owned and controlled, these old-timers would always see him as Samuel's son, his boy.

"I'm saying it doesn't sound like my father," Ash qualified. As much as he would enjoy calling these jackasses out right to their faces, he had no doubt the evening would end in bloodshed if he did.

"But it doesn't really matter. The Annex is mine and will always stay mine. I don't need or want partners. I thought I had made myself clear after my father died."

He had made it perfectly clear. Crystal, in fact, when he dropped out of all the dealings his father held. He didn't accept any money from the garbage contracts, and he pulled all his interest and support from the underground gambling ring they ran.

"I heard there was some trouble at the party last night," Komisky said, looking as though he'd just found the way into a secret laboratory.

"Nothing that wasn't handled."

"Marcus told me what took place." He shook his head. "Seems as though maybe your Annex can't handle the number of girls you have, or cater to some of the buyers' more unsavory tastes."

Ash leaned forward. "If you're talking about your son's fucked-up tastes, then no. We don't offer rape as a product. We also don't force our girls to wear a fucking diaper and breast feed in front of the buyer while he jerks off on her if she doesn't agree to it."

Jansen visibly shrank back while Bertucci's eyebrows knitted together in disgust.

"Is that what your son wanted?" Bertucci asked with a pointed finger.

"His tastes are his own. My point is the Annex could expand, and we could all become even richer."

Ash shook his head. "I took this meeting as a courtesy. Again." He gave a pointed glance at Komisky. "You were good friends to my father." The lie tasted like shit sitting on his tongue. "And I've heard you out. I am not in the market for partners or to expand. For those men who can't find what they are looking for with our services, they are free to search elsewhere. I'm sure there is someone out there who does offer them."

"For the second time, you tried to humiliate my son." Komisky's noncommitted smile dropped, and anger bubbled to the surface. "You've insulted him."

Ash rolled his shoulders back and took a deep breath.

"Your son came into my establishment and put his hands on a girl that wasn't his. My girl. Knowing full well she belonged to me and wasn't on the menu. He's lucky I let him leave with both hands still attached."

Jensen and Bertucci exchanged glances.

"Wait. Is this what this is about? Your pervert son didn't get what he wanted at a party? Are you shitting me?" Bertucci stood from the table.

"Expanding the Annex would be profitable for all of us," Komisky argued.

"Yeah, it would. But you heard him. He's not interested. And after hearing what shit you want to bring to the table, I'm not interested, either."

Jansen followed Bertucci's lead and stood, buttoning his jacket as he did so. "Thanks for the meeting, Ashland. I'm sure you have more important things to be do doing with your time than trying to placate a few old men."

Ash rose and accepted Jansen's hand. "Of course. You would do the same for me." He nodded. And they would. He didn't deny their manners, but he would never have business dealings with the other families again.

Jansen didn't speak to Komisky, only giving him a disapproving glare before following Bertucci from the room, leaving Ash with a red-faced Kristoff.

"You fucking asshole." Kristoff burst from his chair. Ash's men were on him in a flash, ready to take the party outside if need be. The club was packed, and making a mess in the back room would be bad for business.

"I think you should follow your partners lead and get out of my club." Ash moved from the table and took up a spot near the door.

"You can't humiliate my son twice and get away with it. Your father never would have allowed it, and I won't, either." What started out as a light crimson soon morphed into a full red rage. "Disrespecting Marcus is disrespecting me."

"Your son put his hands on my girl. The disrespect was given to me, not the other way around. You tell him, he'll have to have his—desires—filled elsewhere. He's not setting foot in the Annex or any of my clubs. He's blackballed."

Since Ash owned nearly all the clubs in the city, he'd just cut Marcus from any society worthy of roaming.

"You don't know what game you're playing, boy."

Ash shrugged. "I don't play games. Now, I think our meeting is done."

Kristoff kicked the chair out of his way and stormed out. Ash gave a nod, and his men followed. If Kristoff decided he wanted to say something else, he would find himself unable to speak.

"Well, that could have gone better," Peter spoke up from the corner. Ash narrowed his eyes.

"How long have you been standing there like some stalker?" Ash swiped his drink from the table and downed the liquor.

Peter laughed. "Long enough. You know that back panel is starting to squeak. I thought for sure they'd hear me. Might want to have maintenance oil it."

"You're an ass. I can handle those fucks."

"Yeah, I know." Peter shrugged. "Kristoff isn't going to let this go. And blackballing his son? That's not going to be the end of it."

"I know." Ash poured himself another drink. "At least it's just Kristoff. Jensen and Bertucci won't go to war with him over this."

"And Ellie?" Peter asked.

"What about her?"

"What happens with her? Kristoff is going to go after her. You just publicly claimed her, Ash. Don't tell me you don't know what that means."

"I'm aware of what it means, Peter." Ash sighed.

"You just put her in danger."

Ash slammed his glass down on the table. "I said I know what the fuck it means. I'll handle Ellie. You just keep the other girls safe. I want earlier curfews for the time being, and I want escorts when they leave the grounds. If there isn't someone available, they stay put until there is."

"Ellie's classes?"

Ash tucked his hair behind his ears and glared at his cousin. He knew he was right, but it only fueled Ash's irritation.

"Daniel can go with her. Stay outside the room. She just has the one class this semester. The other two she picked up don't start until the next term."

"Her father?"

"I don't give a fuck about that asshole. Marcus won't go after him. I'm sure enough of Ellie's story has been rumored and they know her father isn't in contact with her. Going after him wouldn't serve them."

"You're going to war over a woman." Peter didn't laugh when he made his statement. There wasn't an ounce of playfulness in his expression, either.

"I'm defending what's mine. That's it, Peter. Do not make this more than it is." Ash readjusted his jacket and headed for the door. Staring at Peter would piss him off, and Peter would keep needling him if he let him.

Going home and getting into bed would suit him much better. Holding her—that would calm his spirit.

CHAPTER 21

*A*sh was acting weird. Even for Ash, he was being strange. Ellie had breakfast with him every morning, but by the time she finished, he'd head off to a meeting. He returned for dinner every night, though, and demanded she wait for him to eat.

When they were together, he seemed to be present, but by the end of their meal, his mind would wander. It was like he would start enjoying her company and just as he realized he wasn't a brooding ass, he'd shut down and run off.

He always returned to their bed at night, giving her more pleasure than she thought one body should be able to tolerate without exploding before taking his own. Each night he showed her something new. A new toy, a new position, a new part of her body that had more nerve endings than she thought possible.

She learned she didn't like wood implements nearly as much as the leather flogger. And she learned he tasted best after he'd been drinking whiskey.

But, today, he exceeded his strange behavior.

"I have something to show you," he said when she arrived

home after her class. Daniel left them standing in the hallway, eager to get away, she had no doubt. For whatever reason, he'd been standing guard outside her class for the past week. She hadn't bothered to ask, sure he wouldn't answer, and positive Ash would disregard the question altogether.

"Okay, I'll just put these upstairs and—"

He took the books from her and put them on a random table.

"Okay, then."

He turned and walked away. She sighed and rushed to catch up with him. She followed him down the hallway that led to his office, but instead of going there, he opened a door and waved her up a stairwell.

She gave him a curious look, but he still didn't give her a clue. As she climbed up the steps, fear and anticipation mingled. Ash rarely looked joyful, so his scowl didn't put her on edge, but she didn't know where he was taking her.

Had he finally had his fill of her, and was throwing her in a tower to live out her days? Or was this another secret sex room where he'd mess with her head and pleasure her body until she screamed her release loud enough to shake a few shingles loose on the roof.

At the top of the stairs, the room opened before her. A loft. He'd brought her to a loft.

He stepped behind her and flicked a light switch, illuminating the room.

It was a studio.

She sucked in her breath and turned to him. When his blank stare remained unwavering, she walked around to explore.

Easels had already been put up. New, clean canvas perched on both easels. Each station was fully stocked with brushes and paints.

She ran her hand over the brushes and jumped when the shades rolled up and snapped, letting in all the afternoon light. The outside wall of the room wasn't a wall at all. Floor-to-ceiling windows let in the light and gave a beautiful view of the town below.

"This is… Wow, Ash, this room is beautiful." She went to the windows to peer out.

"It's yours."

She spun to face him. "What? Mine?" She laughed. A studio all to herself?

"Yes, yours. My mother used to paint up here. She said the lighting was the best. It was also the only room my father didn't care about since it's so oddly shaped."

At the top of the house, the outside wall angled inward, and the actual floor space of the room wasn't very large. But it would work perfectly for her painting.

"I—" She glanced around, feeling her chest tighten. "Thank you."

He smiled. Not a wide, toothy grin, but a soft, genuine tug of his lips.

"I had most of the paints replaced. I wasn't sure what was still good." He ran his fingertips over the brushes. "But these are all from my mom. She took good care of them."

Ellie watched the hint of sadness show up and fade while he seemed to lose himself in a memory. This room wasn't just a studio. It was a part of him, part of his history, of his life, and he was gifting it to her.

"The brushes are amazing. I'll be sure to keep them in perfect condition." She placed her hand over his. "I promise."

He slipped free and took a step back. "Your class is going well." He changed the subject.

"Are you harassing my professor for my grades?" she teased.

"I don't harass. I ask a question, and he answers."

She laughed. "Are you serious? You asked my professor about how I'm doing? Am I twelve all of a sudden?"

He stepped closer to her. "I asked him to keep me informed, that's all. He sent me an email to let me know the semester project was going to be a big part of your grade."

"Oh. So, you figured I would need a place to work on the project?"

He studied her. Even after all the times he'd done the same thing, his stare still sent an electric shiver down her spine.

"I wanted to be sure you had everything you needed." He picked up a strand of her hair, rubbing it between his fingers. "You don't put your hair up anymore. Why?"

He knew the answer. He had to, otherwise the arrogant look on his face was a skillful deception.

"I asked a question, Ellie." He ran his nail over her jaw up to her ear.

"You said you don't like it up," she confessed softly.

He sank his fingers into her hair, just above her ear, pulling the strands at her scalp and running them through the long auburn tresses. She winced when he caught a small knot, and bit her lip when he didn't stop but rather shoved his fingers through it.

The softness she'd seen in his eyes only moments before hardened. As though a decision had just been made. His hands dove back into her hair, but this time, he took a fistful of it and held her steady by the base of her neck.

"Do you like your studio?" he asked, his voice hoarse and pupils fully dilated. When he pulled her closer to him, she could smell the musk of his cologne.

"Yes, Ash," she whispered into his chest. Wrapping her arms around his waist, she snuggled into him, feeling the war going on, but wanting to hide from it a little longer. "Thank you," she added.

He grunted in response.

"You won't be able to go to class for a few weeks," he said, and tightened his hold on her when she started to push away from him to look up. She needed to see his face, to see what his eyes said.

"Why? You just said you talked with my professor."

"Why?" He yanked her hair. "What's the answer to that, Ellie?"

He was pulling away from her again. They had finally started to make headway, a gentle connection, and he was pushing away.

She sighed. "Because you want it."

"That's right."

But there was more. There had to be more. He wouldn't just yank her from her class. He wasn't even home most of the day, and although she fully knew what went on in the Annex, she hadn't gone back.

"But you said I could attend class. You even made me sign up for two more." She fisted her hands in his shirt when he still wouldn't release her.

He sighed, the hard whoosh of breath parting her hair.

"It's just for a little while. It's not safe for you to leave the estate right now."

"Safe?" She shoved against him, and he relented. She stumbled over her own feet.

"Marcus Komisky is causing me some trouble. It's being dealt with, but it's not going his way, and he might try to use you to get to me. So, you'll have to stay here until I deal with him."

"Marcus? The man from the party?"

This was her fault. If she hadn't been so damn nosy, this wouldn't be happening.

"Yes."

She ran her hands over her face. Any anger over the situation should be aimed at her. She knew that, and he knew it, too.

"What sort of trouble is he causing?"

"Nothing that can't be handled. A few surprise health inspections at the clubs. He's very juvenile in his attack, but it's going to get him even more pissed. And stupid and angry don't make for a safe combination."

Making her way to the windows, she looked down over the city below. The sun started to fade behind the skyline, casting an orange glow between the buildings.

"This is my fault."

"This is being dealt with. All you have to do is what I say, and that's to stay within the estate. No sneaking off, okay?"

His thick arms wrapped her, and she found his body pressed against hers the comfort she needed.

"Now, I think you wanted to thank me appropriately for the studio."

Her arms were swept behind her and pinned with only one of his, while his free hand began to unbutton her blouse.

"Ash." She tried to squirm. "The windows."

He laughed and bit her earlobe. "Do you think I give a fuck if someone sees us? Besides, we're too high up for that."

As each button opened, more of her flesh became exposed. She stopped trying to get free of him; she wouldn't win against his strength. And the urge to best him had diminished over the past week.

"No bra?" he chastised, but with a lightness that told her he was more pleased than surprised. "Such a dirty girl. You went to school today with no bra on? Do you think the other students saw your nipples?"

She scraped her teeth across her lip when he pinched a nipple.

"Do you think some boy across the room watched as they

hardened beneath your blouse? Wanting to suck them and pinch them?"

Again, she didn't answer, and he didn't seem to require one. He moved his hand across her chest to the untouched breast and cupped it.

"Are they allowed to touch your tits, Ellie?" He nipped her earlobe again, and she stiffened.

"No, Ash."

"So, you were teasing them, is that it?"

What answer could she give to please him? Anything she said would be wrong, or twisted.

"Why aren't they allowed to touch these tits, or this ass, or this pussy? Why can't anyone else—including you—touch this body?"

Including her? Maybe he didn't know, but her hands wandered over her pussy almost every morning after he made her scream the night before. Reliving those evenings during her shower made her mad with desire, and she had to let the pressure off or she wouldn't make it through the day.

"I asked a question." He grabbed hold of her nipple and pinched. Hard. Unrelenting.

Her knees buckled, and she struggled, wanting to relieve the pain but not get away from him.

"Answer me, Ellie." He sank his teeth into the tender spot where her neck and shoulder met.

She squealed and twisted, but it only served to increase the pressure on her nipple and scratch her shoulder with his teeth.

"Because I belong to you!" she yelled out, sucking in air when his fingers opened and burning took over from the pressure. She panted as he rolled the sensitive bud with the pad of his thumb. Around and around he went while she regained her breathing and the pain subsided.

"Very good. I was beginning to think you forgot." He chuckled.

Her blouse hung open, but it wasn't enough for him. He swept the material to the side, fully exposing her front before slipping his hand into the elastic of her skirt.

"Now, you were going to thank me," he reminded her, while the tip of his middle finger stroked her clit.

She moaned and rolled her head back.

"I said thank-you."

"Yeah, but those were just words, and I'm looking for more from you."

Keeping her arms pinned behind her, he walked her over to the drawing table. Every muscle pressed against her body warned her she couldn't get away from him, even if she wanted to. And she found she didn't want to.

He pulled free of her skirt and pushed her facedown over the table. Still, she had no use of her arms and couldn't push up or away. All she could do was turn her face to breathe easier.

"This pussy is all mine, isn't that right, Ellie?" His voice sounded darker, more of a growl.

"Yes, Ash. Yours. All yours." She could feel her body responding, feel the emptiness inside her she needed him to fill. The way only he could, the only way she wanted.

The sound of his zipper lowering made her smile. He wasn't angry, or trying to humiliate her. He was taking what was his, and she was his. Had been since the first time he touched her wet pussy.

Her skirt flipped up over her back, and her ass cheeks were pulled wide apart. It was then she realized she could move her arms, but she didn't.

"Hold your cheeks open for me, Ellie. Give me my pussy." He took her hands and put them where he wanted, and she did her best to pry her bottom apart for him.

The burn in her cheeks reminded her she was supposed to be horrified over the action. But the wetness of her pussy contradicted her mind.

"Good girl," he cooed. Pride welled inside of her at his approval.

The head of his cock pressed against her entrance, and she slid her feet wider apart, lifting her ass higher, offering herself to him. Wanting and waiting for him to take her, to take the need away and fill her with everything she wanted from him.

His rough hands gripped her waist, under her skirt.

"I should probably punish you for not wearing panties. What were you thinking going to school like this?" he asked while slowly pushing his hard cock into her.

She sucked in her breath, memorizing the feel of every inch he gave her. This must have been what it felt like to drink for the first time after being lost in a desert.

"Why didn't you wear panties today, Ellie?" he asked, stilling his movements.

She groaned.

"Because." She tried to move back toward him, to take what he wouldn't give. But all she got in return was a sharp slap to her ass.

"No. Bad girl. Stay still."

She groaned again. Although kicking him would be counterproductive at the moment, it seemed like an amazing idea.

"Tell me."

"I was going to find you when I got home." She twisted her neck to look at him. It was the truth. When she got home from school, she'd planned to search him out in his office in the Annex. The plaid skirt and white button-down blouse hadn't been an accidental wardrobe choice that morning.

"You were coming home to seduce me?" He lessened his grip on her hips.

When she found his expression, she saw genuine surprise. He didn't expect that answer. Then again, seeing as she was his prisoner, why would he expect her to be the aggressor? Why would she seek him out to have sex, or any sort of connection? He was the beast who stole her away from her life. She should have gone up to her room and planned his death, not his orgasm.

"I just wanted you. You've been—withdrawn." She didn't let go of her ass, and she realized it made for a strange situation to be having such a discussion, given her current position.

The surprise disappeared, and he flashed a toothy grin. He slapped her hip and plunged into her.

She yelped, the edge of the desk bit into her, but she didn't care.

His fingers clawed at her flesh, and his cock thrust into her over and over again, until all that remained in her mind was the glorious feeling of his body. The sound of their bodies slapping against each other surrounded them, but she didn't care. She couldn't care less that she chanted his name, louder and louder with each thrust.

"Oh! Fuck," she cried out when it was too much. She couldn't bear it another moment.

"Now, Ellie. Now." He reached below her, knowing exactly what she needed.

The feather-like brush of his finger over her clit was enough to shove her into oblivion.

Her screams rose to the rafters, and his own mingled with hers only moments later. She released her hold on herself as he fucked her, causing his release. The table creaked.

She could still feel him inside her, throbbing against her vaginal walls. He'd come hard, so had she, and their breath came fast. He withdrew from her and, before pulling up his pants, he peeled her from the table and held her.

"Fuck, Ellie." The words were weighted with care and genuine softness.

He helped put her together, buttoning her shirt and flattening her skirt back down. She helped button up his jeans and buckle his belt.

While she pulled the leather through the metal clasp and worked the buckle closed, she felt him watching her. But it didn't intimidate her the way it had before.

Something had shifted.

CHAPTER 22

Ash gripped the handle of the studio door, wanting to punch Daniel in the throat for stopping him from getting upstairs to Ellie. He'd been dealing with bullshit inspections and meetings all day because of Komisky.

The asshole couldn't get to him or Ellie to make any actual threats, so he was harassing him through the legal system. Ash had just as many cops on his payroll as Komisky, maybe more, but health inspectors weren't cops. They were annoying little bitches. Easily bought off, but Ash ran his clubs to code. Buyoffs weren't needed.

And after the third inspection of the week, even the inspector was getting annoyed. Komisky may have paid the asshole, but he couldn't find shit that wasn't there. And Ash had a man with him every step of the inspection, so there wouldn't be any planting shit in his clubs.

He ran clean places. If Komisky had a fucking brain in his head, he'd be setting the cops on the trail of the personal loans he gave, or the manner in which he extracted payment. But seeing as his old man, and he, himself, ran the same business, it would only come bite him in the ass.

So instead, Ash wasted his time dealing with inspectors and crossing too many Ts.

All he wanted to do was go up to the studio and watch Ellie paint. But just as he was about to go up and kiss his girl, tease her about the amount of paint she managed to get on her nose and cheek while creating her work, he had to pause to hear out Daniel.

"You have two seconds." Ash gave him a scathing look. Daniel nodded, giving him the satisfaction of half an ounce of fear.

"I went over her calls, Ash." Daniel handed him a piece of paper filled with her cell phone logs. He hadn't asked about them in over a week. Ellie had been content, almost happy. She didn't try to get into the Annex without him, and he'd taken her there a few times in the evening to have fun in a playroom.

"What am I looking at?" Ash barked as he noticed one number was called repeatedly. As she had no actual friends, the call log usually only listed his own number or the house number.

"That's Jason Sawer's phone."

"Jason? Who the fuck is Jason?"

"He's the guy who works at the coffee shop with her dad."

Ellie's phone had been blocked from dialing or receiving calls from her father's home number, the coffee shop, and his cell phone. But Ash hadn't known about this Jason.

"She's been talking to her dad?" Ash's fist crushed the log.

"No. Just him, I think. I don't know. We didn't tap the calls, just keep the log." Daniel swallowed and eyed the door.

"Fine." Ash grabbed the handle again and pulled.

"Ash, we don't know. She could just be talking to this guy about her dad, you know, checking in."

"Checking in? She's not allowed to check in. Remember

what I told you. She isn't to have anything to do with that lowlife of a father."

"I'm just saying, before you go off on her all snarling and shit, hear her out."

Ash couldn't believe what he saw before him. One of his own men was giving him directions and trying to stick up for Ellie. Had she become so big a part of his world that his men felt they could take her side, could protect her from him?

"And I'm just saying she's mine to deal with. Don't forget that."

Daniel nodded. "Yeah. I get it. Right."

"Where's Peter?"

"He's in the Annex. Amber wanted to talk with him about getting on the list for the next party."

That mess didn't need his attention. Peter could handle it. He had his own issue upstairs.

"Fine. Don't you have somewhere to be?" Ash took a step toward him.

"Yeah." Daniel turned and hurried off down the hall, cursing under his breath. He had earned every curse Daniel threw at him. It wasn't him Ash wanted to yell at. It was the girl up in the studio, looking sexy and fuckable.

Throwing the door open, he barged up the stairs to the studio.

She was exactly as he imagined he'd find her. The easel was positioned so he couldn't see what she was working on, but he could see her face. Her red hair was plaited, and smudges of gray and white paint dotted her nose and her jaw, where she'd probably rubbed away an itch.

"Ash? Hey. I didn't think you'd be home until dinner." She peeked around the canvas at him, gifting him with a shining smile. He'd gotten used to the softness of her greetings, but it didn't lessen his irritation.

He held the call log up to her, as though it explained the furiousness of his frown.

She put her brushes down and stepped out from her work space, taking the log from his hand and skimming it.

"Is this my cell phone bill?" she asked, not an ounce of guilt in her expression. But she was. She had to be.

"Who is Jason?" he demanded.

She raised her eyebrows. "He works at the café with my dad. I've known him for years."

"You aren't supposed to be talking with your father." He ripped the bill from her hand and crumpled it up again.

"I'm not. You blocked him from me in every way technology allows." She folded her arms over her chest. "I ask Jason how my dad is, but I don't talk to him. I figured you had my phone bugged." She threw the accusation at him and turned away, picking up a towel and wiping her hands on it.

"So why not just call Jason and then talk with your father?" he pushed.

"I just told you. I figured you had me bugged." She knitted her brows together. "But Jason said Dad's thinking of selling the café. He wants to get the money he owes you." This came out softly. Cautiously. As though she'd been trying to find the right moment to bring up the subject, and this seemed like as good a time as any.

It wasn't.

"He can do whatever the fuck he wants, but it has nothing to do with you. That deal was already worked out." He pointed a finger at her.

She stepped back, as though his words slapped her across the face. It had been weeks since either of them made a comment on why they were together.

"You'd get your money. And then—"

"And then what? You leave?" Did she think he wanted that? Did she want that?

"I didn't say that." She knitted her eyebrows together. "Jason said Dad hasn't gone gambling. He's getting himself together."

Ash saw the hope blooming in her eyes, the shimmering desire for her father to be exactly as every little girl wanted him to be. But her father wasn't like that. Her father had gambled away life savings. Her father lied. Her father put himself ahead of everyone else. Always.

"I'm not talking about your father anymore," he decreed and headed for the stairs. He needed air. He couldn't think straight with her staring at him with so much hope.

"So, I'm just going to be your prisoner forever?" she called after him.

He was halfway down the stairs when she had hurled the words at him. Five more steps and he'd be in the hallway, not hearing the pain, or the sob ready to break free from her chest.

"Ash," Peter called up from the open doorway. "You're needed. Now." Peter looked over his shoulder, and his eyes went cold. "Now."

Work would be good. Work would give him a minute to think. He didn't respond to Ellie, just finished jogging down the stairs and slammed the door behind him.

"What is it?"

"Her dad's here."

"What?" Ash's hands fisted, his blood pressure rose, and if Peter hadn't been standing in front of him, he might have punched the wall again.

He couldn't seem to get away from her father today.

"You should talk with him."

Ash gave a nod and stalked off to his office. Better to deal with the ass while he was still angry. He might be able to let himself put his fist through his throat this time.

"Mr. Stevens." Ash stormed into the office, ignoring the

panic in the old man's face as he moved around to his chair. "You were told never to come back here."

"I have the money. I have all of it." He dropped several stacks of bills onto Ash's desk.

Ash fingered the bills, taking several calming breaths.

"We already settled your debt." Ash pushed the money across the desk at him.

"I need her back. I need Ellie," her father stated, his eyes flashing between the money and Ash.

"How'd you get this money?" Ash asked. The café hadn't sold. He had men keeping an eye on the business. Ellie didn't need to tell him it had been put on the market. He already knew. And so far, no one had even shown a second of interest.

"I sold the coffeehouse," he lied.

Ash ran his tongue over his teeth.

Something was wrong here. Very wrong.

"To who?" Ash asked.

"Um, well."

"To who?" Ash yelled.

The old man shook. "Marcus Komisky."

CHAPTER 23

What an ass! She'd just had a few conversations with Jason over the past week. Wanting to make sure her father was okay, the business was doing well, and Jason himself was in one piece, she had called. She didn't talk with her father. As much as she wanted to, Ellie only asked Jason about him. As far as she knew, her calls were being listened to. Why would she put her father in jeopardy?

Deciding she wasn't going to sulk in the studio while he just got to walk away, she marched down the stairs. The hallway was empty as usual, so she tried to hear if Ash was talking with someone down the hall.

"I need her. I need Ellie."

Her father. Her father was here. In the house. She ran to Ash's office. Surely that's where they were.

The door hadn't shut all the way. It was open enough she could hear but not see them.

"Who did you sell to?" Ash's demanding voice asked.

Her father's voice shook as he responded, "Marcus Komisky."

"Komisky?" Peter's voice entered the conversation.

"You sold your coffeehouse to Marcus?" Ash sounded quiet, not angry. Which only meant he was scathing.

"I... Yes." Her father was lying. She knew that tone.

"Or did you sell Ellie?" Ash asked.

What?

"I would never." Her father lied again. What was he doing? Desperate to find out, she wanted to barge in and demand answers, but she held steady just outside the office.

"You wouldn't? You already did once, didn't you?" Ash continued.

"I didn't sell her to you." Her father sounded indignant, like he was covering up something he'd done.

"No, what was it you said to me? You didn't have to. You said she'd offer herself."

Ellie's heart sank. That's exactly what she had done.

"You said she'd come here and offer herself. Then I could use her in the Annex to earn the money, and no one would have to force her. That's what you told me. Isn't that right?"

Tears filled her eyes. This wasn't true. It couldn't be true. Her father wouldn't do something so horrible.

"I didn't sell her. She sold herself."

"Just like you said she would," Peter added.

"Look. I have the money. I'll buy her back now." There was a slight pause before her father spoke again. "She's still here, right? You didn't sell her to someone who took her away?"

She closed her eyes and sank to her knees.

Her father used her. He knew Ash wouldn't take her from him as payment, he didn't work that way. So, he'd used her against herself. And like a moron, she came running to save him. Offering herself in exchange. She'd whored herself to save him, except it wasn't that. He had sold her.

Her father had sold her.

"Did Marcus buy the shop or her? And don't fucking lie to me again." Ash's voice ricocheted off the walls.

Ellie pushed herself up to her feet and wiped her face with the heels of her hands. She wouldn't be anyone's pawn anymore.

Shoving the door open, she stepped inside. Her father turned and blanched at seeing her. Ash's jaw tensed, and his lips pinched together. Peter stepped away, giving her room.

"You sold me?" She kept her tone steady, though her insides shook.

"Ellie. No. That's not what happened." Her father reached his arms out to her but didn't take a step.

"You knew I'd find you. You knew I'd do whatever it took to save you if I thought you were going to be hurt or killed. You sold me. And now?" She ignored Ash. If she saw him, she might throw up, and she needed to not throw up right now.

"Ellie. Let's go home, and we can talk about it."

"No," Ash and Ellie answered at the same time.

"I'm not going home with you. Ever. What's the deal you made with Marcus? Did he give you that money in exchange for getting me out of here?" She jabbed a finger at the pile of cash on Ash's desk.

Her father's eyes told her everything. She assumed he'd been weak, trying but failing to keep his gambling in check. She thought he used it to cope with the loss of her mother, of his wife. But now she saw him, standing before her, and the truth of his character shone through for the first time.

"That's it, right? Marcus came to you and offered you this money to pay Ash back so you could get me. And then he'd take me until you paid off your debt to him. Jason said you put the café on the market but no one had showed interest yet, so is this what the deal was?"

Her hands fisted. Tears spilled down her cheeks but she

couldn't stop them, couldn't contain the erupting anger from inside her.

"You said need. Not want." She took a shaky breath. "You said you needed me, not wanted me, but needed." How could she have been so fucking blind for so long?

"Ellie—" Her father dropped his hands and lowered his gaze. "I owe him a lot of money. More than I owed Ash. He said he'd wipe it clean if I could get you to leave here and go with him." He quickly added, "Just for a week. Not forever."

"Not forever?" The floor weakened beneath her, or maybe it was her knees. Whatever it was, she could feel herself sinking. Maybe she could disappear altogether. She could just slip away into an abyss. Somewhere her father didn't sell her to cover his debts. Somewhere where Ash didn't just stand there and let her sink away.

"You let him sell me to you? You said you didn't take women against their will." She turned her anger on Ash.

He raised an eyebrow, but she ignored it. He and his eyebrow could go fuck themselves.

"I didn't take you against your will. You came here. You made the offer, and I accepted."

She pointed a finger at him, seeing her body shaking, but unable to do anything about it. "You sent Peter to get him, knowing I'd come here. He told you, didn't he? He told you that's what I would do."

"I sent Peter to get the money from him. He was brought here the same as any other asshole who didn't pay his debt. When he was here then he told me. And not ten minutes later, Peter was walking to the gate to get you." Ash's voice remained steady. His expression relaxed, like they were just having a conversation, and she wasn't finding out everything about the last month of her life had been a humiliating joke.

She took a deep breath, sucking in air, and spun around.

"I'm leaving."

"Ellie," Ash called to her.

"No, Ash. I'm done. I'm not property. I'm not something that can bought and sold like an old fucking couch." She glanced at her father, letting her heart crack another inch at just the panic on his face.

"You aren't worried about me. You're worried Marcus will probably kill you now." She rolled her shoulders back. "I hope he doesn't. But I'm not letting you whore me out again."

Ash called for her again, but she was already running. She ran down the hall, up the large winding staircase, and to their room.

She paused once inside and let out a scream into the empty room that gave some relief to the building bubble inside of her. Tears blinded her, but she didn't care. She knew the room, knew every inch by heart. She moved around, grabbing clothes, books, whatever she could stash in one bag she found in Ash's closet.

Almost nothing of hers remained in the second bedroom anymore. Piece by piece, she'd moved into Ash's room, and his life. Let him into hers.

She zipped the bag and swung it over her shoulder just as the door opened. Ash stood, his hands at his sides, his eyes wild with worry.

"You're still here." He let out a breath, his wide eyes softening.

"I'm leaving, Ash. You can't stop me." Of course he could, but she hoped he wouldn't.

He blinked a few times and for the first time since she met him, he didn't have an immediate answer.

"I don't want to be here anymore." It would have been more meaningful if she hadn't sniffled right after saying it.

"Ellie. I didn't—I wouldn't have—" He shook his head and when his eyes met hers, the fierceness she'd come to expect from him was there. "Marcus could still be a danger."

"I'll handle him."

"Ellie. You can't just run off." His fingers rubbed together at his sides. The tattoos on his knuckles swayed with the movement.

Couldn't she do just that? Shouldn't she have done that weeks ago?

"I don't want to be here, Ash. Didn't you tell me you don't keep women against their will?"

"You're not a girl in the Annex," he stated with a harshness that penetrated through her anger. It wasn't a demand she stay because he'd bought her fair and square. It wasn't a reminder she'd given herself to him. It was a statement meant for her to understand she was different from the women in the Annex. They could come and go because he didn't care what they decided for themselves. He cared about her.

She couldn't think that way. Especially not now. Not with her bag packed, her father downstairs, and Marcus Komisky wanting to use her against Ash. She needed to forget him. Forget this place, and forget how safe she would feel if she only closed the gap between them and buried herself in his arms.

When she moved her gaze back to his, she found him glaring at her, his jaw clenched. The resolve she'd found down in his office returned with a vengeance. She would protect and shield, but this time it would be herself who benefited.

If he was waiting for her to break and run into his arms and beg him to help her, to make her pain go away, he would grow old waiting. It wasn't happening.

"It's dangerous—"

"I don't care. I'm leaving." She took a step toward him.

"Ellie—" He put a hand out to still her, but she sidestepped it. If he touched her, she couldn't promise herself she'd be able to keep moving. And she needed to keep going, or she'd break right there in front of him.

She waited for a reason to throw her bag down. Something to keep her there, something that told her he'd opened more than his bed to her. Maybe then she could release the ball of hurt from her soul.

"What, Ash?" she asked when he still hadn't said anything.

His mouth opened and closed. A soft flare of his nostrils, and after a grimace, he shook his head.

"At least let Daniel drive you. He'll take you to your apartment."

She tensed. "My father stays there."

"He won't be an issue."

She readjusted the bag on her shoulder, the plea on the tip of her tongue. *Don't hurt him.* Even with his betrayal, she couldn't allow harm to come to him.

"He's safe here, Ellie. Don't worry about him."

She clenched her jaw, tightened her joints, willing something more to come, something of substance that could make this moment more bearable.

"Daniel will take you," he repeated, stepping out of the way. He didn't care. He'd finally be able to get rid of her.

"Yeah," she whispered and pushed past him, trying to ignore the scent of him, the feel of him when she brushed his chest.

He followed her to the stairs but stayed at the top while she ran down them to the front door. Daniel was already there, waiting for her. He glanced up at Ash, and when he was given a nod, he opened the door for Ellie.

He was behind her, staring. If she looked back, she'd see him. Maybe she'd see regret. Or she'd see hope. Maybe he'd tell her to stay.

She didn't look back, though. Because, more than likely,

she'd see a blank expression. And her heart barely beat as it was.

She ambled to the car, and got into the back before Daniel had a chance to open the door. He seemed to know where to go, since he didn't ask her when he pulled down the drive.

Closing her eyes, she kept a focused eye ahead of her. Not allowing herself to see the estate fade into the distance. The tears fell faster, and the sob she'd been holding in burst from her chest. She tried to keep quiet as Daniel drove, but the dam had opened.

CHAPTER 24

Ash stood in the center of the studio, hands fisted and jaw clenched, staring out the window as Daniel's car made its way down the drive and through the gates of the estate.

Taking a few steps forward, he pressed his hands to the glass, watching the car Ellie sat in drive off. He could have made her stay. He could have reminded her she had agreed, had given herself to him.

Dammit, she was his.

But he hadn't. He hadn't forced her, hadn't even tried to convince. He told himself she had been unreachable, her anger too consuming to let her listen to reason.

How much pain could he cause her in one afternoon?

He should have stationed a man outside the studio door to keep her from coming out. Especially when Peter told him it was her father in his office. Nothing good was coming next, he'd felt it in his bones. Yet he didn't take the precautions to protect her. And now she knew the truth.

Losing the ideal you've held your father to your entire life could only be compared to having one's intestines laced through their nose. He remembered the feeling. The moment he realized how heartless, how unrelenting his own father was burned into his memory. He wouldn't put that sharp agony on anyone, especially not his Ellie.

So fucking pure. She had come to him, to his big mansion on the hill, demanding her father be returned to her. And when that didn't work, she easily gave herself to keep him safe. And Ash had let her. Knowing full well she probably wouldn't have done it if she knew her father had planned it. Or, maybe she still would have.

He raked his hand through his hair and let out a growl.

"Things didn't go so well?" Peter's voice mimicked the sound of nails dragging over a chalkboard but succeeded in dragging Ash from his berating thoughts.

"What do you want?" He didn't bother to face his cousin. Whatever he wanted, he could spill and get the fuck away from him.

"She's gone."

"No shit, she's gone." Ash spun and stomped across the studio, feeling her still there. He could smell her shampoo, sense her soul standing in front of the easel. She'd been so fucking beautiful working on her painting. Arguing with him when he wanted to see the project. Her smile knocking the breath from him when he gave in and said he'd wait until she finished.

"You could have made her stay."

Ash touched the table with her paints, wanting just a moment of her warmth to still be there.

"I don't do that. You know it."

"She wasn't an employee, Ash. You could have made her stay, could have reminded her about the payment—"

"Fuck off, Peter!" he roared at his cousin.

"Admit it. Will you finally fucking admit you love her? That you let her go because you love her?"

Ash searched the table for something to throw at Peter's head. One good shot and he could knock him down the stairs from where he stood.

"Of course, I fucking love her. That's not the point!" he yelled instead when he couldn't find anything of good weight.

Peter took an exaggerated breath. "It's the only point that matters."

"What the hell are you talking about?"

"You aren't your father. You have never been him, and you never will be. You won't ever treat her the way your mother was treated."

"I'm really not in the mood for a therapy session."

"Fine. What comes next?"

Ash moved around the table of supplies and came to face the canvas with her project. His chest burst, and he stumbled over his feet getting closer to it.

Large brush strokes, dark coloring, and perfection splayed out before him.

It was him.

His hair was loose, covering part of his face, and his jaw chiseled to give him a fierce expression. Except his eyes. In his silvery-blue eyes, she'd shown him, the true him. The part of him he tried desperately to shelter from her. From everyone.

A vulnerability lurked there. Passion and love and intense honor all conveyed by her gentle strokes.

His fingers traced the outline of his jaw.

She'd seen him.

Not just seen his scars or his hair or his tattoos. She'd seen him. Parts of him he locked away from everyone were showcased so easily on the canvas before him.

"Is her father still downstairs?"

"He's in the basement."

"Call Daniel and make sure Ellie got to her apartment okay. Then find out how much that jackass actually owes Komisky and pay it."

"What? You're going to pay that asshole?"

Ash couldn't tear his eyes from the painting. She would be safe. Back in her apartment, far away from all this bullshit, she'd be better off.

"Yes. Then pay her father whatever his asking price for the café is and send him on his way. Make it clear he is not to go back to his apartment. He doesn't live there anymore."

"Ash—"

"Just fucking do it."

"And Ellie?"

"Leave her be. Tell Daniel to put a detail on her for now. Make sure Marcus can't get to her."

After a long pause, Peter agreed and left him to his own mess.

CHAPTER 25

"Ellie, you can't just wallow in here forever." Jason entered the back room of the café with the register drawer.

It had been a busy day. The chilly weather drew larger crowds, and having the community skating rink up and operational only half a block away made them the prime spot for a cup of coffee or hot chocolate.

Two weeks had passed since she made her way home from Ash's estate. She hadn't heard a word from him or his men since Peter knocked on her door a day after she'd left.

He assured her, her father was fine but wouldn't be coming around unless she wanted him to. She had only shaken her head. She wasn't ready to face him, not yet.

She wanted to ask after Ash. Was he okay? Did he even care she was gone? But she didn't.

"I'm not wallowing, I'm working," she shot at Jason, giving him a forced smile, and turned her attention to the bank ledgers.

"Well, you can't work yourself to death, either."

"I'm fine, Jason. I told you. I'm good."

"You haven't told me anything. You were gone for over a month, Ellie. What happened there?"

"Nothing. Ash wasn't as horrible as he looked." She concentrated on the ledger in front of her, not allowing him to see the pain in her eyes.

"I've seen him, Ellie. The man looks like he could squish me like a bug with his fingers."

She nodded with a shrug. "He could."

Jason's mouth dropped open, and she laughed.

"But he wouldn't, is what I'm saying. He's not the beast I thought him to be."

"Well, his goons are still parked across the street." Jason went about tallying up his receipts and balancing his drawer.

"Yeah," she sighed. "They'll go away after he realizes I'm safe."

"And when will that be?" Jason asked.

She turned away from the computer and rubbed her temples. Numbers made her head hurt.

"I don't know."

Could she be safe without her father paying off his debt? And she doubted Marcus would forgive so easily what happened at the party. It was what caused him to go after Ash in the first place.

A part of her wanted to give the proverbial middle finger to the entire situation. After all, she'd been innocent. She'd been used like a toy and sold into the whole mess.

But Ash wouldn't have to be dealing with the fallout of the party if she hadn't been there. That was her doing, and from what Jason told her, it didn't stop at Marcus.

Jason, she came to realize, paid more attention to the goings on of the city than she ever had. He had told her about Mr. Bertucci and Mr. Jansen also talking about Ash. Though he didn't have much more information other than they had wanted to get into business with him, but he declined.

"Are there any customers still out there?" she asked.

"Just the two guys in the corner. They're just finishing their coffees. I told them we were closing."

She nodded. "I'll start closing down the pastry case, then. I'll box them up for you. Take them home. If I do, I'll eat them." And she'd spent the last ten days eating her feelings already. She wouldn't be able to fit into her jeans if she kept it up.

Ash was a passing memory. Whatever she'd dreamt up between them was just that, a dream.

This was real life. The café, her art, school. This is what she would focus on. Because when she stopped, when she gave herself a two-second break, he would drift into her thoughts, and the surrounding world would stop moving. She'd be lost in the tension in her chest, the pounding of her heart, and she would lose all concentration.

Forgetting him was the only way to survive because living with his memory would kill her.

She left Jason counting quarters and went to clear out the pastries. The bakery would be making their delivery early to refill her order, and having empty shelves to stock would make it easier at five in the morning.

The two men Jason mentioned sat in the corner, huddled together, talking quietly. They glanced at her when she started working in the case but returned to their conversation, ignoring her completely.

"Just a little longer and this whole fucking mess will be done," one of the men said. "After it's done, I'm taking a fucking vacation. This shit has me all tied up in knots."

"Yeah. Me, too. Going up against Ashland Titon isn't exactly easy business," his partner complained.

Ellie's heart skidded to a stop. Without glancing over at

them, she moved over in the case, reaching for the peach Danishes and concentrating on their conversation.

"Komisky's an idiot if you ask me. I mean, getting us to harass him a bit with the health inspections fine, it's annoying, but no big deal. But what I hear he's planning tomorrow night? He's either got some big balls or is missing a few screws."

His partner laughed. "I've met the man. He's definitely missing a few cogs in that wheel of his. He doesn't have the business sense like his old man."

"From what I hear, it's his balls that got him all pissed off in the first place. Wanted some piece of ass he couldn't have, or something like that. If you ask me, Ash shoulda just gave him what he wanted. It's not like he's working with a bunch of virgins up in his castle."

Ellie's throat constricted, but she continued working the pastries out of the case.

"You know that's not how he operates," the first man said with some heat. "His dad, sure, but not since Ash took over."

"Look. It doesn't matter. After tomorrow night, he'll either be locked up or dead. For our sakes, dead would be a better option." The larger of the two men threw back his coffee and pushed his cup away from him.

Ellie eased out of the case and stood up, watching the two men, memorizing their features as they stood from their table and put on their coats. Button by button, she committed it all to memory.

Ash was in trouble.

They grabbed their hats and headed for the front door, Ellie's heart still hammering away in her chest. The larger of the two, the one wishing for Ash's demise, opened the door while the second one turned back to her.

"Best cup of coffee in town." He smiled at her.

She swallowed and nodded. "T-thanks. Have a good night."

"Will do." He tipped his hat to her and followed his partner out into the street.

What the fuck was she supposed to do now? Shouldn't she call Ash and warn him? Let him know what was happening?

"What's wrong?" Jason asked, coming out of the back.

"What? Nothing." She closed the pastry case.

Was her father still there? Didn't Ash turn him over to Marcus, or did he still have him locked up in his basement? Or worse.

She should have asked Peter when she saw him. She should have demanded more answers. The hurt of being betrayed by her father had clouded her sense of right and wrong. Her mother wouldn't have wanted her to leave him to die at the hands of those men.

No.

Ash's problems were his own. He was a grown man who made his own decisions, and he could handle whatever came his way.

She wasn't going to run in and try to save him. She wasn't that person anymore. She protected herself. No one else. Just herself.

"Everything's fine, Jason." She closed the box of pastries and put it on the counter. "Here, take this home."

She would go home, read a good book, have a glass—or bottle—of wine and go to sleep.

Ash Titon didn't need or want her.

And she didn't need him.

CHAPTER 26

Ash slammed his office door. Ten days. She'd been gone ten days and not one word from her. What did he expect? He'd just let her walk out of his life, like every step she took out of the door didn't rip his heart a little more out of his chest.

Some of her things were still scattered through their room. Little trinkets of memory. A hairbrush she'd forgotten, a necklace she had taken off the night before she'd run. One of her damn colored pencils sat on the dresser, laughing at him each night as he sat in his bed alone, wondering what she was up to.

He didn't have to wonder, for the most part. His men reported her movements daily. All the woman did was go to work and home. She hadn't even gone to her class; her professor had already emailed him inquiring about it.

The days were running into each other. Nothing other than a new moon separated them, and no matter how immersed he became in work, he couldn't shake her from his mind.

"Ash." Peter stalked into the office with a stack of papers in his hand.

"What?" Ash snapped. He'd lost patience for pretty much everyone around him, and Peter wasn't an exception.

"Don't get pissy with me. You're the one who ordered another party put together so fucking soon." Peter's eyes darkened. He was right, of course. Ash had given the order, and there wasn't much time to put the usual effort in.

"What do you want?" Ash asked again, trying to erase the pain from existence.

"Here's the final guest list with responses. Surprisingly enough, we should be having a good turnout. And the girls who weren't put on longer contracts from the last party have signed up to go on contract this time."

Ash brushed a stack of papers away. "Good. Anything else?"

Peter coughed. "Another inspection at Delilah's. We passed, of course, but the kitchen couldn't serve for the first two hours we were open last night."

"Two hours? What the fuck."

"He was extremely thorough." Peter laughed, but it held no humor. Nothing about it was funny. Every hour the kitchen stayed closed meant money didn't get made. The patrons would tip the dancers, and the drinks would flow, but during the first few hours, the kitchen made the most money.

"Komisky is really starting to piss me off." Ash fisted his hand. It wasn't enough his heart barely recognized life since Ellie left, but he had to be continually annoyed by that prick.

"Do you want to do something about it?" Peter asked. Ash had kept them all on a leash when it came to retaliation for the idiocy of Marcus Komisky, but Peter was right. He needed to be dealt with.

"Let's get through the party then we'll focus on him," Ash agreed.

"Daniel said Dominick has been asking for you again."

Ash laughed and spun around in his chair. "He can wait until this mess is all cleaned up and Ellie is in the clear. Then I'll deal with him."

"You can't keep him locked up forever," Peter stated the obvious.

"I can do whatever the fuck I want." Ash poured himself a drink, his eye catching on the painting on the wall just over the bar. It had been one of Ellie's favorite scenes. At least half a dozen times, he'd caught her in his office, looking at his mother's artwork.

"Have the rest of Ellie's shit removed from my room and the adjoining room. Whatever you find, have it delivered to her. She'll want all her things." He tossed back the liquor, wishing for a stronger burn than it gave.

"Why don't you bring it to her? Maybe see her for yourself?"

Annoyed, Ash yelled, "Why the hell would I do that?"

"Because you need her." Peter didn't retreat when Ash advanced on him. "You need her, and she needs you."

"You don't know anything. Just get the party in order, get her shit out of my room, and do your fucking job." Ash poked a finger into Peter's chest and moved around him to the door, slamming it behind him.

He ignored Daniel who lingered at the end of the hall like he had a question. The men standing at the stairs waiting to talk to him, silently stepped aside so he could get up the stairs.

Couldn't they see how hard it was to breathe? Didn't they feel the Earth dying around them?

Climbing another set of stairs, he made his way to his

personal workout room. He needed weights, and to run, and to put his mind somewhere else. Somewhere Ellie hadn't marked.

Except, everywhere he went, she seemed to still be with him.

CHAPTER 27

The sun started to fade, illuminating the city outside her condo window. Not like the beautiful orange hue she'd seen from the studio on Ash's estate, but still she found serenity in the moment.

Sucking in a deep breath, she took her phone from the pocket of her jeans for the tenth time. She swiped the screen open, found his contact screen, and again her finger hovered over the little envelope icon. She could just send him a text, letting him know what she'd overheard last night.

Then she could get rid of the phone.

She should have gotten rid of it when she got home. Having the link to him only made her keep thinking about him when she should be moving on.

"Oh, fuck it. He's a big boy. He'll be fine." She tossed the phone on the couch and made her way to her father's room.

It was time to clear out his closets. She wouldn't throw his stuff out, but she needed to get a handle on the mess he'd left behind. Maybe, after another week, she'd go out to the detail Ash had stationed outside her apartment and ask them to get the stuff to her father for her.

She'd been home for nearly two weeks, and not once had she set foot in his room. The stale scent of his aftershave probably hung in the air. What she found comforting as a child would only be a reminder of his betrayal. He'd used her. Her own father had bartered her life to save his own. Not once, but twice. How many times had she bailed him out of trouble over the years? How hard she'd worked to scrimp and save just enough to pay for one class at the university, only to have him use her for his own gain in the end.

She was his daughter. He should have been scrimping and saving. He should have gotten a second and third job to provide for them. It was his duty, not hers!

Had she really meant so little to him? Had her mother meant nothing to him? Oh, how devastated her mother would be to see the mess he'd created for himself. And the turmoil Ellie had caused as well.

She could sit and let the past destroy her, but it wouldn't solve anything. The morning would bring bills to be paid. The coffee shop to be managed. Her life still needed to be lived, even if it was to continue on with less vibrant color than before.

So, for the time being, she would take on the mountain of papers.

Her father kept everything: paid bills, old newspapers, it was never ending. But, after two hours of going through one pile and half of another, she came across a red file folder with her name scribbled on the front in her mother's script.

Ellie traced the elaborate loops and pen strokes, letting her fingers touch the places her mother had touched. If her mother had lived, would her father have turned out the way he did—would Ellie have turned out the way she had?

She settled on the bed and opened the file. Her birth certificate, some old school papers her mother had been especially proud of, and business papers.

Just as she was halfway through the file, the doorbell rang, followed by an insistent pounding. She shoved off the bed to get answers.

"Ellie." Jason, breathless and flushed, stood in the doorway once she pulled it open.

"Jason? What's wrong? Is the café okay?" She tugged him into the apartment and shut the door.

"The café's fine. But some guys were just there asking about you. Ellie, they were asking about Ash, too. I recognized one of them. He works at that restaurant on Fifth."

"Restaurant on Fifth?" She tried to think but came up blank. "What restaurant?"

"It's run by the Komisky family."

Her chest clenched. The room chilled ten degrees.

"How do you know that? I mean, what does that have to do with me?" Surely, Marcus would be able to find where she lived easily enough, he wouldn't have to shake down her cashier at the coffee shop.

"They said they were headed to Ash's house next. There's a party, and they were going to settle something with him first. And they wanted to know when you'd be back in. Ellie, what the hell happened when you were gone? What's going on?"

"I don't know. Why would they tell you what they were doing with Ash?" She walked over to the window, pulled the curtain to the side, and looked for the detail. Since she'd moved home, two cars remained parked on either side of the street. "Where are the cars?"

"I think they are going to kill Ash Titon, Ellie, and they'll come for you next." Jason's voice held an unfamiliar edge.

She spun around and went in search of the phone she'd left on the couch. "Okay. It's fine. I'll call him. I'll warn him."

Jason had her phone in his hand. "Of course. Here."

She took it from him, pushing the buttons to bring it to life. Nothing.

"I had it charged. I know I did."

"Here, use mine," he said, offering his phone.

"Thanks." She took his, but realized she didn't know Ash's number. It had been programmed into the phone. She'd never had to look at it.

"Dammit." She gave the phone back to him and ran to the closet to find her shoes. "I have to warn him. I need to get there before those guys do."

"I'll take you." Jason had the front door open before she finished lacing up her shoe.

She had to reach him before anyone else did. If he was having a party, then there'd be a lot of people there. He'd be surrounded. He might not see the threat until too late.

"Fuck the speed limit, Jason. Floor it."

CHAPTER 28

"The girls are ready, and the doors opened twenty minutes ago. What the hell are you doing?" Peter barged into the Annex office.

Ash looked up from his computer screen but disregarded the anger in his cousin's eyes.

"I'm working. Just take care of the announcements for me." Ash waved a hand over the laptop.

"Are you fucked in the head? After what happened with Marcus at the last party, and then you throw another one so soon, and now you aren't going to do the announcements? Do you know what that looks like?"

Annoyed, Ash slammed his hand on his desk. "I don't give a fuck what it looks like, Peter. Just handle it."

Peter's gaze narrowed. "Bertucci is here, Ash. You can't fucking disappear."

Having the party had seemed like the perfect avenue to take. Keep his mind off Ellie, and she'd become a faded memory. Except it wasn't working, and now he had a full room of men waiting to be given the instructions on how to purchase their woman for the evening, or longer. The parties never started without his announcements, and having Peter suddenly step up would give the wrong impression.

"Fine. I'm coming."

He yanked his suit jacket on and closed the laptop. He wasn't getting anywhere in his search anyway.

"After tonight, you are going to Ellie's house. Because I can't take another fucking minute of your brooding," Peter mumbled from behind him as they made their way to the ballroom.

"Ash! Peter!" Daniel came running down the hallway, waving his hand at them.

"What is it? What's wrong?" Ash asked.

"Ellie's detail is gone."

"What?" Ash squared off with him, ready to smash the messenger to alleviate his worry.

"They didn't check in, and when I tried to reach them, no answer. Both cars. Gone."

"This could be Marcus," Peter said. "He could be goading you into leaving the house, going after her."

"Marcus is here." Daniel jerked a thumb behind him. "He just pulled into the front drive. He's with his father."

"Send four men to Ellie's. Make sure she's safe. I want eyes on her." Ash shoved a finger into Daniel's chest.

"I already sent them," Daniel said, holding his ground. "What about Marcus?"

"Why would he come with his father? Especially if Bertucci's here. Are they trying to start a war with the other families?" Peter questioned.

"I have no gripe with Kristoff." Ash ran his knuckles along his jaw. He wanted out of the family shit, away from the old ways, but the assholes just kept worming their way back to him.

"What do you want me to do, Ash?" Daniel asked, phone already in his hand.

Ash looked down the hall at all the hanging pieces of art. He had thought to have Ellie's work there one day. He could hear the murmurs of the partygoers already inside the ballroom, waiting for him to begin the evening. If Ellie had been there, she could be on his arm, walking into the room at his side. If he'd just let her in, that's where she'd be. At his side.

But she wasn't there.

Ash met his cousin's eyes. "Let them come."

CHAPTER 29

*E*llie jumped out of Jason's car two blocks east of the estate. Traffic stood still at the intersection, and she couldn't wait for it to clear. Before Jason had the car shifted into park and scrambled out, she was running up the hill to the gates.

The estate glowed, lights burning in each window. The party had already begun. She ran faster, huffing and ignoring the burn in her lungs as she made her way up the incline.

The gates were open. Several of Ash's men guarded them, but they made no move to stop her.

"Ellie, slow down," Jason urged, but he fell in step with her as they climbed up the steps to the house.

Ash's men milled around outside the front door.

"Ash, where's Ash?" she demanded.

The taller of the group glared at her at first, but recognition must have hit him. He stumbled over his own feet to push the door open.

"Inside. He's in the Annex, his office."

She nodded and shoved past him into the house.

The door to the Annex stood wide open. She moved on, down the hall, past the ballroom full of people.

The doors to his office were closed when she got to them. She tried the handle, but it was locked.

"Ash!" She pounded on the door. "I'm here! Ash. I'm here!" she yelled, smacking the flat of her palm against the door.

It opened slowly, and Peter's face greeted her. His dark expression didn't bring any relief to the tightness in her chest.

"Ellie." Peter looked back over his shoulder. "You shouldn't be here," he whispered.

"I need to talk to Ash." She tried to push past him, but he put his arm out.

"You really can't be here, Ellie. It's not safe."

More annoyed at his arrogance than ever, she fisted her hands. "Fuck safe." With both hands, she shoved at him. The surprise of her attack could be the only explanation for how she got the large brute to move an inch. And it was only an inch, but enough for her to wiggle through the doorway and burst inside.

Ash stood in the center of the room, facing off with Marcus and an older man.

"Ash!" She came to a halt between the men.

Ash didn't take his eyes off Marcus. "Ellie, get out," he ordered in a calm, low voice.

She wanted to touch him, to ease the fury and tension from his body, but she held herself in check. There were rules in Ash's world, and to show any concern for him would be seen as a weakness.

"Can't you just stop?" She unleashed her fury at Marcus. "What is worth all of this? Just because you can't have some girl?"

"Your woman doesn't know how to heel, but I'll teach her." Marcus's sneer oozed over Ellie's skin.

"I let you into my office out of courtesy to your father, but my patience is over. I've let you have your temper tantrum, but it's over now."

"I wouldn't exactly say that." Jason's hard voice caught Ellie off guard, drawing her attention to the door where he stood, pistol in hand.

Marcus and the old man stepped closer together, their expressions relaxed.

"Jason. What the hell? Where'd you get the gun?" Ellie said.

Jason moved through the room, his pistol aimed at her. Ash wouldn't care if it was aimed at him, Peter wouldn't let that stop him, either, but having it trained on her kept them frozen where they stood.

"You sure took your sweet-ass time," Marcus barked, holding his palm up to Jason.

"I told you I'd text when we got in the car, but you didn't wait. Impatient as always, Uncle." Jason reached beneath his coat and produced another pistol, handing it off to Marcus.

"Uncle?" Ellie tried to grasp the situation, but the players of the game weren't known to her. Except Jason. She knew him. Had known him for over a year.

"Ellie, get out of the room. Now," Ash demanded.

But she couldn't. All she could do was focus on the gun pointing at her. The round, black barrel aimed at her chest.

"You wanted me to get you in with your gun." She stared at Jason. Of course. Once again, she'd been fucking played.

"It was the easiest way. We aren't looking for a lot of bloodshed. Besides, the men out there can be useful once everything changes hands. Killing them would only make my ranks smaller." Marcus cocked the gun he held and raised his arm.

"I did give you a chance," the older man said with a shrug. "Sell the business to me, and I won't kill the girl."

"No." Ellie sidestepped, placing herself between Marcus and Ash.

"Ellie, you're being stupid. Move out of the way." Jason jerked the pistol to the side.

"Why would you work at the café if this is your family?" she shot at him.

"You really are naive, Ellie. Your father hired me as a favor to my uncle. Just a part-time job to keep me legit." Jason's lips pulled into a smirk.

Had she been so blind to everything right in front of her?

Marcus spoke up again. "Everything that's here is ours now."

A low laugh bubbled behind Ellie. Peter.

"You really think you can just come in here with a gun and take the place?"

"No. I think I can put a gun to this bitch's head and walk away with everything Ashland Titon owns." Marcus's smirk nauseated Ellie.

"You won't be walking out of here with anything," Ash's voice boomed behind her.

"Well, I suppose we could strike a deal." The older man pushed Marcus gently and came forward. "Give you a cut of the business, a small portion."

"I said you get nothing."

"Killing me won't get him to sell you anything." Ellie stepped toward Jason. "If I'm dead, why would he sell? He has a whole room full of women out there just waiting to fall at his feet. I think you've overplayed your hand." She took another step.

Jason's eyes flicked from her to his uncle. He obviously hadn't planned on her standing up to him.

"Ellie." Just her name, that's all Ash said, but she knew what it meant. He wanted her to stand down. Well, she'd done that too often. Too many times, she'd let things slide, let the little details that didn't make sense go because she didn't want to cause waves by asking questions.

"Or is this all because Ash wouldn't let him have a toy he wanted? He told you, I assume, this all started because he wanted to buy a girl who didn't want to be bought. She didn't want to wear a diaper, be forced to breast feed while your uncle jerked off. And instead of finding a woman who had the same games in mind, he has a hissy fit." She could feel Ash tense behind her. She'd overheard a conversation between two of the girls from the Annex in the garden one afternoon. Ash had no idea she knew about Marcus and Amber, and Ellie had never felt the need to inform him.

"My uncle—"

"Is a dirtbag. Agreed." Ellie nodded and turned her attention to Marcus.

His face burned red.

"All he had to do was pick someone else. Find someone willing to give him what he wanted. But he's a spoiled ass who wants only what he can't have."

"You bitch," Marcus seethed, turning his gun on Ellie. "You fucking bitch." Spittle flew from his mouth, his fat, vulgar face puffed up with anger or embarrassment at having his secret desires laid out for his family to see.

"Marcus." Ash drew his attention from Ellie.

"And you." Marcus swung back.

Ash jerked forward, arm outstretched, but he wasn't quick enough. Marcus aimed his pistol and fired before taking aim.

The blast dulled her hearing. Peter was on Marcus, wrestling him to the ground and getting the gun away from him. Through blurred vison, Ellie witnessed the gun put to Marcus's head.

Another man ran into the room, tackling Jason to the ground, the gun skidding across the room. The old man stumbled in his attempt to flee, falling onto his side near the door.

Not concerned with any of them, Ellie searched out Ash. He wasn't standing in the same spot anymore. He lay on the floor, a dark-red pool of blood beneath him on the floor, a ring of blood spread across his left side. His eyes were closed.

"No," she screamed, rushing to his side, falling to her knees. "Ash. No. Ash!" She yanked his shirt open; buttons popped off and flew, exposing his undershirt. The blood already saturated the cotton material.

"No, Ash. Please." A hard sob shook her as she put her hand over the wound, pushing down, trying to stop the bleeding. "No. You can't. No." Tears fell from her face, mingling with the blood on his chest and on the floor.

This couldn't be happening. He wouldn't leave her. Not like this, not without fighting.

"Please." She rested her forehead on his chest. "Please, Ash." She clung to him with everything she had, listening for a heartbeat. Wanting to feel the familiar pounding of his heart. "Ash. I love you, Ash. So much. Please no." She pressed her cheek to him while keeping pressure on the wound.

A fist gripped her hair. Not pulling but lightly holding her.

"Say it again, Ellie," a hoarse whisper demanded.

CHAPTER 30

Ash's side burned like hell had taken root in his side. He groaned when he twisted his body, trying to move. A light touch on his arm gave him pause.

"Don't move too much," Ellie chastised in a soft voice.

She loved him.

He'd heard her say it.

Once, and then again after he made her repeat herself. The sight of her tears spilling down her face, the horrendous sound of her sobs made him want to get out of the damn bed and chase down Marcus fucking Komisky.

But she loved him, so he stopped fidgeting in the bed.

"Tell me again." He closed his eyes to the pain and grabbed her hand.

She sighed and sat beside him.

He'd been brought home from the hospital the day following being shot. Hospitals were no place to heal, and he wanted to be alone with his Ellie. Where he could be sure she was safe, and his men could protect them while Marcus was being dealt with.

"I love you," she said. He grinned over the annoyance in

her voice. He'd made her repeat the sentence at least a dozen times a day since they'd gotten home from the hospital.

"You shouldn't have come back." He tried to sound firm, but he couldn't. He could either brave the pain in his side, or he could give her the tongue lashing she deserved, and since seeing him in pain upset her so much, he routed his energy down that path.

"You can yell at me later, after you're done healing." She pulled the quilt up his bare chest.

"It's too hot," he argued and shoved the quilt back to where he had it.

"How did you know they would be here?" he asked. Questions roamed his mind for days, but he waited until he could think clearly enough to hear the answers.

She stood and folded her arms over her chest as he pushed himself to sitting up against the headboard.

"Glare all you want, Ellie, I'm not a fucking kid. It's a scratch. I'll let you be bossy for one more day and that's it." He pointed a finger at her.

Truth of the matter, he could stay in bed for another week, but he wouldn't. Business had to be tended to, and he couldn't operate anything from the comfort of his bed. Even if it was exactly where he wanted to be, if Ellie would be with him.

"Now, tell me."

She threw her hands in the air and climbed up onto the bed, careful not to jostle him as she took a seat beside him with her legs crisscrossed.

"Two men were in the coffeehouse the night before talking about you. About how Marcus was going to take you down somehow. The next day, Jason showed up saying they were back and asking about you—about me."

"The night before?"

"I didn't text you because, well." Her face flushed. "I was

still upset. I figured you would take care of it, you'd know anyway, so I let it go."

He didn't respond but continued to stare at her, waiting for all of it.

"I'm sorry, Ash. I should have texted you, warned you."

He put his hand on her knee. "You should have stayed all the way out of it. Marcus could have killed you. He could have turned his gun on you instead of me." Just thinking about it made his anger boil all over again.

"No, I should have come sooner."

"Ellie, what happened was not your fault." He toyed with the ends of her hair, tugging to get her eyes to meet his. "He used you to get his guns in here. My men checked him before he got inside. He needed Jason to get in here and with you leading the charge, it was easy. How could you have known about Jason? This wasn't your fault."

"Still—"

"No, not still. You were trying to protect me, to warn me. You had no idea about Jason. That's not your fault. Barging into the room after Peter told you it was unsafe—that, however, I haven't forgotten, yet."

"Seriously? You're mad about that?" She pulled back from him, taking her hair from his grip.

"Not mad." He scratched his beard. "I want you safe, Ellie. And being here wasn't safe."

"I was trying to protect you!" She poked her finger into his thigh.

"And I had it all under control."

"Yeah, if Jason hadn't gotten the gun in, they would have found another way. He was coming to kill you, Ash. Kill. Not steal, not bother with health code, kill," she pointed out.

He laughed. "You have such little faith in my men?"

She pointed at him. "And the detail you had outside my apartment?"

His mood soured again. "The two guys who were in charge of you that night were found a few miles away from your apartment." Alive, but barely. "They'll be fine." And then they could answer why the hell they were lured away from their posts so easily in order to get the shit kicked out of them.

"And Marcus?" she asked in a hushed tone. She scooted closer to him again. He wanted her to lay her head on his chest, so he could hold her. She'd been hovering over him for two days, and he hadn't been able to comfort her properly. She'd gone through hell, and he couldn't protect her or soothe her from it.

"Peter took care of it."

Her cheeks blanched, and she nodded. "Peter—I mean, Marcus is—"

"Peter has it handled." Ash wouldn't tell her anything more than that. She'd already had too much of her innocence ripped away. He wouldn't be part of shredding another piece in front of her.

"What about Jason?"

The pain written on her face, saying that asshole's name, gave him the energy to bound out of bed and kick his face in. She'd been betrayed by everyone close to her.

"Jason won't be an issue again, and before you ask, Kristoff Komisky has been dealt with as well—and not by us. The other families will deal with him. He went behind their backs, trying to steal what's mine to keep for himself. They had an agreement among them, and he broke it."

"So, what happens now?"

He reached up and brushed her hair over her shoulder. "Now, you fucking kiss me, and tell me again you love me."

"Ash." She shoved his leg. "I'm serious."

"So am I." He yanked on her shirt until she fell forward onto him. He grunted but wouldn't let her move.

Wrapping his hand around the back of her neck, he pulled her to his lips. Fuck, she felt like heaven.

"I love you, too, Ellie," he whispered against her mouth and deepened the kiss. "And as soon as I get the chance, I'm going to show you how fucking much."

She pulled back when he ended the kiss, her face hovering over his.

"But what about us, what happens?"

"We make a new start. You move in here, permanently. Keep the café if you want it, or sell it, I don't care. And you'll work on your art, or you won't. Go to school or don't. Whatever you want is what we do next."

"And the Annex?"

"What about it?" He braced himself for the ultimatum.

"You'll let me help with it?"

He drew his eyebrows together. She hadn't brought up the subject of the Annex after he explained the details of the wing. Probably because she didn't want him to know she knew what was going on with Marcus. His woman could be sneaky; he'd have to keep an eye on her.

"Help how?"

"Work with the girls, business stuff, or whatever? I want to be a part of it if it's part of you."

He kissed her again.

He lowered his voice. "We'll figure something out. But you aren't on the menu, Ellie."

She rolled her eyes. Like she'd ever even consider it, but he wouldn't give her the impression she belonged to anyone other than him.

"And what about my father?"

He tensed and released her.

"I want to talk to him."

He nodded. "Of course." He hadn't decided what to do with him other than to let him go. Nothing mattered as much as Ellie's happiness, and keeping her father locked away didn't seem the way to do that.

Just the topic brought a shadow to her features.

"No more talk about all that for now." He scooted down the bed again until he lay flat. "I'm pretty sure we're in my room."

"Yeah?"

"So, what are you supposed to be wearing in here?" he asked, flipping the hem of her skirt.

She blushed. "Ash, you're wounded."

"A scratch. Now take off those fucking panties, and your skirt. You can keep your shirt on." He pushed at her until she got moving and then he moved to the center of the bed, fixing the pillows beneath his head.

"What are you doing? We can't. I mean, you can't. Seriously, you can't," she argued, but since she was working the button on her skirt, he didn't count it against her.

"I may not be able to fuck you senseless, but there's not a damn thing wrong with my tongue." He caught her hand when she placed it on the mattress. "Get over here and ride my face, Ellie. I want your pussy, and you won't deny me."

Her throat worked, her nostrils flaring with her increased breathing, and her lips parted. With her skirt discarded and her panties tossed aside, she knelt on the bed beside him, giving him a bird's-eye view of her sex.

Taking a deep breath, he grinned up at her. "I can smell how wet you are."

She leaned on her heels, bringing her knees together.

He tsked his displeasure. "No, open those legs." He tapped her knee.

Sliding them apart again, he rolled to his good side, ignoring the fire burning in his left. He lightly touched her pussy lips with his fingers.

"So fucking wet." He showed her the moisture he'd

collected before shoving his fingers into his mouth and moaning over the utopian flavor.

Repositioning himself on the bed, he gave her a stern look. "I wasn't asking, Ellie," he reminded.

"I don't want to hurt you," she whispered but inched closer.

"I'll worry about that. You only worry about getting your pretty pussy licked and sucked until you're screaming my name."

He could sense her apprehension, but she started to move anyway.

"That's my good girl." He moved his arms to give her the space she needed. And licked his lips as she lifted one leg over his body and positioned herself over him.

He inhaled deeply, his cock hardening from the scent of his girl's cunt.

"Hold on to the headboard and don't let go," he ordered, cupping her naked buttocks in his hands. Spreading his fingers across her smooth skin, he lifted his head enough to flick her clit with the pointed tip of his tongue.

She moaned and jerked back, but he held steady and brought her pussy closer to him. He took her clit between his teeth, relishing the groan she gave him for his trouble.

Licking her slowly, he flicked her clit and began again. After several passes, she began to gyrate above him, rubbing her nub into his mouth.

He covered her with his mouth and sucked until she sucked a breath through her teeth, making a hissing sound.

"Ash," she begged when he continued to suck, but not give her clit the attention she wanted.

He opened his eyes, looking up the length of her, and found her darkened green eyes peering down at him, pleading with him. He released her and began to lick again. She closed her eyes and moaned.

"Oh fuck, Ash, fuck," she panted.

"Don't let go of the headboard," he ordered and pried her ass cheeks apart. Her legs stiffened, and her ass clenched, but he wouldn't be denied.

He was the patient, after all, and didn't he deserve to have exactly what he wanted?

"No, don't clench. I'm having my way here. Just enjoy it." He dipped his forefinger into her cunt, thrusting into her while he paid special attention to her clit, and once she was lost in the pleasure again, he removed his finger and began to press it against her asshole.

"Ash." She clenched tight, but one slap to her hip and she relaxed.

His tongue lavished attention to her pussy while his finger pushed into her ass, past the tight ring until he was up to his knuckle.

"Oh fuck," she panted, and he smiled against her pussy.

"Come, Ellie. Come for me," he urged, and began to thrust in and out of her ass while licking, sucking, and savoring every inch of her pussy.

"Ash," she cried out, and her hips moved toward his hand, toward his tongue. She couldn't seem to decide where she wanted the pressure.

Her thighs tensed and shook beside him. He bit her clit and pushed fully inside her.

She screamed his name. Her orgasm ripped through her body. He could feel the shivers. Her ass clenched again, and she rubbed her pussy over his tongue like she was riding for the gold medal.

As she slowed her movements, he removed his finger and gently stroked her ass. Her breathing slowed, and finally she moved away from him. Not sitting on his chest, but not getting off him, either.

"Fuck, Ash." She flung her leg over him and flopped on

the bed next to him, resting her head on his chest. He wiped his hand across his mouth, still enjoying the smell and taste of her on him.

At a knock on the door, she hurtled off the bed before he could stop her. She pulled on her skirt and tucked her panties into her palm just as the door flew open and Peter walked in.

His obvious concern for his cousin wrinkled his brow when he eyed the bed then her standing beside it. Relief softened his features.

"Seriously. You couldn't wait?" He shot the accusation at Ash.

"You wouldn't, either." Ash winked and shoved himself to sit against the headboard.

"I have to…check on something." Ellie didn't make eye contact with Peter as she rushed past him, and flung the door closed behind her.

"You didn't need to make her run off."

"You shouldn't be fucking around like that. Your stitches."

"Fuck off, my stitches. If you had a girl like Ellie, you wouldn't give a shit about some thread stuck in your skin, either. Now what do you want?"

"Bertucci called. It's done."

"What about everything else?"

"What else? The girls are all accounted for and safe. The guests from the party have already inquired about when the next will be held, so he didn't get to fuck that up for you. The only thing left to deal with is the old man rotting in the basement."

Ash nodded. "Ellie wants to talk to him. After that, we'll decide."

Peter grabbed the door handle and started to back out of the room. "You're a lucky son of a bitch. You know that, right?"

"I'm well aware, yes."

"Good. 'Cause if you hurt her, I think you'll have a mutiny on your hands. The men heard how she came running in there to try to warn you, to save you. If they didn't already like her before, they would lay their lives down to save hers now."

Ash waved him off. "I know the feeling. Now, get the fuck out of here. I feel like someone set my skin on fire."

Peter laughed. "Serves you right." He was gone before the pillow Ash threw at him hit the door.

CHAPTER 31

"I'm sorry! I'm sorry, Sir! Really!" a high-pitched voice echoed in the hallway just before the sharp snap of leather against flesh.

Ellie tensed and pressed herself against the wall. The door across from her stood slightly ajar, but enough she could see the red bottom being strapped. Not envious of the punishment taking place, she stepped closer to the door, trying to find the disciplinarian.

Ash had told her he never touched the girls in the Annex, but he might not see this activity as touching.

"I don't want to see you in here again, Lorie. You know better, and if we have to discuss the safety protocol again, you'll find the cane more uncomfortable than my belt. Am I clear?" Peter's voice carried.

"Yes, Sir." A sniffling woman moved out of position and dropped her skirt down over the crimson glow of her ass.

Ellie leaned forward, trying to hear Peter's next words only to have the door swept open, exposing her crime.

"Shit." She stumbled forward, catching herself on the doorjamb before embarrassing herself further.

Peter grinned. "You really never learn, do you? You just keep putting your nose in places it doesn't belong."

She gave him a wary glance before taking notice of the short blonde smoothing out her clothing.

"Sorry. I thought—I mean, I was looking for Ash."

Lorie smiled. "It's okay." She turned to Peter. "May I go now?"

Peter nodded. "You have a shift at Sampson's tonight, but since those marks won't be faded by then, you're on cocktail duty."

She looked ready to argue, but seemed to think better of it and nodded. "Fine."

Ellie moved aside to let her exit the room and make her way down the hall to the apartments. She ignored Peter's grin as he slipped his belt through the loops of his trousers.

"You enjoy spanking them," she stated flatly.

"I enjoy being a disciplinarian, yes. I even enjoy watching a woman's ass bounce while my belt dances over it. But I do not enjoy being disobeyed or having to waste a good time by dishing out punishment."

Not exactly sure what to say to that, she changed the subject. "Do you punish all the girls?"

Peter buckled his belt and leaned against the doorframe with his arms over his chest. "No. Just the ones who break the rules. The women here aren't like other women. They enjoy being submissive. They like the structure and boundaries. They agree to the punishments before they sign up to live in the Annex."

"And if they don't agree?"

Peter shrugged. "It's never happened, but I suppose they'd have some other form of consequence."

Somehow, that made it better.

"I didn't mean to interrupt you. I really am looking for Ash."

"Well, I think he found you." Peter pointed behind her, with a Cheshire grin that always grated on her.

"Ellie, I told you I'd come get you," Ash stated, walking up to them. He moved with less grimace, but he had to still be sore.

She tried not to remember the gunshot, seeing him bleeding, feeling him slip away from her, but sometimes she couldn't help it. She'd been a breath away from losing him.

"I didn't want you to have to come all the way to the main house when I am perfectly capable of meeting you here." She tried to smile, but his irritation didn't lesson.

"When I tell you to wait for me, wait for me. Nothing's changed on that end." He stepped closer, lowering himself until he pressed her against the wall. "Just because I love you doesn't mean I won't bare your ass and show you my displeasure."

She swallowed and licked her lips. "Well, can it wait until after you let me see my father?"

He growled and pushed away from the wall. "You think you aren't intimidated by me anymore, but it's because I've become soft. That ends."

She wanted to laugh, no longer terrified at what he would do to her and anticipating the next time he did put his hand to her ass. She couldn't find a morsel of fear toward him.

"Do you want me to bring him up?" Peter interrupted.

"No." Ash waved him off. "We'll go down there." He slid his fingers through Ellie's. "Are you sure you want to do this?"

"Yes." She nodded. It was more of a have-to situation than a want to, but it didn't matter.

Ash led her toward the stairs to the lower level. He didn't talk about what was down there, but she had a good sense of what she'd be walking into.

"What were you and Peter talking about?" he asked, probably to distract her from the nerves in her stomach.

"I saw him belting Lorie."

"You were eavesdropping again." He squeezed her hand. "I would have thought you'd learned your lesson on that."

"Would you ever let Peter punish me? I mean, like the other girls."

As they came to the door, he spun her around and captured her face in his hands. "How many times do I have to tell you this. The other women here are employees. You aren't an employee. You are mine."

"So that's a no?"

"I think you're trying to provoke me into giving you a spanking. I think it's been too many weeks since your ass has been on fire."

She wouldn't deny it. Nor would she agree.

"Tonight, I'll meet you in our room at ten o'clock. And you remember how I expect you to be when I meet you?"

The growling sound of his voice softened the fluttering in her body.

"Naked and on my knees," she whispered.

"Yes." He kissed her, a short, hard kiss and released her. "Are you calm enough to do this? Are you sure?"

He studied her with the same concern as he had when she told him why she wanted to meet with her father. What she wanted to ask him.

"Yes, Ash. I'm ready." It was mostly true. But not entirely. How could anyone be ready to face their father for the last time.

As he led her down the steps, her heart hammered against her ribs, shaking her stomach and giving her the very real impression she was going to lose her lunch in the stairwell.

The air chilled as they made their way down the spiral

staircase. A part of her expected a medieval set up, so when all she found was more of the same as the other floors, she was a little surprised.

Ash grabbed her hand as she stepped off the stairs, and he walked her down the hallway again. A shorter hallway, with several doors on each side, each with small viewing windows at the top.

"Is this where you would have put me if I hadn't—I mean when my father,,,"

Ash stopped in front of a room. "You never would have been kept down here." He pulled a set of keys from his pocket and unlocked the door. "He's in here. Do you want me to go with you?" It sounded rhetorical, but she answered anyway.

"I can handle this."

"Do you want me in there?" he asked with more force.

"Can you keep quiet?" she asked.

"Probably not. If he hurts you—"

"He won't. He can't. I mean, he did, but not now." She surveyed the entrance. "Okay, you can come in, but please let me handle it."

He nodded and pushed the door open.

Her father stood facing them, probably anticipating whatever was coming through the doorway when he heard the keys from outside. He hadn't shaved, and a fuzzy gray beard had taken over his face. The short haircut he normally sported had grown out a bit over the past few weeks, giving him an even older appearance. He hadn't lost weight, though, she noticed immediately. He was clean and had a healthy glow about him.

"Ellie!" Her father grinned.

There was a chill in the air. Crisper than in the hall, but her father didn't seem to notice. His arms were outstretched, welcoming her to hug him.

She stood several steps away from him, arms wrapped around her middle.

"What's wrong?" her father asked, dropping his arms to his sides and moving his gaze to Ash briefly before moving them back to her. "What has he told you? Where have you been?" His voice darkened with each question, until finally the accusation came through. "You've been living upstairs while you let your father rot down here."

"You don't look like you've rotted much." She raised her chin. All the years she'd tried to help him, to cover his debt, she couldn't remember a single time he'd thanked her.

"He let me shower today."

Ellie reached back and touched Ash's hand when she felt him starting to tense behind her. Her father was lying. She could see the signs now, much clearer than months ago.

She took a long moment to survey the room. Comfortable. Nothing like the cell in a dungeon she pictured him sitting in. Concrete walls, but a rug covered the floor, and a bed was pushed against the wall in the corner. There was even a small dinette set and a couch.

"I came to say goodbye." Though she tried to keep herself from shaking, the tremor came through her voice.

"Ellie. No." Her father took a step toward her but stopped with a glance over her shoulder at Ash.

"For years, I took care of you. When Mom got sick, when she was too sick to help at the coffeehouse, when she died." Her stomach twisted at the memory. A long-ago faded image of her mother in the hospital.

"But I can't anymore. I won't."

"Ellie, we're family. We take care of each other," he repeated the mantra he'd quoted over the years of her sacrifices made for him.

"No. I took care of you. When you couldn't make rent, I got a second job. When you owed Jose more than we had in the bank, I sold a piece of Mom's jewelry. You never took care of me."

"That's not true!"

"How many art fairs in high school did you forget to come to because you had a poker game you had to be at? Or parent teacher conferences you didn't attend because you had spent the night at the casino and weren't awake in time?" She clenched her hands to keep them from shaking, but nothing could stop her insides from quaking. Every moment of her childhood he'd failed her pushed forward in her mind.

"I was doing my best. When your mother died, it was so hard," he said. No emotion laced his words. It was as though he'd given himself, and her, the same excuse for so long, it just fell out of his mouth without thought or meaning.

"Yeah, Dad. It was hard. For both of us. But you didn't face it, you just buried yourself in your gambling. I was twelve! By the time I was in high school, I was working night shifts at the coffeehouse, and taking extra jobs on the days we were closed to make ends meet."

"Don't be so dramatic. I was taking care of you. I was putting a roof over your head."

"My head?" She yelled the words, anger replaced the hurt she'd felt moments before. He didn't see it. After all the years, after the last month, he still didn't see how his actions hurt her.

"We almost lost the roof over *my* head three times because of your gambling." She took a deep breath, feeling the tears burn her eyes but not caring to wipe them away. "You sold me, Dad. You knew I'd come here to save you, and I did. Like an idiot, I came and protected you one more time. But, you knew I would. You were betting on it."

Ash moved closer. The heat of his body behind her gave her the strength to push on.

"You know, I always thought you wouldn't sell the coffeehouse because it was Mom's big dream. That's what you told me. You told me she had put everything into the place and selling it would be like cutting her out of our hearts."

She stepped over to him.

"I found the papers, Dad." Calling him that felt heavy. He didn't deserve the title. "You never sold it because Mom put the coffeehouse in my name. You were executor until I was eighteen, and then it turned over to me. You didn't sell it because you weren't able to. She knew what you would do. She knew you'd sell it or gamble it away."

"Your mother was looking out for you, but that's not—"

"She was getting ready to divorce you when she got sick!" A hard sob grabbed her. Reading the divorce filing had been like sticking a knife directly through her heart. "She wanted out. She was going to take me away from you, and you would have been alone. No one to save you anymore. But she got sick and didn't go forward with it."

Her father's face contorted with a rage she'd not witnessed in her life.

"The coffeehouse was as much mine as it was hers. She had no right to do that." He clenched his jaw, his eyes darkening.

"No. It wasn't. Mom bought it before you two met."

Ellie dragged the back of her hand across her wet cheeks. The ache in her chest swelled when her father, the man who was supposed to be her protector and provider, stared at her blankly. But what else was there to say? She already knew everything, and he had nothing to offer in his defense.

"Ellie." His voice softened again, the same tone he used when he was about to let her down again. "We have to figure out what comes next, here. You can't think to stay with him. He'll keep me locked up forever, or kill me."

"You didn't think he was all that bad when you decided to exchange me for your debt."

"I-I was finding a way to pay him, I just needed some time."

"And you found the time by selling me to him, and then you got Marcus Komisky involved. Your solution was to sell me to him in order to pay off Ash. Do you have any idea how crazy that is?" Her voice rose.

Taking a deep breath, she steeled herself. This was the end of her worry, of her heartache over her father's carelessness, his thoughtlessness. She was finally putting herself first. She was taking care of herself and putting him away from here, where he couldn't hurt her again.

"I'm selling the coffeehouse. A condo has been purchased for you. Your things have already been moved there. There's a bank account in your name that will have a small allowance deposited every month."

"An allowance? How much?" her father asked, not giving Ash a glance, or a word. But what had she really expected from him than more greed? Maybe she wanted him to beg her forgiveness and plead with her not to walk out on him. But she wouldn't get those things from him.

She stepped back, feeling Ash's hands on her shoulders.

"I never want to hear from you again. If you run out of money, don't come asking for more. There won't be any. If you run up a debt you can't pay, I won't help."

Her jaw ached, but she kept talking.

"When I first met Ash, I called him a beast. He seemed cruel and heartless. But I was wrong. You're the monster. You're the one with no heart or soul. And I'm done with you." Not wanting to hear any reply he might conjure up, she turned on her heel and left the room.

"If you contact her, I will kill you. Make no mistake, Dominick. I will kill you with my bare hands if need be before I let you hurt her ever again." Ash's voice carried outside the door, where Ellie leaned against the chilled concrete walls.

"Yeah. Okay. I got it," her father said, without remorse or sadness. Her father, for the second time, simply gave her up.

CHAPTER 32

Ellie slept peacefully in their bed beneath the quilt, snuggled up to Ash's pillow. He stood over his sleeping beauty, tempted to let her continue napping. But the beast in him won out.

"Ellie." He shook her shoulder, rousing her.

She wiped her eyes and looked to the clock on the nightstand. "Oh." She quickly shuffled from under the covers and ran into the bathroom.

"Two minutes!" he called after her and left the bedroom to give her space.

Hanging out in the hallway, he listened to her shuffle around the bedroom. He couldn't help but grin when she cursed a split moment after he heard a thunk. She'd hit her toe on the armchair half a dozen times already.

His girl needed tonight. She needed his beast.

Deciding he'd been kind enough, he reentered the room to find her kneeling beside the bed in the correct position. Her naked body was displayed before him, making his already-hard cock stiffen more.

"You remembered your positioning well enough," he

praised, noting the little hitch in her breathing. Her shoulders tensed. She was trying not to look up at him, but she wanted to. Badly. She wanted his pleasure. But not yet.

He walked past her, careful not to touch her naked form, and opened the drawer of his toy box. Picking out the thickest flogger he had in his room, he turned back to her, dragging the leather falls through his fingers.

"Put your face to the floor and stick your ass up in the air," he ordered, running the flogger over her back to let her know what was coming. She could try to anticipate his next moves, but she'd be wrong.

He noticed she'd brushed her hair out while in the washroom, leaving the thick, auburn smoothed down her back. It spilled to either side of her as she moved into position, exposing the creamy skin of her backside.

Stepping to her left side, he ran the flogger over her upturned ass. First to the right then the left, before letting it fall between her legs, brushing against her pussy and running up the length of her spread cheeks.

Her inhale of breath caught him off guard. His girl was sensitive already.

"Did you touch yourself?" he asked, holding the flogger over her ass. "Did you? When you were napping?"

She muttered a curse low enough she probably thought he hadn't heard. He grinned at her. Oh, the beast in him was going to like this.

"Change of plans for my naughty girl." He dropped the flogger and bent down. Pulling her up by her hair, he led her to the bed. "Punishment first." He pushed her face into the mattress and, before she had a chance to get comfortable, he began spanking her ass.

She wiggled and cried with each slap to her cheeks, but he wouldn't stop. Not until the creamy-white ass before him glowed red. And only when she finally stopped begging for mercy she didn't really want any more than he was willing to give, did he slow in his swats.

"You played with your pussy."

"Yes. I'm sorry," she yapped when his hand struck her pussy. Her legs had spread during the spanking, giving him the perfect target.

"How am I supposed to give you an orgasm if you've already stolen one?" he asked with another swat to her thigh.

"You don't have to, Ash," she answered with a seriousness that belonged more in a boardroom than the bedroom.

He yanked her to her feet, turning her around until his eyes could lock on hers. Unshed tears sparkled in her eyes, but the smile she blessed him with soothed away some of his snark.

"I don't have to?"

"No. You don't have to give me an orgasm, or give me a flogging. I just want to be here with you." She licked her dry lips. "I just want to be yours."

Well. Fuck.

He pulled her to his chest and held her tight.

"So, if I push you down and just take your body?"

"I won't stop you. I'll spread my legs wide for you."

"And if I want to tie you to the cross and flog your back until we are both exhausted?"

She kissed his neck. "I'll hold out as long as I can and take every lash you give me."

His eyes nearly crossed.

"And if I say I want you to put a ring on your finger and be mine forever?" He didn't let her pull away. Exposing his vulnerability to her would be too much.

"I'd say let's start forever right now."

"I fucking love you, Ellie," he growled, and picked her up and tossed her onto the mattress, stripping out of his clothes as quickly as his fingers would allow.

"Prove it." She gave him a daring smile and moved back just in time for him to jump on the bed.

There was no need for preamble. He thrust into her wanting body and took her hard. Her nails scratched down his arms and back, pushing him deeper into his arousal.

She arched, grabbing at him when she screamed her release. He didn't wait any longer than the first wave of her orgasm before he plowed into her once more and let his own release steal him away.

Once he caught his breath, he yanked on the quilt and covered them both up. Her head rested on his chest, and he ran his fingers lightly over her shoulder.

"I meant it, Ellie. Be my wife."

She pushed up onto her arm and stared at him, large green eyes dancing with an energy he adored in her.

"I meant it, too. Let's do it right away."

"Demanding woman, aren't you?" He rolled his eyes and laughed. "Once that ring is on your finger, you can bet I'll be keeping you tied to this bed for days at a time."

"Since when do you need a ring for that?" She snuggled into his chest, playing with the hair there.

"True enough," he agreed. "I have some rope in my drawer." He started to roll over, but she playfully swatted his arm.

He growled and rolled on top of her, kissing her hard and trapping her against the pillows.

"You think to hit me, woman?"

"Of course not. I think to make you get the extra rope from downstairs." She giggled.

He kissed her again and bit her lower lip.

"You really are a beast, Ash." She laughed.

"And you're definitely my beauty, and I suppose this is as close to a fairy tale either of us will ever get."

"Because we live happily ever after."

"Fuck yeah, we do. Now, don't move. I'm getting the rope."

He kissed her soundly.

And they lived—mostly—happily ever after.

* * *

Thank you for reading BEAST! I hope you loved meeting Ash and Ellie! They'd love to meet all the people, so please spread the word- tell a friend about these books!

You've met Hunter and Jaelynn here in Hound, but do you know their story? No? Keep reading for a glimpse into the novella Daddy Ever After.

Want more dark romance from Measha Stone? Subscribe to Measha's Email List and find out all the information plus exclusive giveaways and freebies!

DADDY EVER AFTER

AN EVER AFTER NOVELLA

Candles burned in their sconces along the outer walls of the ball room. Jaelynn stood in the far corner, watching everyone. Her stomach had finally stopped twisting into intricate knots, but that probably had more to do with the two shots of amaretto she'd taken before leaving her room and coming down for the party.

Drinking was forbidden for the girls of the Annex right before a party, but amaretto wasn't really liquor, was it? Sure, it had some alcohol content, but it wasn't tequila. Not that she would ever make an attempt at a shot of tequila. In fact, she was pretty sure amaretto wasn't really a shot type liquor, but it had done the job, so she wouldn't dwell on it.

Ashland Titon, owner of the Annex, had already given his speech laying out the ground rules for the evening. Most of them were put in place to keep the girls safe. But she still wasn't all that sure any woman would be safe around Ash, or any of the men milling around the room.

Power flowed through the air. Then again, it could have just been her imagination. She had a way of doing that. Seeing things that weren't there, feeling things that weren't realistic. And she'd made a fool of herself one too many times. Some called it anxiety, she called it life.

But it was the power she sought out at the moment. From one man in particular. If she could just find him, get close enough to him, she could get the job done and be rid of the Annex. But for the time being, until she could make her move, she'd have to keep playing submissive to the alpha assholes who came looking for a good time. At least they paid well.

"Jaelynn, let's go. You have to socialize." Jeffrey, the man assigned to escort her through the room, jerked a thumb at the room.

"Right." She nodded and smoothed out the skirt of her dress, taking a deep breath. "Let's do this." With a nod she pushed herself to start mingling among the rich and powerful.

Though catching the glance of a man looking more terrified than she felt, she wondered how powerful some of them might be.

"You're going to do fine. Just remember, anyone makes an offer, you direct them to me. Peter will have final say since this is your first party." Jeffrey rambled on while she made her way across the room. What was she supposed to do exactly? She couldn't just pace the room like a piece of pie in a rotating case at a diner.

An older man, old enough to be her grandfather, licked his lips as she passed him. She lowered her gaze and picked up her pace. Hopefully he saw the gesture as her being a skittish submissive. If she were to insult one of the guests unprovoked she'd be meeting with Peter again. And she would rather not meet up with the disciplinarian again any time soon.

Once she reached the opposite end of the room, she turned on her heel and started walking back to her original position. She'd make a round after that, she promised herself. Eventually, she would need to actually try to meet up with one of the men in the room, while searching out her prey.

Taking on a man for the night or weekend wouldn't be the worst thing. She had every confidence that Ashland wouldn't allow anyone access to one of his parties without being thoroughly vetted and deemed safe. And she had been assured she had final say on what went into her contracts. If she said no sex, there wouldn't be sex. Which worked well, since she wasn't sure how easily she could fuck a stranger. Playing a little slap and tickle was one thing, and she even enjoyed it to a point, but having some man she didn't even know huffing and puffing over her didn't make the cut. She'd be checking no in that box.

But if she was lucky, she'd find the man she was doing all this for. If she could get him to buy her for the night, she would be able to get close enough to sink her knife into his throat.

If he showed up. It was a hit or miss situation with him and the catalogue parties. Being older now, he didn't partake as often, but she knew he'd come. Eventually, he would, and she could get to him.

Until then, she'd continue working in the Annex, biding her time.

"Jaelynn, I need to get to the front door. There's a problem. You are to stay right over here." Jeffrey grabbed her arm and pulled her to the corner near the bar. "Stephan, I have to step out. Keep an eye out for her, okay?"

The man behind the bar pouring a glass of wine nodded. "Sure thing. Jae, just hang here, okay? I can't leave the bar right now."

"No problem, Stephan." She leaned against the bar and let out a relaxing breath. Who knew putting yourself on a display rack would be so intense. It was like eyes were on her every time she moved.

Specifically, at the moment, she could feel it, the warm stare of a man. Sweeping her gaze around the room, she didn't see anyone ogling her from a distance. Most of the men were already mingling with the girls or engrossed in conversation with each other. Some of the girls had warned her that the guys usually just hang out for a while at first and don't start picking any of them out until toward the end of the night.

The sensation didn't go away once she looked around. If anything, it grew more intense. A heat washed over her. She wasn't just being watched, she was being hunted.

Standing in the corner only made the feeling more intense. She had nowhere to go, nowhere to hide. Not that she should.

Justice—her mantra, but it wasn't working in that moment. Whoever had her locked in his sights was giving her a chill.

"Stephan, I'm just going to walk over there," she tried to tell him. But he was busy pouring drinks.

"Jaelynn, no. Stay," he said when she started to walk away. *Stay.* Like she was just going to obey him on command. He could still see her if he looked up from pouring, and if she was approached she'd bring the gentleman back toward the bar so Stephan would be in hearing range.

Once she was in the open area again, her breathing came more naturally. The heated sensation of being stalked eased away.

She checked the time on the delicate gold chain watch on her left wrist and sighed. Only another four hours before Ash would call the evening to a close. It wouldn't be enough to entertain a few men with conversation throughout the night; she had to eventually find someone to play with. She couldn't let Ash or Peter get the idea she wasn't there for the work.

Being distracted in her own thoughts, she didn't notice a man step up beside her. Her body tensed when she got a whiff of his aftershave. Musk, a woodsy leathery scent. It was almost calming, until she brought her eyes up to meet his.

Dark. Everything about this man screamed run. The severity of his stare, the tightness of his chiseled jaw. The black swirling tattoos that crept up from under his shirt collar and spread over his throat. Around his neck. He rubbed his chin while she continued to gawk at him; more tats. All over his hands. Did any inch of him not have ink?

"I don't think you're supposed to be over here." His deep voice cut through her mental observations.

"What?" She blinked. Her mind had blanked out on her. "Oh. Yes. No. It's okay," she assured him, taking a small step to the left. She couldn't see Stephan with the way this stranger positioned himself between her and the bar.

"Ash made it clear none of the women were to be unescorted. I don't see your escort." His dark eyes never left hers.

"He had to see to something. It's okay."

"Not a rule follower?" he asked with an arched brow. What was the right answer, what did he want to hear? If she said she was, maybe he would find her boring, but if she said she wasn't, maybe he wouldn't find her submissive enough.

"I, I'm Jaelynn." She threw her hand out toward him. Maybe if she drew the conversation back to the beginning she could get him to stop glowering at her.

"Yes, I know." He grabbed her hand, but not to shake it. Instead he cradled it, running the rough tips of his fingers across her palm. "We get a catalogue when we respond to the invitation for the party," he explained when she kept silent.

Yes. That's right. Catalogue. Party. She was supposed to

be finding him. Justice. Yes. It was all coming back to her now.

"This is your first party," he added. "You know, Ashland does a good job of vetting all of these men, but it doesn't mean they are all safe. They won't hurt you anymore than whatever terms they agree to, but they aren't nice men."

If he was trying to warn her away from being at the party, it wouldn't work. She was already there, and she already had her goal.

"And you? Are you a nice man?" She threw on a soft smile, tilting her head a little. Maybe some playfulness would smooth out his edges.

"No," he answered bluntly.

Her smile dropped. The chill that went up and down her spine earlier at the feeling of being watched returned with fervor. He'd been the one. He'd been watching her.

"What's your name?" she asked, still trying to see around him to Stephan. Why hadn't he come to look for her? And where the hell was Jeffrey? He shouldn't be away for this long. If Peter was going to take his belt to her ass for talking to this man without her handler, then Jeffrey better be right beside her.

"Hunter," he said, still not giving her any room to move. "I think we'll stay here until Peter or your handler bothers to find you," he said, his voice full of promise and danger.

Her heart started to patter away. She needed to get around him, back to the open area. She couldn't be blocked like this.

"Why?" she asked softly.

"Because I'm taking you home and I believe Peter will have the final signature since it's your first party."

"You're taking me home? I haven't agreed." She clenched her hands at her sides. How arrogant. Hot, maybe, but fucking arrogant as hell.

"You will."

"Jaelynn." Peter's hard voice crawled over Hunter's back to get to her. Hunter's lips twisted up into a smile and he finally stepped aside to give her room to move.

Peter's fierce expression landed on her as soon as Hunter cleared the way. It might be better if Hunter went back to blocking her. Peter was pissed.

"Peter, I—"

He waved a hand for her to keep her mouth shut. "You were doing exactly what you aren't supposed to be doing. Stephan called me, saying you disappeared into the party and he couldn't see you."

"Jeffrey left—"

"Jeffrey left you with Stephan and you were told to stay put." Peter pressed forward. Giving her one harder glare, he turned to Hunter. "Hunter," he said with some surprise to his tone. "I didn't realize that was you."

Peter extended a hand as did Hunter, and they shook, exchanging greetings.

"I saw her over here, and figured she was probably not supposed to be," Hunter said, no longer looking at her at all. "But I was just starting to negotiate terms with her, so it's probably better you're here."

Peter glanced quickly down at Jaelynn, and she held his stare for a brief moment. What did that mean? Was he approving or not?

"What terms?" Peter asked.

"Whole weekend. Full time. Complete submission. Discipline when needed," Hunter stated and Peter nodded along. Were they going to include her in any way?

"Sex?" Peter asked.

"Yes," Hunter nodded.

"No," Jae said at the same time.

Peter raised an eyebrow. "She does still have final say, even if she's been disobedient this evening."

"Define sex." Hunter posed the question to Jaelynn.

"Excuse me?" If he didn't know, maybe he was in the wrong place.

"Define what sex means to you." Hunter pushed again, his intense stare still winding up her body.

"Sex. Penetration." She started to say more but Hunter already turned back to Peter.

"Okay, I'll agree to no vaginal penetration unless she changes her mind." She wasn't sure the way he said that made it better. Unless she changed her mind? Not likely. Sex wasn't something she was willing to give away to just anyone. Just because she was contracting her body out for other play didn't mean she would open her legs for anyone.

"Anal?" Peter asked Jae the question.

"No," she said, hard.

"That's fine. A weekend doesn't really give me time to train her properly for it anyway," Hunter agreed.

Train her properly? Heat rose up her neck. She'd played this moment out before in her mind. A man negotiating what he could and couldn't do to her body, but this wasn't playing out right. They barely let her into the conversation.

Once they had finished, Peter turned to her. "Anything you want to add? I have your hard lists already and he's agreed to them."

"No. I guess not. What about pay?" she asked, getting to the heart of the matter. She should at least pretend the money was what brought her there.

"Twenty-five hundred for the weekend," Peter said.

"Five thousand," she countered. Twenty percent went to the Annex for a booking fee; no way she'd be low-balling herself. Not when she was giving up her chance to be there when her prey finally showed.

Hunter sighed. "Fine."

"Okay, I'll have this drawn up, and you can meet her for the signatures. I need to take her for a few minutes before you leave." Peter waved over Jeffrey, who finally showed back up. "Here's the details for the paperwork. Please escort Mr. Bianucci to have this drawn up and signed. I'm taking Jae to my office for a few minutes."

Jeffrey glanced at Jae and shook his head. Peter's office meant she would be getting a few licks of his belt before she was sent off.

"I'd rather not be delayed," Hunter interjected.

"She was unescorted when you spoke with her. It's against the rules and she knew it. She was told to stay at the bar with Stephan while her handler was busy. If she isn't dealt with, it sets a bad example," Peter explained.

"Like I said, I'd rather not be delayed. I am more than happy to see to her discipline when we get home."

A new tingling drove through her spine with the smooth and hard way he said those words.

"Peter." Jae stepped forward. "I only walked away for a minute. I just couldn't stand over there, there was too many people. I did tell Stephan," she explained.

"And he told you to wait," Peter countered.

"I don't want her marked," Hunter stated bluntly.

After a long pause, Peter relented. "Mr. Bianucci will see to your punishment." Peter leaned closer to her, his dark smile increasing as he spoke. "But if you think you're getting off lightly, you're wrong. I've seen him punish his girls before. You'll wish you'd let me handle it."

She swallowed.

"Let's get the papers done," Peter said and dismissed Jeffrey.

Hunter flattened his hand against her back and firmly led

her to where she would sign away her freedom for the weekend.

Two full days of being completely Hunter's.

Why wasn't she terrified?

You can read Daddy Ever After right now on Amazon.

ABOUT THE AUTHOR

USA Today Bestselling Author Measha Stone is a lover of all things erotic and fun who writes kinky romantic suspense and dark romance novels. She won the 2018 Golden Flogger award in two categories, Best Advanced BDSM and Best Anthology. She's hit #1 on Amazon in multiple categories in the U.S. and the U.K. When she's not typing away on her computer, she can be found nestled up with a cup of tea and her kindle.

https://meashastone.com

ALSO BY MEASHA STONE

EVER AFTER

Beast

Tower

Red

Hound

GIRLS OF THE ANNEX

Daddy Ever After

Obediently Ever After

DARK LACE SERIES

Club Dark Lace (Boxset)

Unzoned

Until Daddy

DARK ROMANCE STANDALONES

Valor

Kristoff

Dolly

Finding His Strength

Simmer

The Mob Boss' Pet

OWNED AND PROTECTED

Protecting His Pet

Protecting His Runaway

His Captive Pet
His Captive Kitten
Becoming His Pet
Training His Pet

STASZEK FAMILY
Taken By Him

BLACK LIGHT SERIES
Black Light Valentine Roulette
Black Light Cuffed
Black Light Roulette Redux
Black Light Suspicion
Black Light Celebrity Roulette
Black Light Roulette War

Windy City SERIES
Hidden Heart
Secured Heart
Indebted Heart
Liberated Heart
Daddy's Heart

Made in the USA
Coppell, TX
01 July 2022